Kitty Catches Kismet

A Pride and Prejudice Variation

Jaime Marie Lang

Idle Musings Publishing

Book Cover by Jaime Marie Lang

Editing by Bailey and Bloom Ink

Prologue

CATHERINE LOOKED OUT THE window at the passing scenery. She was grateful the other occupants of the carriage had nodded off, granting her a moment to contemplate just how much her life had changed, and the new opportunities that awaited her in London.

Having spent most of her childhood in hiding, she never thought much about her future, let alone her first season. Her father had been a despicable man and cared nothing for his property, his tenants, or even his wife and daughters. Gaining his attention was not a desirable outcome, as it often resulted in insult and emotional injury. Catherine had attempted to stay out of his way, out of everyone's way.

Her sisters and mother had to rely on each other closely to endure her father's tyranny. Their bond had grown stronger over time and no matter how hard Mr. Bennet tried to tear down the ladies of his household, he never managed to succeed.

From Jane to Lydia, her sisters and mother had tried to instill in her the confidence to chart her own course despite their father. Their efforts seemed futile until a dastard named Wickham had tried to drag her injured sister away. Unable to stand aside or hide as she typically would have, Catherine had made use of the archery lessons

Elizabeth insisted she took and shot Wickham. The memory of her triumph filled Catherine with a warm sense of satisfaction, a smile spreading across her face.

In the end, her father had failed in his attempts to rule over Longbourn and his family with disdain and he had been forced to sign away his control over his wife and daughters. They were stuck in their unhappy situation simply because they were female and lacked the rights to change their circumstances. If their father had not signed his rights away, they would have been forced to return to him, according to the law. With his rights gone, they were finally able to leave Longbourn without facing the consequences he had always threatened.

Within a year of their liberation, Mr. Bennet had truly gotten his comeuppance. His preference for the pleasures of his book room and a good glass of port left him unable or unwilling to maintain the profitability of his estate, and once Longbourn was no longer aided by the Bennet ladies, it had quickly gone bankrupt. Unfortunately for him, things went from bad to worse, and he passed away shortly thereafter.

Lizzie and Mr. Darcy, who insisted she call him William, had brought them all to Pemberley after their marriage and turned them in to family. The first year there had been lovely, as they finally had the freedom to pursue their own interests and endeavors. Jane had gone around visiting all the tenants with Elizabeth, eager to see to their care. Both sisters excelled in these tasks, as they were innately compassionate and dedicated to taking care of others. Mary had worked on the school she wanted to set up for Pemberley's tenant children. While the allure of the gardens at Pemberly had captivated Lydia, and William had given her permission to design a new garden. She could often be spotted diligently working alongside the gardeners, eager to absorb their knowledge. They had all helped mentor Georgiana on how to assist the tenants.

They had all taken pleasure in meeting the many families around Pemberley, both the tenants and neighbors. Mr. Bertram Hawkins was one of Mr. Darcy's long-time neighbors. He often visited the shops in Lambton, with the bookstore being a particular favorite, as he was an ardent bibliophile. A widower with no children, she had thought him nice, but paid him no mind until he proposed to her mother weeks after they had learned of Mr. Bennet's death.

While her sisters and herself had been slightly shocked by the turn of events, they were ecstatic when they learned their mother had fallen in love with him. She had suffered through more than twenty-two years of marriage to a capricious and cruel man; they were happy that she would finally have love. Though they were even more stunned by the news of their mother's pregnancy six months into her new marriage than they were by her remarriage.

Catherine knew she should not have been surprised by her mother's pregnancy as she was not an old woman—her mother had married Mr. Bennet at the tender age of sixteen. She had been remarried to the love of her life and welcoming her new baby boy Mathew by forty.

She was going to miss both her mother and her new baby brother while she was in London. She had not had a season the year before because of her father's death, so this would be her first season. She was nervous as she headed into the city to confront the throngs of people journeying to London to see and be seen.

It was also going to be Georgiana's first season as well, so at least that was something. She would not be doing it alone. Actually, between all the people who were going to be staying at Darcy House, she was definitely not going to be alone.

Mary had not yet married, so she would be participating in the season, and Mrs. Ansley, who had started out as Georgiana's companion but now served them all, would be an invaluable presence. Lydia was going to be there as well, even though she was not yet out. In fact, Jane would be her only sister missing from the fun because, like their mother, she was going to be staying at her own estate with her husband and new baby.

Of course, Lizzie, William, and their darling little son were going to be there. It would be nice to be able to play with little Artie when she needed a break from all the pretentious ladies of the ton.

Catherine knew she was participating in the season because it was expected of women her age in order to find husbands. But did she even want a husband? She was just starting to realize her own strength and capabilities, and although she desired a husband and children, she was in no hurry to make it happen. She knew what she wanted in a marriage partner, and it was love. Nothing less would do. Her desire was not for a love that was fleeting, but the kind of love that endured, like the love she saw between her sister Lizzie and William.

With everything going on during the season, finding a love like that seemed impossible. She knew love was unpredictable and sometimes you had to fight for it. Should she be so lucky that love did show up in her life, she would grasp it tightly with both hands, refusing to let it escape. Despite that belief, that hope she wasn't sure she was willing to even admit to herself, she worried of ever finding someone with whom she could develop that sort of love. But she told herself not to fret. This year, she had decided she would merely try to enjoy the season and the opportunities to visit the theater and other delights only to be had in London.

Feeling settled, she closed her eyes and decided that she would join the others in a bit of a nap. It would be quite a while before they reached their next stop and if her childhood had taught her anything, it was that there was no use worrying about things beyond her control.

Love was a possibility, and the odds were in someone's favor. The only question was whose favor?

Chapter One

Every night Theodore dreamt it was the same, and he knew that morning would be no different. Upon waking with a start, he laid there, shivering from the dampness of his sweat-soaked sheets. He desperately fought the lingering panic that clung to him in a suffocating embrace. Kicking futilely at the tangled sheets, Theodore growled in frustration. He had fought hard to survive the many battles he had experienced while in the regulars. Few people ever saw the scars that crisscrossed his hardened body, and even fewer knew of the scars that were etched deep in his psyche. His nights were often spent in a fight against his own mind.

Staring at the ceiling above him, Theodore attempted to catch his breath and ground himself in reality. He was in London, in his brother's home, not a smoky battlefield full of the moans of the dying. His hair was matted with sweat, making it sticky and uncomfortable against his scalp. He ignored it and scrubbed at his face in frustration. Forcing himself to sit up, he threw the damp sheets back from his body.

He would start the day as he always did to regain some of his equanimity. Going to the table by his bed, Theodore poured some water from the ewer to the basin before leaning over to splash his face.

He cleaned up and dressed to go out. Looking in the mirror, he noted that despite his best efforts, he couldn't hide the redness in his eyes. He left his room while still fiddling with his cravat. It had been over a year since he had served, but he was still trying to adjust to a different wardrobe. Heading downstairs, he went in search of something to sustain him for the exercise that he desperately needed.

He knew that Mrs. Goodwin would have put out coffee for him. The cook at Matlock House had always found little ways to support and pamper him. With her way of seeing to the fact that he was always served his favorites, was it any wonder that he preferred her nature to the housekeeper? Knowing he was an early riser; she brewed a fresh pot of coffee for him to start his day. As a child, he had thought she must be some sort of witch, for she always seemed to know what he was up to. Hiding spots and plots, foibles and fears, she knew about them all. Her discovery of his morning coffee dependence intrigued him and made him wonder what other new secrets she had uncovered.

He did not even bother to sit to drink his cup of coffee. Gulping it down so quickly that he almost burnt his mouth, he headed out the door. The bitter taste on his tongue helped him orient himself to the day ahead as he made his way to Hyde Park. The sun was rising as he arrived, and he savored the tranquility of the early hour, undisturbed by the hustle and bustle of the day.

Choosing his direction, he took off at a brisk pace. Scenes from his past stalked him night and day. He was not, however, a willing or obliging victim. He kept himself busy, for movement was an ally in the silent war he fought within himself.

***

THE SUN WAS FULLY risen by the time he walked down the street to return home. He normally stayed across the square at his cousin Darcy's home, which was usually the epitome of comfort, but with so many debutantes filling the space, Theodore opted for Matlock House instead. Between Georgiana, Mary, Catherine, and Lydia, there were too many young unmarried women at Darcy House, and he could not stay there with the eager gossips in London for the season. They were like a plague, spreading their toxic tales and destroying reputations. And so here he was, gazing at the imposing building that was his own family's home in London, trying to muster the desire to go in.

Walking up the steps, Theodore bit back a curse as his leg tried to give out on him in protest of his earlier exercise. He grabbed the railing and waited until his leg decided to obey. He could handle pain; it was the intermittent weakness that frustrated Theodore more than anything. Finally able to stand, he went in with his shoulders back, ready for whatever the day might bring.

If he had his druthers, he would be anywhere else doing anything else. His choice would not be to be in London, having to deal with his family and the more annoying people from society. Entering the morning room, he spotted his mother sitting at the end of the table with a cup of tea and toast. His brother was not in the room yet, and Theodore nearly turned around and walked out.

He had spent little time at all with his mother. She rarely visited him in the schoolroom and then after that he was at Eton, Cambridge, and away with an active unit of the regulars. Since returning from the continent, he had realized that they had little in common. She was quite fond of the status quo, but it was something he never bothered to give a second thought to. He had met soldiers from noble families that were utter cowards, liars, and cheats. On the other hand, he knew men from the lowest of families that had more integrity and compassion than their king. Status quo would never truly sway him, and so he stood in the doorway watching his mother pick at her food. Somehow, even as a battle-hardened ex-soldier, he did not want to face his mother alone.

"You went in public wearing *that*, I see," she said with a sigh. "I can only imagine what they will say. I do not know how I was cursed with two so unnatural sons. Your father, if he was alive, would be so disappointed in you both." Lady Matlock quickly followed her complaint with a theatrical sob into her handkerchief.

Aside from looking down at his clothing in confusion, he ignored her insults out of habit. She had, for the most part, ignored him, and he was too worn to try to engage in her ploy for attention. Besides, he could not figure out what she meant about what he was wearing. He had only been going to the park. So what if he was not dressed to the nines? Going to the sideboard, he pushed his confusion aside as he contemplated the eggs and scones. Should he get sausage or bacon? Both?

Meanwhile, his mother's emotional outburst showed no signs of abating. Exaggerated sniffles and peeking at him from behind her handkerchief were only part of her morning routine. From the corner of his vision, he observed her, wondering if she truly believed her behavior could sway him. And if so, what did she expect him to change about himself? Moving to the table, he put his plate down before returning to the sideboard to get a cup of tea. He wished for more coffee, but his mother had declared it gauche and refused to have it served when she was present.

"Mother, it is too early for your theatrics. Your life is not the Cheltenham tragedy you make it out to be. If you want to conduct yourself in such a manner, please do so in the confines of your room," a familiar voice said from the doorway. "Otherwise, we would be happy to enjoy a pleasant morning with you."

Turning to greet his brother, Theodore smiled, "Good morning, Cedric." It was a welcome relief to have him there. Theodore's military training, which involved barking commands at people who were misbehaving, was not useful when communicating with his mother. The last time he had tried to cut off one of her diatribes had been futile. Her screaming and recriminations had only continued, seemingly on end. Comparatively, his brother, with his experience in parliament, was more adept at managing her theatrical displays. Cedric had honed his people skills, making it easier to influence their mother with no outward resistance. Despite his aversion to using his brother as a buffer, his exhaustion from yet another restless night rendered him incapable of responding to her adequately.

His mother stopped mid sob and narrowed her eyes before straightening to stir her tea. Clearing her throat, she tried what appeared to be another tactic. "I expect that you both are anticipating the ball this evening. Lady Lavinia will be in attendance. She will be reserving two dances for you, Cedric. Such a lovely girl. If I am not mistaken, she will be this season's most notable diamond due to her demure and lovely demeanor."

Cedric had gotten himself a cup of tea before sitting down at the head of the table opposite his mother. Just as his teacup was almost to his mouth, Lady Lavinia's name was mentioned, causing him to halt. Putting his teacup down, he briefly pinched the bridge of his nose before responding. "I wish you would not encourage girls to expect my favor. I shall not show her preference any more than I did Miss Julia last year, or Lady Helena from the year before. We have had this discussion. I will not marry one of your proteges."

"You've had your fun, Cedric, but you are in your thirties, for goodness' sake," their mother admonished. "It is beyond the time you should have set up your nursery. Start thinking about your future family. You are the Earl of Matlock. The responsibility of carrying on the family name and legacy falls on you, and it is important that you choose a suitable wife and beget heirs." Glancing at Theodore, Lady Matlock wrinkled her nose, as if detecting a faint, unpleasant scent. "Heaven forbid it falls to your soldier brother. He has not trained to take over the role as you have. Should you pass away without an heir, it would be a *catastrophe*."

"Mother, I will not have you disparaging Theodore!" Cedric snapped harshly.

Looking contrite, Lady Matlock waved her hand as if to wipe away her former misspeaking. "It is not that I dislike your brother. It is simply...or rather, both of you must admit he is not at all qualified for the position you hold." Biting her lip, she looked at Cedric in concern.

"That is enough, Mother. Beyond enough. I have told you that your presence in my home is reliant on your ability to be civil to everyone who enters. Servants, guests, and most of all, family. That I have to remind you to be polite to your own son is disgraceful." Cedric's stare was unyielding, leaving his mother with no hope of getting her own way. "Barring a horribly, terrible accident, I am not going anywhere, anytime soon. Additionally, I am *certain* that Theodore can accomplish anything he sets his mind to; he has my complete support. I happen to think he would make an astoundingly amazing earl."

"I must get myself ready to make calls. I will see you both at the ball tonight." Lady Cecilla Imogen Matlock got up, her heels clicking against the polished wooden floor as she left the room with her chin lifted high in what Theodore recognized as defiance of her two children.

***

CEDRIC STOOD UP AND shut the door behind his mother, closing her out of the morning room. At least with her gone, he could eat his breakfast in peace. He loaded his plate with a hearty breakfast of ham and eggs and couldn't resist adding a slice of delicious ginger cake. Taking his plate back to the table, he watched his brother push the food around on his plate. It was evident Theodore was suffering from some kind of malaise.

Theodore's well-being weighed heavily on him, and it was not a new feeling for Cedric. He had worried for his younger brother since the day he realized his parents had set him up as a carrier in the regulars. Most noble families provided a small estate for their second sons. Not his parents. They told Theodore at the age of twelve that he would join the regulars as soon as he was done with Eton and Cambridge. Though Theodore seemed accepting of the directive, Cedric had been angry on his behalf. Though at fifteen, he had no authority to do anything to stop his parents, even if he was a viscount.

It had been a couple of years since Theodore's original injury at Badajoz had brought him home. The wound to his thigh had festered during his journey back from Spain, and they nearly lost him. During the extended fever, he could not distinguish reality from his fevered dreams. From what Cedric had heard of Theodore's ramblings, the battle had been a living hell, but it was afterward that tormented his brother. Apparently, the aftermath of the battle was far worse than the fight itself. Cedric had worried his brother would never recover from such an experience. The process was slow, but Theodore had finally healed and could resume his daily activities—*civilian* activities.

His injury had been severe enough to end his military career. As a cavalry officer, he had to be able to wield a sword or fire a weapon, and that required expert control over his horse with his legs. Despite being able to ride again, he lacked the thigh strength and stamina necessary for battle. Theodore's future had always revolved around the military, so when that future was taken away, he was left adrift.

Cedric felt relieved at first when his brother seemed to accept the change, but he couldn't shake the feeling that something was off now. Theodore had gone to Hertfordshire to visit Darcy shortly after his recovery. In the small town of Meryton, he ended up discovering a new fight to take on. It had helped for a time. Theodore had been doing fairly well, but recently there was a listlessness about him that Cedric did not like. "Was your morning walk any help at all?"

Theodore's tired eyes flickered towards his brother, and a grimace crossed his face. "I should have known you would see what she did not. It went as well as it ever does." He leaned back in his chair, his fork abandoned on the plate, and let out a tired sigh before rubbing his face.

Cedric knew that he had to take a risk and confront the problem. Letting his brother come to him was clearly not working. After weeks of waiting, he was disheartened to see that his brother's condition hadn't improved. "I know you are feeling at a loss to come up with something to do with your life."

Theodore's eyes widened in shock. He licked his lips before questioning. "How did you know that has been bothering me?"

"I am fairly logical, and I can put pieces together as fast as the next man. You thought you were going to spend the rest of your life at war and now you are not. You have been moping. Moving from one thing to another with no genuine interest since you helped save the Bennet ladies." Cedric watched the surprise filter across Theodore's face, and he reveled in the satisfaction of catching his brother off guard. "Now you are stuck in London trying to help Darcy with the season and the three ladies here for marriage mart events. The events you have been attending lack purpose, leaving you unfocused and dissatisfied."

Standing up from his spot at the table, Theodore paced. "I feel like I failed at the mission I had committed to. Despite the hardships of life in the regulars, I found fulfillment knowing that I had a clear purpose and was highly proficient in my duties. Losing my place in the regulars has left me feeling as if the skills I have do not align with the world I am being forced to live in. More than that, I am mooching off all my family members for my support."

Cedric watched Theodore slow his pacing and waited for him to look at him before continuing. "Ignoring your statement about mooching off family, because we have had and will continue to have that fight. If you want to make it worth it, find something of significance to do. You helped the Bennet ladies. Look what good you did there. You have always been a knight looking to do good in the world. Find that good that needs to be done."

"That will be harder to do than one might suppose. London is all style and little substance. It is one dance after another. Even time at the park is spent seeing and being seen." Returning to his seat at the table, Theodore began eating his breakfast, but his disinterest in the meal was clear.

Looking down at his own plate, Cedric took a bite of his ham. It was an excellent breakfast, despite his brother's disregard. "Charities would be a good place to start. There are plenty in London. Beyond that, you can find people in need of help in unexpected places if you are observant. I know it is not the thrill of the battlefield, but there are even people to help at those dances." Pointing his fork at his brother, Cedric added, "I suppose you will be going to the ball tonight."

"Of course. Georgiana is my ward. I would not miss her first season if I could help it. You know how badly Darcy does at social engagements," Theodore grinned, shaking his head at their cousin's incompetence when it came to social gatherings. "He will need help, and Bingley is still at his estate with his wife and new baby. Elizabeth will be there, but they will have their hands full between Mary, Catherine, and Georgiana all out."

"Our poor cousin is quite outnumbered by eligible females." Cedric couldn't help but smile, picturing Darcy's attempts to navigate it all.

With a look of contentment finally on his face, Theodore took a bite of his meal before commenting, "Yes, I know Darcy's mother-in-law would have come if she could, but she is still recovering from the birth of her son. I can understand her new husband's hesitation in bringing her and the new babe to London. The air is often horrid. It is much better that she and the child stay at his estate in Derbyshire."

"I am still surprised by the development of Mrs. Hawkins's swift marriage and pregnancy. It progressed so quickly after we learned of the death of Mr. Bennet, too. She seems to be happy, though," Cedric observed. He remembered meeting his cousin's mother-in-law shortly before her wedding. Cedric had never met a woman more unlike his own mother before. She was all strength and no-nonsense compassion. It was no wonder her daughters were so unique.

Looking over at his brother, eyebrows raised in clear warning, Theodore said, "She is only seven years older than you, and she was married to a horrible man for far too long. I am glad she was able to find the happiness she deserves." Then grinning, he asked, "Are you going to the dance as commanded by our lovely mother?"

"Yes, I will be in attendance, but not at her command." Cedric finished his eggs and took a bite of his ginger cake. The estate in Wales was finally ready for his mother to move in, should she ever need to, and he felt a sense of relief knowing she would be taken care of. She received the right to live in the estate for life in her settlement, and he wanted to have all his bases covered once he married. He would have no wife of his forced to deal with his mother's hostility.

Theo looked at his brother in that penetrating way of his. "Are you finally looking to settle down?"

Playing with his empty teacup, Cedric considered exactly how much to disclose to his younger brother. "I wanted to make sure that I had somewhere to send mother if she refused to behave. The estate she received in her jointure is in Wales, but it was so dilapidated that I would never send a cat there. It's been renovated, and now it's in excellent condition. I have asked our mother to treat others with respect and grace. If she is unable to do so, then she can choose to live elsewhere. I am not a monster. Mother can behave how she wants as long as it is not at the expense of the people I love." Cedric locked eyes with his brother, silently urging him to realize that he fell into that group of people. He still regretted his inability to prevent Theodore from being forced into the regulars all those years ago, but he was grateful he now had the chance to help his brother find his way in a world without death and bloodshed.

***

Catherine looked out the window of the carriage at the shadowy figures going about their business. Taking deep breaths, she tried to settle her stomach and smoothed out the skirt her gown. It was easy to appreciate her evening dress if only for a moment. Despite its typical debutante white coloring the beautiful imperial crepe overlay made it a pleasure to wear. Even such a wonderful dress could not completely distract her from her nausea. If it was simply riding in the carriage that had turned her stomach, she hoped things would improve once they reached their destination. Though even as she accepted a ginger candy from Mrs. Ansley, tendrils of dread continued to take hold. They had only just settled into Darcy House a couple of weeks ago and were already on their way to the third ball of the season.

Shortly after coming out, Catherine had quickly realized her distaste for all the social outings that were required. Her presentation before the queen had gone well enough, though she was glad she would not need to do that again. Musical evenings were nice enough and she loved visiting the opera or the theater, but she had found that she was not at all a fond of balls. Of course, she had only been to two other balls before, but she had enjoyed neither. There was far too much posturing and backhanded compliments that reminded her of her father's cruel tendencies.

Sucking on the candy, Catherine distracted herself by looking across the carriage at William and Elizabeth. Despite the responsibilities of Pemberley and caring for a toddler, their love for each other burned just as brightly as when they first fell in love. Elizabeth was snuggled into William's side, both of her arms wrapped around one of his. Leaning up, Elizabeth whispered something to William that made him smile. Catherine suspected they did not at all mind the carriage's close quarters because it allowed them to cuddle.

What would it be like to have such a love? The more eligible men she met, the less likely it seemed that she would ever find it. So far, the season had only provided the kind of gentlemen she would deem unsuitable. Maybe the type of man she was looking for did not like balls and eschewed them for other pursuits?

Catherine knew William was not looking forward to the ball either. He only attended to help support Catherine, Georgiana, and Mary during their seasons, and it made sense that a man with similar character would have other, more interesting pursuits. At least she would not be alone in her discomfort. With effort, Catherine would make it through the night. At least she could look forward to practicing archery later in the week.

Sooner than she was ready for, the carriage stopped and the door opened. Though Catherine longed to tell them to shut the door and drive her back to Darcy House, she refrained. Straightening her shoulders and holding her head high, she took the groom's offered hand and descended the steps, ready for whatever the night might bring.

Chapter Two

THEODORE SCANNED THE BALLROOM from his spot near the entrance. Lavish decorations and candles seemed to be everywhere. Colorful dresses swirled around the room, almost as if they were dancing to the sound of the gossip that seemed louder than the music. His brother was further in the room, studiously avoiding Lady Lavinia's mother. A smile tugged at the corners of Theodore's mouth at his brother's predicament. With his substantial wealth and noble title, many families vied for Cedric's attention, and the wives of his cohorts from parliament were eager to introduce him to their daughters. Theodore suspected his brother longed for a woman who appreciated him for who he was, rather than his title and wealth. Theodore hoped Cedric would find that unique woman who would do that for him. Elizabeth and her sisters had proven it was possible.

Turning his gaze back to the ballroom, he looked for Darcy and all the ladies he was trying to shepherd. His cousin would need help in the nest of vipers that was the London season. Eventually, he spotted Darcy seated at a table across the room with Elizabeth next to him, her arm linked with his. He could see several people staring at Darcy's grin, clearly stunned by the shift in his demeanor.

If people were being polite, they would say that Darcy was brisk and reserved at social gatherings. If they were being rude, they described him as proud and severe, always hovering on the edges and frowning, making no effort to interact with others. Some people present had probably never seen his smile or the dimples that his young wife seemed to delight in provoking.

Making his way over to them, he greeted and chatted with many people. The latest on-dits were oft repeated, and he wondered at the inanity of the social season. No one seemed to have an original thought in their head. He knew it was the social norm, but he could not brush it away as he usually did. Who enjoyed such surface-level conversations repeated over and over?

At the sound of a joyous laugh behind him, he paused to find the source. Several young debutantes were chatting and hiding their blushes behind their fans. Noting that Mary and Catherine were in the group, he smiled. At least there was someone enjoying tonight's event.

***

PLANTING A PRACTICED SMILE on her face, Catherine hoped no one could decipher her distaste with the event. Being judged at every turn and forced to laugh, or at least smile when people spoke of others' faux pas, was not something she could enjoy. She was certain if something did not change soon, she would say something she truly meant. Telling the lady across from her that she thought her hat an insult to the birds that had worn the feathers first would never do. So she held her tongue with ever-increasing frustration.

These balls were interminable, and the season had just started. Whoever thought up this method of finding a mate clearly had different criteria for a husband than she did. It was frowned upon to talk about serious subjects. How did one find out anything besides the fact that a gentleman had learned how to dance and could dress with style? No one thus far had been willing to talk of anything of note, and she had failed to uncover anything about anyone's true character. For no reason that she could determine, people constantly judged one another. Perhaps it was utter boredom? Or spite?

She turned to Mary, who had been out longer and seemed more accustomed to the critical stares. Her sister kept glancing around the room, probably searching for Mr. Goulding who had promised to be there this evening. Catherine was happy that he had come to London for the season. Mr. Goulding valued her sister's opinion enough to engage in deep conversations beyond the superficial topics of gossip and decor.

Catherine could not say the same thing about her own dance partners. Most were preening puppies who expected her to have nothing between her ears but lace and idle nonsense. Elizabeth had gotten William to sign her dance card, so that was something, at least. Looking further afield, she hoped to spot either Theodore or Cedric. Not only were they willing to dance with her, but they were also gentlemen who would treat her with respect on the dance floor.

"Miss Catherine, that is a lovely dress. Just who is your modiste?"

Dragging her attention back to the conversation at hand with a faint blush, Catherine focused on the speaker. Miss Eliss was a somewhat pretty girl that Catherine could not quite pin down. She said all the right things, but Catherine had never felt any warmth from her, no matter how much she claimed to be her friend. "My sisters and I use a modiste named Mrs. Barclay. We all find her designs lovely."

Miss Eliss smiled, though it did not reach her eyes. "Really? I would have assumed Mr. Darcy would want the best for his sisters. Mrs. Bell is all the rage right now, but I understand it is hard to get in to see her."

"We did not find Mrs. Bell to our taste. My sisters and I found a modiste who is more deserving of our patronage." Edging closer to Catherine's side, Mary's voice cut through the gathered debutantes like a blade. "While others might not be as discerning as my family, we found the poor treatment of her staff prevented us from supporting Mrs. Bell's establishment." It was a good idea to remind others of the unbreakable bond between sisters. Trying to belittle one of the Bennet sisters was never wise, as it would invite the others to close ranks. "It has been lovely chatting with you, Miss Eliss, but we really must be getting back to our sister, Mrs. Darcy, before the dancing starts."

While Miss Eliss never lost her smile, her eyes went flat as she glanced at Mary. They stared at one another for a moment, both with bland smiles on their faces, neither seeming to give in to whatever the battle of wills represented. After half a beat, Mary and Catherine curtsied and Miss Eliss was forced to reciprocate. Turning, Mary and

Catherine left the group, with Catherine feeling as though she had accidentally survived an ambush.

Waiting until they were out of earshot, Catherine finally spoke. "I know she says she is our friend, but I cannot see it. I'll have to find new friends elsewhere if this is the kind of company society can offer."

"You must not pay her petty words any mind, Kitty," Mary spoke softly as they walked away. "I have faith that as time passes, you will find good friends. Even though these settings often encourage superficiality, some people manage to stay genuine."

Taking Mary's arm in her own, Catherine squeezed it. "Well, I will just have to rely on you for company until that day."

Walking arm in arm, Catherine and Mary approached Elizabeth and William and she felt her previous frustrations dissipate. Not only was Catherine delighted to be free of the shallow conversation, but watching Lizzie and William together always brought a smile to her face. They were such a happy couple, so in tune with one another. Her sister's laughter and the twinkle in her eye were evidence of her true happiness with her husband.

Colonel Theodore Fitzwilliam had found them and was chatting enthusiastically with them both, though as she looked him over, she noticed that his usual vigor was somewhat diminished. She was uncertain of what had changed in him, but something had—he appeared tired and worn. He had been of much help to her, and she only wished he would allow her to return the favor. But would he allow a younger woman such as herself into his world to help him with his struggles?

He played a crucial role in helping her and the women of her family escape from her father's narcissistic grip when she was seventeen. She had idolized him for a time after that. The colonel had been there to share the news of her father's demise. He had been there to celebrate both of her sisters' weddings, and oddly enough, her mother's marriage to Mr. Hawkins. Lizzie even paid tribute to the close relationship with the brave man by naming her son Arthur Theodore.

It did something to Catherine to notice that he was somehow less than himself. She would simply have to try to do something to help him. Reaching the group, Catherine turned to him and spoke up with a sly smile. "Colonel Fitzwilliam, I beg your assistance, kind sir."

Bowing with a flair that was more like himself, he responded to her comment in kind. "Oh, magnificent Artemis, how may a humble soldier such as me assist a goddess such as yourself?"

Catherine was glad to see the improvement in his countenance, even if she knew it was only temporary. It had been some time since he had called her Artemis and she enjoyed hearing him refer to her as such. When she had brought down the weasel Wickham all that time ago with a well-placed arrow, he had called her Artemis for months. It was the greatest endearment she knew. To hear it again made her smile widen. "I implore you, sir, to join me in a dance. Only then can you save me from the posturing puppies that are so eager for my time. Though it may only be one set, I will be forever grateful for the respite you will provide."

The colonel's eyes widened for a moment, but he quickly masked his surprise with a smile. "I would fight hordes of puppies for the honor to dance with a goddess of such skill. I wonder why you wouldn't opt for a more direct approach and simply slay them as needed. Your ability to handle such a task is beyond doubt. I know you have the skill to hold off their advances on your own," he smiled knowingly.

"Alas, the hostess would never forgive me if I stained her marble floors with that much bloodshed. She took such trouble to decorate so nicely that it simply would not be polite." Catherine grinned at the bark of laughter that erupted from Colonel Fitzwilliam. She remained shy around strangers, but in the company of those she trusted, she displayed a sharp wit she credited to Lizzie's influence.

"You won't have to worry about the preening puppies, and the hostess won't have to complain about her ruined floors, as I shall be your dance partner." Reaching out, he took her dance card and assigned his name to the supper set.

***

ON THE DANCE FLOOR, Catherine found herself falling back into the pattern from her childhood she had grown to hate. She knew she was avoiding eye contact and was not responding to his comments as she truly wished. She spoke in a monotone, barely inflecting her voice, using as few words as possible to respond to his questions. Yet she knew of no other way of coping with how uncomfortable her current dance partner made her feel.

At first glance, Young Viscount Deerhurst was everything Catherine might want in a husband. A title was something most families sought. He had an unencumbered estate and appeared to be without debt, but that was never certain. Although he was older than her, it was not unusual in society to marry someone older. His fashion sense was always on point, even though he didn't necessarily dress like a dandy. His exacting standards were apparent in the way he dressed, with every item perfectly coordinated. He had well-formed features to go with black hair and eyes so dark brown they seemed to be black in the low light of the ballroom. So what if his dark coloring was not her preference?

She couldn't quite put her finger on it, but there was something in his black eyes that made her uneasy. He didn't seem to care about her unease and instead appeared captivated by it. Catherine knew he was an eligible gentleman and was viewed as a tremendous catch by most of the ton, but she could not like him. Her instincts told her to escape, yet she would have to endure as it would cause quite the scandal if she ran from the dance floor.

"Miss Catherine, you are truly the most beautiful debutante to grace London for many a season." Smiling smugly, he clutched her hand tighter than called for.

"You are too kind, Lord Deerhurst." How could he say such things with a straight face? Catherine knew she was not exactly plain, but she certainly was not as handsome as Jane, who had her come out not two years ago. Why this very season, she knew of several debutantes considered to be more classically beautiful. Attempting not to roll her eyes, Catherine cursed her frozen tongue that kept her from demanding he stop pouring the butter boat over her head.

"So modest. You are such a—"

Thankfully, the turn of the dance drew them apart, and she was not required to listen to whatever else he had thought to say. Allowing her face a moment to lose its forced smile, Catherine glanced around to see where her family was. She spotted Mary further down the line, dancing with some unknown gentleman. He seemed timid and unassuming, and Mary was clearly doing her best to set him at ease. Georgiana was dancing as well, though this time she was dancing with a younger son to Pemberley's largest neighboring estate. Elizabeth and Darcy were sitting out the dance, stealing glances at each other while speaking to a dowager in a feathered turban.

When the dance moved her back in to Lord Deerhurst's sphere, she forced her bland smile firmly back in place. Catherine knew that it was crucial to avoid displaying authentic emotions to maintain a refined image. Heaven forfend if the debutantes present showed their actual feelings while in public view.

"I heard the most interesting story this morning…"

Catherine had heard the tale that afternoon at the round of calls she made with Lizzie. Finding that a mere nod of her head encouraged him to continue without expressing her distaste for the tale, she allowed him to ramble while her mind wandered. A group of lads visiting London on break from Cambridge had raced down a well-used road in town to see who was the best curricle driver. The part of the story that caught his attention was when the poorest of the boys won the race. Apparently, the lad should have allowed one of his betters to win. Deerhurst omitted the fact that the race had resulted in numerous injuries and extensive damage. So much so that the aftermath of the destruction left several vendors in tears and many people shaken.

She thought she was free from his grasp as the dance ended, but he quickly grabbed her by the arm. His smile growing wide, he leaned down to speak to her. She knew he was presenting the image of a romantic couple, but nothing was farther from the truth.

"My dear, you appear rather flushed. Let us head to the balcony so that you may cool off." His smile was just a facade—his eyes revealed his true feelings.

Catherine's fingers itched for her bow. He would not endeavor to bother her after she had aimed a few warning shots at his person. She had become so skilled that she was certain she could target any part of his body. Surely he could get by with a limp. As she thought of her bow, she could almost feel the familiar weight in her hand and the confidence it gave her. "No sir, I am fine. I would be obliged if you would take me to my family now."

"Do not be so silly. I can tell you would do well to have some crisp, cool air. We will enjoy it together." Pulling her away from the crowd and towards the doors that went to the balcony, he began to lose his smile. Cursing the smooth-soled shoes that allowed him to pull her along without any trouble at all, she wished for a means to stop his forward progress. For a moment, Catherine flashed back to the look in her father's eye as he sneered at her mother. Was this how all men of society treated women? She had not come this far just to find herself in a situation akin to her mother's, where she would be diminished and under the thumb of a ruthless man. Her quest for love would not come at the expense of her independence.

Her anger flared like a flame, melting away the timidity that had gripped her like ice. Dropping all pretense of a smile, her nostrils flared, and she allowed her steely determination to show through the clenching of her jaw and the tilt of her chin. "No, you are mistaken. I will take myself back to my family now." Catherine attempted to wrench her arm from his grasp without causing a scene, but felt his fingers tighten into talons.

"Come now, do not be missish. It is a lovely night. You will enjoy it." His brows furrowed, and he tilted his head, puzzled by her resistance. Why would she not want to accompany him on to the balcony?

"It is a foggy London night, cold and damp. It is not my definition of a lovely night. If you want to go out into the fetid fog, be my guest, but I will not be accompanying you." Catherine watched his eyes widen as she spoke. His lips tightened, and she could see the fury building inside him. Casting her gaze around, she spotted what might be of use to her. In a quick motion, she grabbed a glass of punch that was on a nearby table.

Before the lord had time to react as he she knew he might, she splashed him with the bright liquid. He was known for his style, which was the perfect balance of elegance and grandeur, with no expense spared in creating a look of luxury. His cravat was tied with such intricacy that it looked like a work of art, and his bottle green jacket was impeccably tailored to his form, but it was all ruined when the red liquid soaked into the fabric. His reaction was exactly as she wished it to be.

"You... You! My cravat! Do you know how many hours it took to dress for this evening?" Letting her arm go, he furiously wiped at the punch on his face.

Immediately, she took two steps back to get out of his reach. "Oh, you poor dear. I tripped when you so ungentlemanly pulled on my arm. You really should do something about that. I think it might very well stain if you are not careful."

"You will regret—"

"Lord Deerhurst, you were always so clumsy at school, but I did not expect you to spill your drink in such a fashion. You really should leave so that you may take care of that." Colonel Fitzwilliam's droll comment had a sharp edge that belied the simple words. Despite not being on active duty, he possessed the same unwavering drive and determination that characterized a soldier.

Deerhurst opened his mouth, only to snap it shut when he saw the dangerous glare that was coming from the colonel. He stormed off with such determination that he almost knocked over a nearby matron. More than one person turned to stare when they heard his disgruntled mutterings. His behavior today had the potential to reveal his true nature to society. Then again, society forgave much when it came to gentlemen, and they excused many unfortunate behaviors as youthful indiscretions.

"At least I found a good use for that punch. I was not really a fan of the taste. Too sweet." A nervous laugh left Catherine as she tried to tell her legs that it was not the time to turn to jelly.

The colonel's eyes seem to scan her for anything amiss. "Miss Catherine, I was coming your way, but it seems my gallantry was unneeded. If I had known that some of these puppies were more...troublesome than others, I would have stayed closer."

She took a deep breath, trying to shake off the residual tension from the past half hour. Through archery, she had learned the power of deep, steady breathing and drew in another shaky breath, before releasing it slowly. She sensed Colonel Fitzwilliam's watchful eyes on her, yet she was confident he would understand her desire to recenter herself. "Well, that one was less preening puppy and more vile vermin. They are certainly the more dangerous of the two, but had the punch not worked, a swift kick would have been a possibility."

"Why don't we get you another drink? You did not enjoy the punch, but I have heard good things about the lemonade. My lady?" He offered his arm to Catherine. Then, with a reassuring pat on her hand, he escorted her to the refreshments table.

"I noticed you reserved the supper set. I will have to get creative and come up with some entertaining things to talk about. Your offer of aid was so gallant that it would pain me to have you bored throughout your meal. Do you perchance enjoy talking about lace and feathers?" His chuckle led to her own, and this time it felt more sincere than before. The feel of the cold glass in her hand and the taste of the sweet lemonade he handed her helped her to feel like herself again. When she looked up into his blue gaze, a peculiar excitement coursed through her. Catherine was uncertain what it was, but she certainly looked forward to supper.

Chapter Three

WALKING AWAY FROM THE refreshment table, they moved back to where Darcy and Elizabeth had been sitting. Theodore felt himself losing his own composure as he watched Miss Catherine take deep, calming breaths. She had handled Viscount Deerhurst with grace and a clear head. It had ended well, but he was angry to know that even the most proper ballrooms were unsafe for young ladies like Miss Catherine. Cedric had said he should look for places to do good. The ballroom was the last place he expected to find an opportunity to do good in the world, but there it was.

Suddenly, the cheery ballroom had a darker, more ominous aspect to it. Looking around, he saw no overt danger, but he had been a soldier long enough to know that sometime danger was there even if you could not see it. Turning his attention back to Miss Catherine, he looked her over carefully. "Are you certain he did you no harm?"

Looking down at her arm, she grimaced. "Mostly it was just an unpleasant half hour. If there is any damage, it will be covered by my long gloves."

Zeroing in on the arm she looked at, Theodore could note some redness just above the edge of the glove that ended above her elbow. Once again, his temper flared. "I am truly sorry I was not there to stop him earlier, but you handled him remarkably. Though I am not surprised you did so well. You have always had that sort of strength about you."

Avoiding his gaze, she worried her lip, and when she finally spoke, it was evident that her frustration had overwhelmed her. "Not always. Even this evening, when I realized just the sort of man I danced with, I was too timid to say anything until I saw he was determined to bring me out onto the balcony."

Pained by her self-criticism, he spoke up to offer reassurance. "You need to look at what matters—you were able to act when you had to. Take it from an old, wounded soldier. It is not the fear that matters, it is how you act when the situation demands it."

His words seemed to draw Miss Catherine's gaze back to him. Her sea-green eyes widened momentarily at his encouragement before she smiled softly. "Thank you for the reassurance. I will try to think about that. However, I question part of what you said." Tilting her head, she gazed at him with a slight crease between her eyebrows. "I am uncertain about accepting your portrayal of yourself as an old, wounded soldier. You have a marvelous talent for dancing, and your injury has not hindered your performance. You were perfectly capable enough to come to my aid."

Grinning despite himself, Theodore appreciated her depiction of him. The loss of his military career, along with the expectations of how his life would go, wore on him. The fact that she did not consider it to be the bane that he did meant something to him. With a mischievous glint in his eye, he playfully teased Miss Catherine. "Ah, that may be, but I am still rather old."

"Though older than I, you are by no means on the shelf, so to speak. Society has suggested gentlemen much older than you as potential matches for me. You are not even thirty. Frankly, I would say you are currently in your prime." As Miss Catherine finished her speech, she seemed to realize what exactly she said, and a hot blush raced up her cheeks.

He was genuinely stumped on how to respond but managed a grateful, "Thank you."

"I think our dance will start soon. I expect you to dance with the grace that I know you possess. No dragging your feet." Miss Catherine flashed a compelling smile at him.

It startled Theodore to notice how her smile hit him. His anger over earlier events slowly dissipated, replaced somehow with a sense of warmth and hope. Giving his head a swift shake, he once again offered his arm so they could head to the dance floor. She was a remarkable young lady, and deserved all the best things in the world. Of course, he would dance with her and look out for her as he would Georgiana. She was like his cousin.

***

CATHERINE FOUND THE SUPPER set so much more enjoyable than her dance with Lord Deerhurst. For one thing, Colonel Fitzwilliam looked at her with genuine respect. When he smiled, it reached his eyes in a way that did not leave her wanting to run and hide. She found herself eager for the dance to bring him back around so that she could chat with him. They spoke of nothing specific, just the usual chatter that they had enjoyed many times since they met.

As the dance once again separated them, Catherine discreetly watched him from afar. She could not quite put her finger on what she was feeling. She wanted to say that she was comfortable with him, but that was not quite right. If she was truly comfortable with him, why did she feel an overwhelming tension when he drew close to her in the dance?

Moving through the pattern, the colonel was back at her side and Catherine found herself unable to notice anything but the warmth of his hand on her shoulder. She managed to maintain their conversation, but she knew not what they spoke of. Only the years of dance lessons kept her from tripping when he chuckled. The sound of his laugh had certainly never done that to her stomach before. Looking up him, she studied his expression for any hints of suspicion, but he simply smiled back at her. There was something about the look in his eyes that made her breath catch in her throat.

No, comfortable was definitely not the word for what she was feeling. But it wasn't entirely unpleasant.

***

As Theodore approached Catherine with her plate, he couldn't help but smile at the sight of her chatting animatedly with Cedric's dance partner. Their dance had been an enjoyable interlude. Once he had managed to pull his thoughts away from Miss

Catherine's smile, he was able to relax and enjoy the company of someone he found engaging.

"Lady Derby has a gathering most Thursdays, early in the morning. Well, before calls. My sisters and I attend whenever we are able." Miss Catherine's voice could be heard as she spoke to the other woman.

"I would love to join you all. Though I have never attempted archery, I always relish an outdoor activity." The woman's voice was soft but seemed genuine in her enthusiasm.

"Then you would get along well with my older sister, Mrs. Darcy. She loves her estate in Derbyshire and is always out rambling. Though I am fond of nature, and I relish the opportunity to practice my archery, painting is where my heart truly lies." Looking up, Catherine saw his approach and smiled. "Miss Burgess, have you been introduced to Colonel Fitzwilliam?"

"I do not believe that I have," the woman, who seemed to be older than Catherine, replied. She was not the classic blonde beauty that seemed all the rage that season. In fact, she had curly black hair that seemed to form a halo around her face.

Cedric came up to them with a plate for Miss Burgess as well as his own and sat down. "Miss Selene Burgess, my baby brother, Colonel Theodore Fitzwilliam. Brother, Miss Burgess."

"I told you to stop introducing me as your baby brother, Cedric," Theodore said, his annoyance laced with humor.

"Well, last time I introduced you as my little brother, you pointed out that you are taller than me. You will always be my baby brother.

You cannot outgrow younger." Cedric smirked at Theodore before taking a bite of food.

Leaning over to Catherine, Miss Burgess mock whispered, "It is nice to see that brothers act the same way wherever you find them. My brother would say the same thing were he here. Though I am older by thirty minutes, I am not allowed to call him my little brother. But to be fair, he is very much taller than me."

Catherine's melodious laughter spilled out before she said, "I have only recently begun studying brothers as I have none of my own. Lizzie's recent marriage has gifted me a taste of what you must enjoy."

Both girls laughed softly, and Theodore felt drawn by Catherine's smile once again. Lost in thought, his brother startled him by stomping on his foot under the table. Looking up, he saw Cedric gesture to Miss Burgess and realized what he was implying. "I know I did not say so before, but it is a pleasure to meet you, Miss Burgess. It is nice to have a second moon goddess seated at the table. I am sure Artemis will love the company."

Tilting her head, Miss Burgess looked at Catherine before asking, "Oh, should I assume you are Artemis? Something to do with your love for archery?"

"The colonel was witness to a very good shot of mine a couple of years ago and has referred to me as Artemis ever since," Catherine replied, while a blush spread over her cheeks.

After taking a bite of his meal, Theodore washed it down with some of the lukewarm lemonade. "An excellent shot indeed. You shot him in the hand at thirty yards. I know soldiers who are not that accurate with their rifles."

Miss Burgess's eyes widened in astonishment and there was a piece of asparagus speared on her fork, paused midway to her mouth. "You shot someone? I think I am missing the full story here."

Catherine sighed, but Theodore caught how she seemed to sit taller before she responded. "There was someone on our estate that was trying to harm one of my sisters. He happened to make the ill-conceived attempt while I was practicing my archery. I am not sure if he realized the error of his ways, but he suffered some painful consequences. Without going into details I will only say that someone swiftly took him away, and he became someone else's problem." Turning to glare at Theodore, she called him out for his behavior. "If you keep bringing things like this up, people will get all sorts of ideas about me. If you continue along this line, I am going to have to force you to learn archery in compensation."

The laughter of everyone at the table, including his brother Cedric, made Theodore smile as well. For as horrible as his day had started, he was happy that it had improved as much as it had. It was nice to be able to experience the camaraderie, even if the food was subpar and the drinks warm.

***

THEODORE STOOD BY THE edge of the dancing with his brother, watching Georgiana, Mary, and Catherine dance. He suspected his brother was watching Miss Burgess dance. "I enjoyed meeting Miss Burgess. How long have you been hiding her and how come I never noticed?"

Cedric tugged at his cravat with a finger. Seeing Theodore's quirked eyebrow at the action, he sighed and responded to the query. "It appears your keen observational skills have dulled, but you have not been quite yourself lately. I met her at the start of the season but have been biding my time." Watching the woman in question dance with some young buck, he frowned. "This is her third season. Her father is a viscount in Northumberland. Her twin brother is his heir. I think you would like him. I met him at Gentleman Jack's, and he has a remarkable right hook."

Scrubbing his face with his hand, Theodore wondered where his mind had been. Lost in his struggle to rebuild his life and haunted by nightmares, he now found himself failing his brother. "I know I was off, but that is a lot to be missing. I am sorry I have not been paying attention lately."

Cedric shook his head and grabbed his brother by the shoulder. "I am only encouraged to see you doing better this evening. After all, you are my baby brother. I only want you to find your way to happiness."

Despite the odd pressure in his chest from the comment, Theodore smiled at his brother. "So, is Miss Burgess your way to happiness?"

"She might just be, though I have had to be careful. It would not do for Mother to catch wind and turn nasty. You know she only wants weak-willed, timid things for us so that she may maintain her position. I asked a friend of mine to see to it that she was invited to play cards. She is thoroughly distracted and did not notice us eating together." Cedric's smile was practically triumphant. It appeared that he was rather proud of his schemes regarding their mother.

Theodore looked at his brother in consideration. He was grateful that Cedric seemed to be finding happiness. His life as an earl was not conducive to finding those who genuinely cared for him, and Theodore was glad that he was making the effort to protect that. Cedric certainly had a handle on their mother that Theodore did not feel he himself possessed. "I have to give it to you, Cedric. You fight an entirely different battle than I am used to. Point me at an enemy that I can attack outright, and I am confident in my ability to win the day. You have an amazing ability to confront problems in a roundabout way."

Shrugging, Cedric smiled sardonically. "I have been immersed in society since I left Cambridge. While you were off fighting and figuring out how to stay alive while people were shooting at you, I was here. I was studying how to sway people's opinions without causing any friction or hostility."

As he gripped his brother's shoulder, a playful chuckle escaped his lips, filling the air with warmth and laughter. "I must say you have succeeded. You are a master at it. You handle people like a chess master handles his chess pieces. Each of your moves is calculated and intentional."

"Yes, you could look at the maneuverings in the ton and see the similarities to chess. In fact, people like our mother look at people like pawns to be manipulated and cast aside at her whim." Cedric looked over to the doorway that led to the card room. Their mother would be occupied there for some time but would eventually come out to gossip with her friends.

Shaking his head, Theodore watched the swirl of glittering gaiety with palpable distaste. "I cannot like it. Since Badajoz, my time has been mostly dedicated to recovering or being in the country. I have lost touch with what you have been having to deal with. How have you endured *society* so long?"

"I use what I have learned to help those that I can. There are always people that need help when you look for it." Cedric cast a glance at his brother.

"I think I am beginning to see what you mean. We might need to keep an eye on Deerhurst. He was trying to pull Miss Catherine out on to the balcony." The recollection of the rogue's despicable actions made Theodore's pulse quicken.

Cedric swiftly looked at Miss Catherine, seeming to also check her over for harm. Theodore followed his gaze and noticed that she was smiling kindly while moving through the motions of the dance. Her partner appeared slightly clumsy, though she was reassuring the lad despite his latest misstep. "You must have come to her aid in time. She looks to be well enough."

"She intentionally ruined his perfectly tied cravat with a glass of red punch, forcing him to release her. He left to attend to the stain. I think, however, that he will try to make trouble for her, or at the very least, other young debutantes, in the future." Theodore's voice seemed to end in a growl. He told himself his anger that someone would try something against Miss Catherine was not completely unexpected. He was very protective of those under his care.

"It's evident that the Bennet ladies are not to be underestimated when it comes to their ability to defend themselves and each other." Smiling, Cedric turned his attention back to Theodore.

Theodore did not look at his brother, but out at the dancers instead. One dancer in particular. "Yes, but she is only a girl. She should not have to fight to protect herself while at a ball."

"At nineteen, she's no longer a girl but a young woman. Actually, she's participating in the season to find a husband, so she's not just a young woman, but will soon be someone's wife." Cedric's laughter towards his brother's confusion was inexplicable, or at least Theodore thought it was. Seeming to take pity on his younger brother, he composed himself. Then, looking serious, Cedric stared off in thought for a moment. "But yes, no one should have to worry about their safety while enjoying the festivities of the season. I will have to make sure the viscount is not making a nuisance of himself."

"And how, pray tell, will you be doing that?" Theodore knew his brother was all about connections, but what connection could help him with a dastard like Deerhurst?

"His father, who holds a seat in parliament, is an acquaintance of mine. He controls the purse strings. If that does not work, I have other connections that might be useful."

Theodore abandoned his reply as his attention caught on Darcy rushing towards them with a worried frown. "Darcy, what is wrong?" he questioned.

"Someone delivered a message just now that Artie has developed a fever. I am taking Elizabeth home so we can care for him. I know his nanny is a wonderful woman who adores him, but we would like to see to him ourselves." Looking out to the dance floor, he spotted his charges all in the middle of the dance. "I do not want to disrupt the night for Georgiana, Mary, and Catherine. Mrs. Ansley is here to chaperone them, but I would feel better if you could escort them home. If you are willing, Theodore, I will send my carriage back for you to use once we get home."

"Of course. You get home to my little namesake. Do not worry too much if you can help it, for Artie is a tough little tike. I am sure he will quickly recover from whatever this is," Theodore reassured him, hating to see his cousin's panic.

After Darcy expressed his gratitude and rushed off, Cedric spoke up. "I am not certain Artie could quite be called your namesake. His name is Arthur."

"His name is Arthur *Theodore*," Theodore proudly clarified. "He is my namesake and will most likely be the closest I will come to a legacy."

"At least until you have children of your own," Cedric said with a certainty Theodore certainly didn't share.

Shaking his head, Theodore denied the possibility. "I do not know if I will ever have children. Who would have me? I am a discarded soldier. I have no estate, and no true prospects for my future."

"You are not yet thirty. Soon, but not yet, and you are the brother of an earl. That means a lot to many people. I know both Darcy and I have attempted to give you an estate, but you have repeatedly turned us down," Cedric pointed out, clearly attempting to dismantle Theodore's argument with one swift speech. "You are an intelligent man and I know that with time, you will find your own way to establish yourself. Despite your assertions, I have hope for your prospects yet and will be here to support you along the way."

***

ELIZABETH TOOK ADVANTAGE OF the empty carriage to lay her head on William's shoulder, snuggling her forehead into his neck. She needed the comfort his presence gave her and knew he would appreciate her closeness as well. "I know he will be fine, but I cannot help but worry."

"That is because you are a good mother." William laced their fingers together, his thumb stroking her skin in reassurance. "We still have some time before we can see him for ourselves. Let us talk of something else before you start worrying yourself about possibilities. What did you think of Theodore's behavior at the ball? He has been...off lately."

Sighing, Elizabeth tried to force her muscles to relax, and thought back to recall what she had seen of the colonel. "Theodore seemed well enough, but you are right. During his unguarded moments, he appeared more pensive than usual."

"I have always pictured Theodore as the perfect knight-errant roaming the countryside, looking for battles to win and people to save. In the regulars he had a purpose, and I think he is somewhat lost without it." Leaning his head down to rest on Elizabeth's, he continued, "London society is not something he fits into well. He has always had a distaste for superficial drama."

"I would not worry about him too much. I'm sure he will find his way and you will help him. Besides, did you see him at supper? He looked to be enjoying himself with Catherine and Cedric." Elizabeth closed her eyes, savoring the comfort of being held by William.

"I will trust your faith in him." After being silent for a moment, he asked, "Did you see Mary with Goulding?"

"Yes, I did. He always tries to dance the supper set with her when they are at a dance together." Laughing with an undignified snort, she continued, "I do not think either of them realize how obvious they are to us. He should be finishing Oxford soon. I wonder how long it will take for him to propose."

Chuckling softly, William pressed a kiss into Elizabeth's hair. "Ah, to be young, though he does not have the best of prospects."

Leaning back, Elizabeth looked at her husband, her eyes narrowed. "Fitzwilliam Darcy, you know Mary does not care about prospects and we could very well provide a number of places for them to live. One of your satellite estates, or even Pemberley. Mary would live in a hovel if she felt she was loved."

William leaned in and nuzzled Elizabeth's nose with his own. "I very well know that Mary would live anywhere if there was love in her life. I was simply worried about Goulding. Young men are often proud, you know, and he may hesitate to propose if he feels he cannot offer her what he thinks she deserves."

Elizabeth giggled with a roll of her eyes. "Oh, you young men and your pride."

***

HEADING AWAY FROM THE gaiety of the ball and into the hallway with Georgiana and Mary, Catherine tried not to worry for Artie. It was rather silly that William would think they would want to stay and enjoy themselves while their little nephew was home sick. Besides her dance with Colonel Fitzwilliam, she could have done without the whole experience.

Between the pettiness of women like Miss Eliss and the vile actions of Lord Deerhurst, the evening was a complete waste of time and a good dress. Thinking about the dance with the viscount made Catherine suppress a shudder. Just what percentage of the men she met would prove themselves more like him than the more stellar examples of their kind?

For a moment, she considered the possibility of wearing shoes with a better grip to the next ball. Perhaps with some kind of reinforcement in the top of the shoe? That way, she would be better protected from clumsy dancers stepping on her feet, not to mention they would certainly make a better weapon if she was forced to kick someone. Grinning, Catherine rolled her eyes at the absurdity of her thoughts.

Looking ahead, she saw the colonel standing in a pool of light at the entrance speaking with his brother and hoped the candlelight would conceal her blush. Though she could easily do without most of the experiences she had that night, she would never have traded away her time with Colonel Fitzwilliam. The time with him was something she would cherish, even if she wasn't sure what to make of that realization.

He had come to her aid and reassured her. Supper had been thoroughly enjoyable and chatting away with everyone made for a special meal. The dance, however, had been something else altogether. Never before had a dance evoked such feelings. She knew debutantes who absolutely loved to dance and though she had always found it enjoyable, she would not have pined had she missed the opportunity to dance.

She couldn't quite put her finger on it, but there was an unmistakable shift in the experience that made her feel off-balance. His eyes held a mischievous glint, and the way his deep chuckle reverberated through her left her stomach in a constant state of flutter. Somehow, the dance had created a thrilling anticipation within her, leaving her uncertain of her desires. Did she hope those new feelings would gradually fade away? Or did she want them to intensify?

***

STANDING AT THE ENTRANCE of the building, Theodore spoke with his brother, who wanted to leave before his mother made herself a nuisance. "You go ahead, Cedric. I am sure Darcy's carriage will be here shortly, and then I will see you at home. All these lovely ladies will keep me company while we wait. Isn't that right, Mrs. Ansley?"

"More like keep you in line," Catherine's cheery response came from where she stood between Georgiana and Mary.

Seemingly reassured, Cedric bowed elegantly in their direction. "Ladies," he said as way of farewell before turning his gaze to his brother. "I will see you at home, Theodore. Please tell Darcy that I hope young Artie recovers swiftly." Climbing into his carriage, he disappeared into the foggy London night.

Wringing her hands, Georgianna peered into the darkness as if trying to spot their carriage. "I hope Artie is all right. I could never stay and enjoy myself, knowing that he was unwell."

"We will be home shortly, and you can check on him yourself. Between all the maternal figures in his life, I am sure that he will have plenty of arms to hold and care for him," Mrs. Ansley reassured Georgiana.

Mary wrapped an arm around Georgiana's shoulders in a comforting gesture. "Children are always coming down with one thing or another. I am sure he is fine."

It was only a matter of minutes before their carriage arrived and they all piled in. Conversation was quiet as the hour was late, and despite their concern, they were all tired. Sitting in the quiet allowed Theodore to contemplate the evening. While he would never say that he enjoyed balls, the night had progressed better than he had hoped.

Spending time with Catherine had managed to tip the scales towards something he hadn't felt in quite some time: hope. Their dance had been delightful, and the supper conversation had been fun in a way that he hadn't experienced in a while. Seeing Cedric happy with Miss Selene had been a wonderful surprise, and he was thrilled she had managed to make his brother laugh.

While he would never want to spend more time in society than he had to, perhaps a dance here or there with the right people could be bearable. He knew that as an earl, his brother had to attend more events than Theodore could ever manage without pulling out his hair. He had previously wondered how he would manage the season and help shepherd the girls, but after tonight, he mused that attending events with Cedric, Darcy, and his gaggle of ladies was probably something he could handle after all.

The steady pace they had been taking came to an abrupt halt, pulling Theodore from his thoughts. There was a commotion in the distance that made the horses stomp uneasily. An unusual screaming filled the air. There was a seriously injured horse somewhere at the front of the line of stopped carriages. Theodore could recognize it from his time in the Calvary.

Sticking his head out the window of the carriage, Theodore asked, "Can you see what is going on?"

The footman sitting beside the driver looked back at Theodore. "There has been an accident, sir. It looks like a carriage has been overturned."

Hopping down from the carriage, Theodore felt a familiar quiver run through his leg on impact. At least it had not given out on him. Amidst the cacophony of the horse's cries and the searing ache in his leg, fleeting memories of past battles flickered in his mind. He did not know if the memories brought the pain, or if it was the pain that brought the memories, but the familiar rush that came with going to someone in need helped him move beyond the horrors of his past.

Cedric was right, he needed to find ways to help people, and this was just the kind of opportunity he had been needing. Not only did he have the experience necessary to help with the horses, but he also knew how to treat injuries in a pinch. Looking back up into the carriage, he said, "Ladies, stay in the carriage. I am going to see if someone needs assistance. Please do not go haring off trying to help. It is late and I do not want any of you to get injured." With that, he rushed off towards the sounds of commotion, weaving his way through the dark street.

***

TRYING TO BLOCK OUT the screaming of the injured horse and the cries of alarm, Cedric closed his eyes. The accident had turned his carriage into a chaotic mess, and he found himself lying against what used to be the side of the carriage but was now the floor. The bumps and imperfections of the material were a comfort of sorts, for at least he could feel them on his cheek. He had tried to get up to help whoever was screaming earlier, only to come to realize that he could not move.

A heavy sense of dread settled in his chest as he accepted the grim reality that the situation was beyond his control. He could still blink, which was good because it meant he could blink the blood out of his eyes as it dripped down his face. It was clear that he had a head wound, though he guessed it was probably not the only wound he had sustained. At least he was mostly free of pain.

As time passed in an odd, disjointed haze, he felt his mind drifting. The dance he had shared with Selene had been lovely. He almost smiled, thinking that it was good to end things on such a pleasant evening. She had been all that he was looking for in a dance partner, and spending time talking with her at supper had been a delight. She did not fawn over him and his title and had expressed several interesting opinions. It was a pity he would never dance with her again.

He was not going to lie to himself. He knew that the situation indicated his end. No one who had become paralyzed at the neck lived for very long. He most likely had other injuries that would only complicate matters, and he was weary, feeling as though time was slipping away.

There was a shout that pulled him from his hazy contemplations. The familiar voice, filled with a distinct sense of authority, had been Theo. His poor baby brother. It would all fall to him now, and while Cedric had every confidence in him, his only remaining worry was whether his brother was happy. Everything else faded into insignificance. He heard the door to his carriage fly open.

"Cedric, my God," Theo cried from above him.

After a few grunts, Theo was before him, and he could see his brother's terrified face. Cedric realized he really must look horrible if his battle-hardened brother was that pale. He knew in his final moments that there was not much he could do to help Theo, but he felt that he must find a way. It would be so hard for his brother now, with so much to take on. Summoning reserves he did not know he possessed, he managed a faint smile. "Find your happiness."

Chapter Four

THE HAIR-RAISING SOUND OF the horse's scream that filled the air was so foreign to her that she had trouble comprehending what was happening. Almost as disturbing was the silence following the single shot that echoed in the distance.

Mary, Catherine, and Georgiana sat shoulder to shoulder in the carriage, their hands clasped tightly together as they tried to steady their shivering bodies. The darkness of the night seemed to be closing in, suffocating and heavy with foreboding. Despite her composed facade, Mrs. Ansley's charges could detect a subtle sense of nervousness in her mannerisms.

After an interlude of waiting for Colonel Fitzwilliam to return, Mrs. Ansley spoke to the groomsman. "Is there any sign of movement?"

Trying to stand on the seat with the assistance of his comrade, he replied, "Some carriages seem to be inching forward at a snail's pace. It appears they have been able to maneuver around the accident."

"Can you see the colonel?" Miss Catherine was concerned about his extended absence. If it had been a simple issue, he would have been back already. It felt as if she was waiting for some horrible news. As time went on, the likelihood of people having been horribly injured in the accident became more and more probable.

"No, there are people moving around, but it is too dark to tell them apart," came his response.

Even as they started moving again, they were stuck in limbo, waiting for more information before they could make any decisions about how to proceed. If the accident was bad enough, they were not that far from Darcy and Matlock Houses and could aways send back help.

The driver gasped as they got closer. "I think the carriage is familiar, Mrs. Ansley. I hope I am wrong, but...I think it is the Matlock carriage."

"Good Lord, how far back are we?" cried Mrs. Ansley.

"Maybe five carriages back now."

Catherine stuck her head out of the window, straining her eyes as she tried to see anything in the dark, foggy night. Everything was shadowy and without detail and she could not tell one carriage form another. "Jameson, can you run to Darcy House? I fear that Colonel Fitzwilliam will be in need of assistance if that is his brother's carriage."

"Yes miss, I will be back with help as swiftly as possible." The groom climbed down from his perch and took off into the darkness.

Looking back to those inside the carriage, Catherine could see Georgiana burst into tears. Mary's grip on Georgiana tightened, clearly trying to soothe the younger woman as she cried. Catherine reached out and gripped Georgiana's free hand as she sat numbly in the night.

***

The colonel's devastation was palpable, and it broke her heart to see him that way. When they had pulled even with the accident, Catherine had jumped out of the carriage and gone in search of Theodore. He had been issuing commands, sending people for supplies and instructing how to move the carriage further out of the way of traffic. Despite watching him take control of the scene, she could see the cracks forming in the facade that he was presenting to the world. She could hear his breath hitch every time his eyes drifted towards the silhouette of the blanket-covered body.

It was enough for her to know with a sickening feeling who was under the blanket and just how horrible the accident had been. She had asked in a halting voice how she could help him. His only response was a shake of his head and pursed lips, as if he could not even vocalize what he needed.

Reaching out, she had attempted to clasp his hand in comfort. He allowed it for a time, but not for long. Regrettably, he abandoned the moment and redirected his attention towards overseeing things. The Matlock carriage had to be brought somewhere to possibly be repaired and a single horse laid in front of the ruined carriage. Catherine's stomach turned at the sight of the animal, its limb twisted at an unnatural angle. The poor creature's suffering had come to an end with the sound of the shot she heard. It was evident that the only surviving horse was agitated by the accident and the chaos that unfolded. It was frantic, shaking its head and stomping in an unhappy fashion.

Part of her had wished that she could help, but in the end, she had gone back to the carriage and rode on to Darcy House. There were several injured people, but there were also more than enough people to help them. A man was moving among them with a medical bag dispensing aid and wrapping injuries. There was no need for her to stay, and she was aware that her presence would probably slow down the demanding work that lay ahead.

As she arrived at Darcy House, she could hear people bustling around, gathering items to aid in the accident. Elizabeth was there to gather Georgiana to her and hold her while she cried. After some time, she began guiding Georgiana up the stairs toward her room.

"He is gone, Lizzie. Cedric is gone." Georgiana's pain spilled out of her as easily as the tears that streamed down her cheeks.

The group followed behind Elizabeth as she led Georgiana to her room, the air thick with grief. "Oh darling, I am so sorry. Let me help you get out of those clothes and into something comfortable."

Georgiana looked at Elizabeth with concern. "But what about Artie? Is he all right?"

Smoothing the blonde hair away from Georgiana's face, Elizabeth reassured her. "He has a fever and is congested, but they have him breathing steam. Lydia has taken over the nursery and is directing everything for his care. He will be fine for a few minutes while I am with you."

"Where is William? Does he know?" The sorrow that consumed Georgiana seemed to have physically diminished her, leaving her looking smaller and fragile.

"He went to go be with Theodore." Elizabeth's voice, while quiet, was still strong. It was a strength that they were all going to need.

Catherine watched them go into Georgiana's room, and she moved to her own only two doors down. She shared a sitting room with Georgiana while Mary shared one with Mrs. Ansley. Her maid, Lambert, was there waiting for her to help her get ready for bed. She mechanically went through her bedtime routine, knowing full well she wouldn't be able to sleep. Even the tea her maid brought her, the relaxing tea Jane always prepared for the family, did not help.

The night dissolved into a tapestry of violet and lavender, as she couldn't shake off the painful memories of the evening, which wrapped around her mind like a veil. Despite her desire to sleep, to momentarily escape the tragedy that would haunt her and her family, Catherine was still staring at the ceiling above her bed hours later. The night had been long and difficult, and the day promised to be no better. She could not recall sleeping, only tossing and turning, and her bed was a tangle of blankets and sheets, thrown about in a disorderly fashion.

Eventually she had given up and got out of bed. There was no point in lying in the dark any longer. She slipped into her simple gray gown unassisted as she did not want to call for her maid. Solitude allowed her mind to untangle the mess of thoughts and emotions whirling around inside her. Putting her hair up in a simple knot, she went downstairs to see who was about.

The morning room was set with coffee and tea and various breakfast foods. Despite the early hour, William and Elizabeth were sitting at the table, speaking softly. They clasped each other's hands as they always did, but this time their grip was tighter, as if seeking comfort in each other's touch during this difficult time.

Passing up the tea that she desperately knew she needed, she went to Elizabeth and gave her a hug. She craved the human connection even more than the hot cup of comfort. Wrapped in Elizabeth's warm embrace, she felt protected and safe from the turbulent sea of her emotions. At least until she stepped back and had to face the cruel reality of the day.

"Did you manage to sleep at all, Kitty?" Elizabeth looked at her in concern, always looking out for others. Despite the grim circumstances, Catherine smiled faintly at the use of her sisters' nickname for her. Though some people might look askance at such a nickname, Catherine cherished it. She had often been told the story of how the nickname came to be. Somehow, when Lydia started talking, she had gone from Catherine to Cat to Kitty, not that she remembered it much.

"I do not think so, but I could not lie there any longer." Catherine shook her head and moved to get herself a cup of tea. She added a liberal dash of milk and several lumps of sugar, feeling she would need it for the day before her. It had not even been twelve hours since she ate supper with Cedric. He had been so happy and now he was gone.

"I think we will find that most everyone had trouble sleeping. It will be a rough day," Elizabeth spoke quietly while she stirred her coffee.

"How is Artie doing this morning?" Catherine queried as she moved to sit with her tea.

"He had a surprisingly good night's sleep, and this morning his fever has all but disappeared, but he is still struggling with a stuffy nose. I am glad it is not worse. As it is, it is heartbreaking to see him suffering, especially when he can't communicate what he needs." Elizabeth put on a brave smile, but no one doubted how much she worried for her little boy. Little Arthur was just over a year old and he already had everyone wrapped around his tiny fingers. Elizabeth was an exemplary mother, taking care of him herself as much as she was able despite it not being a popular idea amongst society.

Catherine took a sip of her tea, feeling the warmth spread through her body, bolstering her for the difficult conversation ahead. "William, how are you this morning? I cannot imagine how you must be feeling right now."

Looking up at Catherine, Darcy gave a wan smile. He had deep shadows under both his eyes, suggesting he had not slept at all either. "Thank you for your concern, Catherine. I was not as close to Cedric as I am to Theodore, but I am still deeply affected by his death." He briefly glanced at the ceiling, as if trying to make sense of it all, before shaking his head. "It has been a tremendous shock."

"I wish I knew the right words to say to make things better." Catherine glanced at Elizabeth as she put her arm around her husband, offering the comfort that he needed.

Darcy held his wife's gaze for a moment before turning back to Catherine. "The fact that you want to be here for me is enough."

Despite the circumstances, Catherine couldn't help but feel a twinge of envy towards her sister's loving relationship. She felt a pang of longing as she realized that watching them might be the closest she ever came to experiencing something like it. She had felt nothing remotely like it with any of the gentlemen she met at the various dances and social events she was required to attend. As she gazed into her cup, she couldn't help but contemplate how being surrounded by babies, with Elizabeth, Jane, and her mother all experiencing the joy of motherhood within a short span of time, offered her a sense of purpose. There was sure to be more too, especially since William and Elizabeth seemed to be unable to stay away from one another. There would at least always be the need for someone to help tend them.

Catherine took another fortifying sip of tea before broaching the topic that had been worrying her all night. "How was Colonel Fitzwilliam when you saw him last night?"

Rubbing his face, William responded with a pained air. "There was something about him that was not himself. Despite the surrounding chaos, he remained composed and handled everything efficiently. From checking on people to tending to injuries, he made sure everyone was taken care of with great diligence. He even made sure that the carriage was hauled safely to a blacksmith, though I doubt it can be salvaged." With a sigh, Darcy shook his head. "Theodore managed to hold back his grief until he reached home with Cedric's body, but once there, it consumed him entirely."

"I worry about him. He held his brother in high regard and never aspired to the position of earl," Elizabeth spoke into the somber room.

Catherine felt a deep ache in her chest, knowing how much Colonel Fitzwilliam must be suffering. Was it only the night before that he had brought so much light into her evening? He treated her with respect, valuing her opinions and allowing her to freely express herself regardless of her gender. It was ironic that he, who was always so eager to help, was now the one in desperate need of assistance. She worried he would not see the need to accept it. "I worry about him too."

***

Catherine sat alone in her sitting room. She had retreated from a household that was alive with preparations. Despite the frenzied atmosphere, there was a clear sense of order and purpose in the house. The servants moved swiftly and efficiently, each one knowing exactly what needed to be done. Becoming a house in mourning was not such a simple thing. Plans for the funeral were being discussed and black dresses were being found for all the ladies.

Taking up her paper and pencils, she positioned herself at the desk in front of the window that looked over the courtyard. Instead of admiring the beautiful sight, she turned her attention inward, as she often did before working on a creative project. Her fingers itched to create, and she found solace in the texture of charcoal and pencils, ink and paint. She had to bring a stability of some kind to the staggering feeling of grief she was lost in. There was a way to bring some kind of positivity to all the negative that surrounded her. There had to be.

A memory came to her from the night before. The moment was filled with laughter and smiles, creating a bright and cheery atmosphere. It had happened before the night had turned so dark and hopeless with an accident that would change so much. Her hand moved instinctively, as if guided by the memory of love and light. She drew out what she wanted to appear on the page and submerged herself in her work. With single-minded determination, she allowed only the image in her mind to remain, blocking out all other distractions.

She spent the next hour ignoring all that was going on outside of the drawing that she was creating. Ignoring how her fingers became soiled and her nose gained a smudge of its own, she worked hard on her creation. Though she had planned to add colors later, she couldn't help but pause when she finally saw the picture as she envisioned it. The anticipation of what was to come filled her with excitement, and she hoped it would provide solace for the colonel.

Chapter Five

THE GROUND HAD BEEN cold and unyielding, as if the earth itself did not want to accept Cedric's death. The funeral was over, and Theodore was forever separated from his brother. He would never again see him or his smile, and he found himself wondering if he could find a way to bear it all.

Darcy had stood beside him, silently supporting him through it all. Despite his dislike of crowds, Darcy was a bulwark protecting him from the numbers of unknown well-wishers. So many gentlemen had shown trying to gain favor with the new Earl of Matlock. He found himself wishing for the people in his life that society would not allow at the funeral—the women. Catherine and her sisters would have been so much more comforting than the posturing men that had shown.

It was all a hazy, surreal dream to Theodore. He had gotten used to waking up from his nightmares sweat-soaked and shaking, but this time he found he did not have the power to wake up from the madness that was his reality. How could his brother be dead, and from a carriage accident no less?

His brother was only thirty-four and healthy. He was actually doing things with his life. Despite the chaos of parliament, he remained resolute in his mission to fix things for the greater good. He was making changes in the world to help people, and it had seemed as though he had finally found a woman he could like as a wife. Given enough time, he could possibly love her, and now he was dead? With no regard for his hopes and dreams, and how much he meant to everyone. No regard to how much Theodore depended on him.

"My lord, there are callers." A noise penetrated the fog in his mind. "My lord?"

It took a moment for Theodore to register that someone was speaking. It took much longer for him to realize that someone was speaking to him. Why was he being called *my lord*? That was not his title. He was a sir, a colonel, or if they were family, people called him Theodore or Theo. Why did people insist on calling him lord? That was not him. That was his brother. He had not been raised to be an earl. He was the spare and had been raised to be sent off to war.

His duty was to the regulars, and he had always expected to die on the field of battle. While he had healed from his injuries at Badajoz, it hadn't been enough to return to war and so he was stuck being the failure who could not return to his assigned task. It left him in an odd limbo, trying to find his place in a world that he was unfamiliar with. He knew war and dirt and grime and pain; he did not know the grandeur and expectations and lies that filled society. It was a battlefield he was not ready for.

Life had thrust him into the role of earl following his brother's untimely death, and Theodore felt the impossible weight of his brother's legacy on his shoulders. The task ahead of him was far beyond his expertise, but he could not fail his brother, so he gritted his teeth and endured. He had experience with endurance. He could recognize that, at least. Turning to the voice, he focused on the person who spoke. "I'm sorry, I was lost in thought. Did you need me for something, Barnes?"

"My apologies for disturbing you, my lord, but there are callers. Are you at home?" Barnes stood with a slight forward lean and a wrinkled brow. After years of being Theodore's batman on the continent, Barnes made the commitment to stay with him, even when Theodore had to part ways with the regulars. They had been through a lot together.

"I will come down. Do I look presentable?" Theodore stood and smoothed down his waistcoat. He always remembered his brother being perfectly turned out and looked down at what he wore. He was suddenly concerned that he might not measure up to the expectations of Cedric's friends and wanted to avoid any missteps.

"You are entirely presentable."

"Thank you, Barnes." Leaving the sitting room, Theodore went down to speak with the people who had called to offer their condolences. It was going to be a long day.

***

CATHERINE WATCHED ELIZABETH BRING Lady Matlock a cup of tea where she sat by the fireplace. She had never understood the custom that prevented women from attending funerals. She had once heard that a woman's sensibilities were too delicate to attend a funeral, no matter how close you were to the deceased.

Were men afraid that the women would cry? So what if they cried? Catherine was not ashamed of the tears she shed for poor Cedric. Looking at the ceiling, Catherine worried for Theodore. He had gone up to his room without saying a word after the funeral.

"Lady Matlock, you really must eat something. Why don't you have a biscuit with your tea." Elizabeth was kneeling next to Lady Matlock, trying to remind her to take care of herself. "Callers will be coming. I know you want to represent Cedric well, but you cannot do that if let yourself grow weak."

Catherine suppressed a smile at the way Elizabeth was able to get Lady Matlock to listen. She suspected very few people would be successful in such an endeavor. Looking around the room, Catherine tried to see if there was anything she could help with. Georgiana was sitting on a settee in the corner being comforted by Mary. The sideboard was covered with finger foods and an urn of coffee. Things seemed to be well in hand.

Motion in the doorway drew her attention where one of the servants stood looking anxious. Looking around, she did not see William, so she went to speak with him. "What is the matter?"

The well-dressed footman looked at Lady Matlock who had not spoken anything in some time before speaking softly. "There are callers, Miss Catherine, but the earl is not down yet."

Glancing at her sister who had finally gotten Lady Matlock to drink some tea and eat half a biscuit, she made a judgment call. "He will be down as soon as he can. For now, feel free to let the callers in. Lady Matlock is as ready as she will ever be."

"As you wish, Miss Catherine." Bowing, the footman left.

Standing close to the door, Catherine readied herself for the people coming to offer condolences to the family. She greeted them briefly as they trickled through before they moved on to speak with Lady Matlock. Oddly enough, though she had not spoken to anyone since Catherine arrived, she spoke to all of the guests.

Lady Matlock gripped the hand of the woman in front of her. "Yes, I miss my dear Cedric so. He was the best of sons. You have no idea how I suffer here with no other ladies in the family to comfort me." She began chatting with the others who came in, soaking up their sympathy like a sponge.

Soon enough the Bennet ladies were on the periphery, serving tea and chatting with those who Lady Matlock did not draw in. Catherine was perfectly happy standing to the side and being ignored by most of the visitors. She strategically stood by the entrance so she could watch the stairs.

Her wait was rewarded when a bleak Colonel Fitzwilliam descended the stairs. She knew he was now Theodore Fitzwilliam, Earl of Matlock, but he would not feel comfortable with the title yet. Somehow, she knew it was too soon. Slipping out of the room, she went to him as he reached the bottom of the stairs.

Looking up into his eyes, she knew that there was nothing she could say, that his pain was too great for mere words to help. Guiding him over to the nearby settee she got him to sit down and sitting next to him she took one of his large, calloused hands in one of hers. They sat in silence while he tightly gripped at the lifeline she offered.

Eventually visitors noticed him sitting at the side of the room and approached to speak with the new earl and Catherine was forced to move away. She knew she could not stay; it would look unseemly holding his hand, but she ached for him. How did one recover from the loss of a dear sibling? Was it even possible for him to recover from such a shock?

***

SITTING AT THE HEAD of the table felt wrong to Theodore. He gazed down the table to his mother sitting at the other end, nothing but empty seats between them, and was overwhelmed with a sense of loneliness. He couldn't help but notice that the dish in front of him was made up entirely of his favorite foods. It was apparent that Mrs. Goodwin had noted his lack of appetite, and she wanted him to eat, tempting him with all the food she knew he liked. He idly wondered if she would serve syllabub with dinner.

"It was nice of the Baldwins to come and offer their condolences," his mother spoke up between bites of food.

"Yes, I was not aware that Cedric knew the marquess." The sea of people coming in and out all day seemed never ending. It was a shock to him when he realized the number of titled people present at any given time, though it probably should not have surprised him. His brother had spent most of his time in parliament with many of the members of the titled class. The titles meant nothing to Theodore though, for he had only found comfort with one visitor. "It was nice of the Bennet ladies to lend their support today."

"Yes, well, your brother spent his time cultivating many *important* relationships. He was always attending one gathering or another.

So important." Taking up her handkerchief, she dabbed at her eyes. She looked tired and worn out, as if the last few days had aged her prematurely. The shock of losing her oldest son had visibly been hard on her, so much so that he refrained from mentioning her lack of appreciation for the Bennets.

"Cedric was an amazing man." He swallowed, attempting to keep his emotions at bay. "I think I will always miss him."

"He really loved you. His loss has been so hard on me, on us. I realize there were so many things that I had never properly considered. I have regrets, so many regrets." His mother paused and placed her hand over her mouth, blinking several times before continuing. "I am so glad I have you still and that you will uphold everything he held dear."

While it took a moment for Theodore to process what his mother had said, he was wary of where his mother was going with the conversation. He had always known her to be self-centered and conceited though he had hoped that she loved both of her sons, albeit in her own way. Was it possible that the horrible loss they were experiencing could bring them closer? He was afraid to wish for such a thing, though it sounded as though she was on the verge of saying that she was pleased with him. "I want to do my part in ensuring that his legacy lives on."

"Despite what I may have said before, you are a good boy. I am sure that you will do a fine job. You spoke so pleasingly to everyone that came after the funeral." As her eyes met his from across the table, a gentle smile appeared on her lips with what appeared to be a hint of pride. "You were away from home for so long that I think I forgot how capable you are."

As he watched his mother, Theodore was left speechless. Maybe he was right, and his mother had a heart after all? Who knew his brother's death would potentially thaw her icy demeanor? Would he finally have a mother worthy of the title, or would he continue to be disappointed?

***

DARCY COULD SEE THEODORE's hands tremble as he sat down at Cedric's desk, and the sight of his cousin in such anguish caused his heart to ache. It had only been a few days since the funeral, but reality was already crashing in on Theodore's grief. From experience, Darcy knew that bills still needed to be paid and stewards still needed instruction no matter how much grief weighed you down. Volunteering to help Theodore sort through the mess of Cedric's desk had been a simple matter for Darcy. Theodore had always been there for Darcy, trying to support him despite what the rest of his family saw as deficiency. Now, with Cedric's death, Theodore was being shoved into a role that he had never been prepared for.

At least when Darcy had gained the responsibility of Pemberley, he had expected it would be his duty at some point. Theodore had expected a completely different life—a life of battle and blood, not of estates and ballrooms. Not only was Theodore grieving his brother's death, but he also had his entire world turned upside down.

"It does not feel right sitting here," Theodore finally creaked out. "I do not want to sit here. It makes it too real."

"I do not think Cedric would ever begrudge you anything, and he would certainly never begrudge you his chair." Watching Theodore hang his head, Darcy offered a solution. "Would it feel better if you switched chairs? There are plenty of chairs in this room. We could move them around."

Standing, Theodore pulled Cedric's chair back from the desk and pulled it over to the fireplace. He then grabbed another chair, seemingly at random, and placed it behind the desk before sitting down again. Darcy waited patiently as Theodore rubbed his hands on the wood of the desk. Suddenly his hands stopped moving, and he leaned into the wood, as if trying to channel his strength. When Theodore finally looked up at him, Darcy could not quite read his expression.

At first, Theodore's lips pressed together so tightly they were turning white, but then he blew out a breath and spoke. "Thank you for coming, Darcy. I know I have so much to learn. I do not even know what I should be asking."

"My purpose is to provide support for you. We can talk about Cedric if you want, or we could talk about what it means to run an estate." Darcy leaned back in his chair, patiently waiting for Theodore as he visibly struggled to process his emotions, let alone put them into words.

"Even after I came home, Cedric never asked for help with anything. I know there was a lot he did, but it all ran so smoothly that I do not know what needs to be seen to. This is not a battle I am adequately prepared for, Darcy." Speaking so openly seemed to be a struggle for Theodore. The clenching of his jaw caused his words to come out clipped and sharp, and he maintained a strained, tense expression, even around his eyes.

"You do not have to rush headlong into everything. Cedric had several competent and faithful stewards, and they will continue to run things as needed. I am here and I will not leave you alone in this," Darcy assured him, but worried Theodore was so lost in his anguish that he didn't believe him.

***

THEODORE WONDERED IF NOT sleeping at all was better than the nightmares. Rolling over, he punched his pillow in frustration. Sleep was no refuge from the persistent anxiety that plagued him. He was faced with the daunting task of continuing his brother's work without any knowledge of what it entailed.

He had only grown more and more confused the longer he had tried to decipher all the papers strewn all over his brother's desk. Darcy had helped, or had tried to, but eventually Theodore had sent him away. Despite claiming exhaustion, Theodore had gone back to try to sort things out once Darcy was out of sight. He knew that Darcy offered help, but he had his own house to take care of. Why had he never been taught how to do anything of use outside of the military?

If there was one thing he had learned from what he had reviewed so far, it was that his brother had been trying to do too much yet never once had asked for help. Why did Cedric not show him anything? Of course, Theodore had never assumed anything like this would happen, but at least then he would have had some idea of what to do now.

One thing he found perplexing was he had known his brother owned several properties, yet he had not realized Cedric had at least five that he found evidence of. That was not even considering the one in Wales that his mother received from her jointure. He knew his brother had jokingly offered him an estate, but he had never taken it seriously. Theodore had never learned how to take care of a *single* estate. How did one oversee five or more?

Had Darcy mentioned stewards? It seemed improbable that his brother had visited all his estates and instead spent the majority of his time in London tending to parliamentary matters. He knew his brother was passionate about many things he put forth in parliament, but Theodore only knew about a fraction of them. He knew nothing about how his brother went about accomplishing what he set out to do. Would people expect him to pursue the same course of action? What if people expected him to take his brother's seat in parliament?

And so, it continued—more and more questions and the anger that seemed to build with the lack of answers. Sleep would never come. As the hours ticked by, Theodore remained wide awake, the cracks on the ceiling his only company.

***

THEODORE DRESSED HIMSELF WITH even more attention to detail than usual before sneaking out of the house. In the weeks since his brother's death, people had started realizing who he was, and he hated their judging stares when they spotted him. While he had never been one for popular fashion, he did not want them to judge Cedric for having a brother who was less than he needed to be.

He wanted to move. He needed to move. And despite feeling like punching something, he decided to forgo Gentleman Jack's and instead chose to take a brisk walk. With the sun barely peeking over the horizon, he relished in the sensation of the cool morning air on his skin and headed to the park.

The sky was a hazy lavender blushing into pink. He knew it was beautiful, but he could not find it within himself to appreciate it as he once might have. Another night without enough sleep seemed to have drained him even more than normal. It had been almost a month since his brother had died and he still struggled to sleep at night. When he noticed he was entirely alone in a secluded part of the park, he quickened his pace to a jog, despite his heavy fatigue. Pushing his body physically seemed to keep the questions and the anguish at bay.

He was careful to stop before the sun had risen too high in the sky. Leaning over with his hands on his knees, he caught his breath before taking out his handkerchief to blot at the sweat on his forehead in attempt to make himself presentable. Though his thigh ached, it was still cooperating, which he attributed to his frequent morning exercise.

Heading back home, he weaved through the crowds and caught snippets of conversations along the way. The street was alive with activity as vendors and hawkers hustled to set up their shops for the day. It felt surreal that the world had not changed despite his brother's death. The reality remained that people still needed to earn a living and support their loved ones.

Despite the pain he felt over the loss of his brother, the world continued spinning and the sun continued to rise and set. Upon reaching his opulent home, he couldn't help but feel a wave of sadness as he saw the hatchment on the front door, signaling his brother's death. He was greeted by the footman who had gotten used to his early morning rambles. Making his way to his room, he found Barnes waiting for him with a hot bath. "Thank you, Barnes," Theodore sighed gratefully. If there was one thing he had come to appreciate from becoming an earl, it was the fact that there always seemed to be hot water waiting for him.

After arranging the towels, his longtime batman turned to him, appearing to scrutinize his appearance with a critical eye. Barnes always seemed to worry about Theodore's condition, regardless of if Theodore cared about it himself. He was worse than a governess in some ways. "Did you enjoy your run this morning, my lord?"

"I remain unable to sleep through the night, but I feel more settled after my exercise." Theodore loosened his black neckcloth as he spoke. Sitting down, he began to pull at one of his boots before

Barnes was there to help him remove them both. "How is the state of the house? Anything to be concerned about?"

Theodore watched as Barnes pondered his inquiries. One reason he appreciated Barnes so much was his innate ability to ferret out issues that needed to be addressed. His skills at reconnaissance were second to none.

"Your brother was well loved by the staff. He treated them well and they all seem to be mourning his passing. Your brother's valet is looking for another position, but that was to be expected. Jones has been concerned of late, but he is staying attentive to his duties."

Coming out of his fog upon hearing there was a need he might be able to help with, he looked to Barnes. "Oh, what is his concern? Is there anything we can do to assist him?"

"It seems that he has developed feelings for a maid named Sally, who works across the square, and she has been ducking the advances of the master's son. He is rather worried that she is in an unsafe position. He does not make enough to support them both yet and so they are waiting to marry while praying she can find a new position."

"No one should be forced to stay in such a situation. Speak with Timmins, I am sure we can find some sort of position for her," Theodore said thoughtfully. "Then it will be possible for them to marry all the sooner."

"I will do so. I believe that Jones will be very pleased to learn of it." Getting up off the floor, Barnes carried the boots to the side of the room and opened the clothes cupboard. He began to rummage around for Theodore's outfit for the day. Taking a dark waistcoat in hand, he laid it out on Theodore's bed. "I will set out your clothes, unless there is something specific you want to wear?"

"I am only going over more paperwork with Darcy today, and maybe go to Whites later. Nothing special."

Nodding his head, Barnes went back to composing the rest of an outfit, always meticulous about selecting each piece. "It will be good for you to get out of the house, my lord. Do you have something planned for the evening?"

"No, but I assume that Elizabeth will want me to come over for dinner. Despite the season, and it being Georgiana and Miss Catherine's first season at that, they are staying closer to home since Cedric died."

"They are a fine family." Completing his tasks, Barnes moved to the door.

"Yes, they are," Theodore agreed with a tired smile. "They've been inviting Mother, but she has refused, stating the need for solitude. Thank you for readying everything."

Barnes left the room, allowing Theodore to bathe in peace. Theodore was aware that earls and other powerful men had valets to aid them in bathing and dressing, but he couldn't fathom the idea of being dependent on someone for such basic tasks. Stripping his clothes, he stepped into the hot water and sighed. Resting his head against the back of the metal tub, he closed his eyes, reveling in the fact that relaxing in the tub was so much easier than in bed lately.

∗∗∗

THE PIANO'S LAST NOTES hung in the air before everyone broke out into applause. Over the last several years, Catherine had honed her skills to a remarkable degree. While Georgiana's pieces were flawless, Catherine's had a certain charm and warmth that were hard to replicate.

"Wonderful, Kitty. I told you that you could do that piece justice," Georgiana commended her from her chair by the fireplace.

"Thank you. I had to push myself to get started, but once I did, I found the challenge quite enjoyable." Getting up from the piano, she approached Theodore and sat next to him on the settee.

"You did very well, Miss Catherine. It is a remarkable piece." Theodore smiled at Miss Catherine as he spoke. It was an odd sensation to recognize that his own smile felt slightly stiff. He used to be such a jovial person—when had that changed?

Thinking back, he wondered when he had last felt most like himself. He had enjoyed staying at Netherfield and then afterwards, he was fine at Pemberley when Darcy married. London seemed to have sucked the laughter out of him but since his brother's death, he struggled to even find anything to smile about.

"Yes, though challenging, I enjoy most of Haydn's works." His smile was mirrored by Catherine, although her eyes seemed to hold a silent inquiry. "I have a request to make of you, Colonel."

Surprised that she would request anything of him, Theodore sat up straighter. "And what would that be, Miss Catherine? Is my cousin overlooking something he should have in your care?"

"Lydia and I typically go to Lady Derby's to practice our archery with Elizabeth, but she is unable to accompany us tomorrow. Would you be willing to accompany us?"

It felt like an age since he had done anything so carefree and though he would not do something so frivolous on his own account, he would not hesitate to help Elizabeth's younger sisters. "Of course, I do not mind. Who would object to watching a goddess practice her sport?" Maybe it was time to step out of the dark, if only for a morning.

Chapter Six

HER PLAN WAS IN place, and Catherine was happy that it was. Getting the opportunity to speak with Theodore the night before had been a wonderful opportunity to get the ball rolling so to speak. Cedric's death had caused Theodore to change, and she watched as he drifted further and further away from who he used to be. It had to stop. She was uncertain why watching him flounder hurt her as badly as it did, but she could take it no longer.

She had found her strength on the archery field, and she had thought perhaps he could find his own there too. Thanking her maid for her help in preparing for the day, she left her room to join the others in the morning room for breakfast. "Good morning, everyone."

"Good morning, Kitty," came the swift reply from Lydia, who stood by the sideboard collecting her breakfast. "I am so happy you got Theodore to accompany us to archery. Archery is not something I would want to miss if I can help it."

"I am sorry to not be able to go with you today, but I could not avoid the appointment," Elizabeth spoke from her spot at the table where she was drinking her morning coffee. "Apparently, the charity that I am supporting is having some kind of issue. I need to meet with some of the other ladies to oversee some changes."

"I do not mind in the least. You have responsibilities that you need to see to and besides, I am quite proud of my solution. Two birds with one stone and all that," Catherine replied on her way to the sideboard to get some toast and marmalade. Gathering her plate, she put it on the table and went back for some tea. She noticed how Lydia had so casually said *Theodore*. For some reason, even referring to him as Theodore in her mind felt odd to Catherine, but Colonel Fitzwilliam felt too cold now, and Lord Matlock was even worse. She supposed that only left Theodore.

"Whatever do you mean?" The words were somewhat muffled as Lydia spoke while chewing on a piece of toast. Catherine watched as her sister caught the disapproving look on Ansley's face and swallowed hard. Hastily wiping her mouth, Lydia whispered an apology.

Catherine loved her little sister dearly. In a different world, one without all the individualized attention Elizabeth gave her to counteract her father's cruelty, she could have been her bolder sister's shadow, imitating Lydia's every move. Despite that, Catherine was glad she managed to find the way to be her own person. "I have been worried about Colonel Theodore and am hoping that by getting him out of the house, we can help him. Archery has been a source of strength and development for me, and I hope he will also find it to be a positive experience. I do not know why exactly, but it's painful for me to witness him so disheartened. He was not meant for it."

"That is very kind of you, Kitty. I think we have all noticed how much Cedric's death has affected him. I hope you are able to bring some light into his life," Elizabeth said before looking up to see a maid entering the room with a tray containing the mail. "Oh, thank you, Jemma."

Mary and Georgiana bid them all good morning as they entered the room moments later, and after they sat down with their own breakfast selections, Elizabeth announced, "We received letters from Mama and Jane this morning."

"Do read them to us. I hope the babies are doing well. I still find it hard to believe that little Artie got a cousin and an uncle in the same week," Lydia said, this time making a visible effort to ensure her mouth was entirely free of food before speaking.

"Mama says..."

Catherine settled more comfortably in her chair, happy to hear some positive news from her mother about her baby brother Matthew. Their lives had been shrouded in sadness, but she prayed her mother's words would bring some much-needed light and cheerfulness.

***

"I AM EVER SO grateful that you were willing to accompany us to archery practice. I think you will enjoy it," Lydia gushed, her excitement palpable as they rode in the carriage.

"I have watched you ladies practice archery before." Theodore smiled at Lydia, clearly enjoying her enthusiasm.

Catherine was happy to see Theodore smile. He needed to smile more. "Yes, but this time you will be able to meet Lady Derby. She is the one that convinced Elizabeth to take up archery," Catherine said.

"Let me get this straight. Your Aunt Gardiner's cousin is Countess Derby? So the woman who Miss Bingley was so nasty about was really Lady Derby?" Theodore burst out laughing upon hearing the information. "I love it. How is your Aunt Gardiner connected to Lady Derby?"

"You may not know of a man named Baron Wallace, but he has property about a day's journey from Pemberley," Catherine explained. "He had several sons and many grandsons, but only two granddaughters. His oldest son had a daughter named Amelia and his youngest son had a daughter named Matilda. Amelia married an earl, becoming Countess Derby. The younger son was a vicar in Lambton and his daughter Matilda met, fell in love with and married my Uncle Gardiner. They shared a special bond as the only granddaughters of Baron Wallace and spent much of their childhood together. They are still close friends." Catherine was fond of her aunt's cousin. Her exalted position did not diminish her kindness and strength, qualities which she shared with her beloved Aunt Gardiner.

"It was probably a good thing Miss Bingley did not know who she was insulting." A warm smile spread across Theodore's face.

When they arrived, there were already several other ladies gathered, spread out between the various targets. The targets were closer than at Pemberley, but the goal was to hit the center every time with a tight grouping of arrows. Here they focused not on distance, but close-range accuracy.

Lady Derby saw them escorted in by the butler and hurried to greet them. Giving both the girls a hug, she cheerfully welcomed them. "I am so happy you could make it. When Elizabeth told me something had come up with one of her charities, I was afraid I would not see you. I see you managed to find someone to bring you instead."

"Lady Derby, may I present Colonel Theodore Fitzwilliam, the Earl of Matlock. He is Mr. Darcy's cousin," Catherine introduced the two. "Colonel Theodore, may I introduce Lady Amelia Stanley, Countess of Derby."

Colonel Theodore bowed and upon rising said, "It is a pleasure to meet you, my lady. You have done remarkable work encouraging the Bennet ladies to learn archery. It has done wonders for them."

"Oh, I simply enjoy the sport so much I cannot imagine anyone else not benefiting from it." Turning to the girls, she encouraged them to a spot at the end of the line. "I saved a target for you at the end there. Go on and start warming up. Maybe later we can show off for the earl if I can steal him away from his duties."

***

LADY DERBY WATCHED THE Bennet girls head to their spot at the end. They were wonderful girls, and she was proud of the outstanding women they were becoming. When Madeline had told her that she had inherited five nieces with her marriage to Mr. Gardiner, Lady Darby had wondered about who the girls would be. Now she hoped that her own two daughters would grow up to be as strong and self-assured as they were proving to be.

Turning to her guest, she looked him over. He was dressed appropriately but not in any of the foppish styles of the day. He was a colonel, though, so that would explain some of the simpleness of his attire. The black arm band showed his mourning status as well as his black cravat. She was most intrigued, but the grimace that he had displayed when she had called him earl spoke volumes. "I want to offer my condolences on the loss of your brother. As someone who has lost a sibling myself, I know the agony that you must be experiencing. I can only imagine how hard it must be to take up the mantle of earl unexpectedly while dealing with that grief."

His eyes widened slightly, as if surprised by her comment. "Thank you. Losing my brother was a shock indeed and it has been a struggle every day since. I was raised for the military, not the earldom."

Lady Derby considered him, her heart aching for the young man. "Though it might be presumptuous, I have some hard-earned advice. Take it as you will. Do not let your grief or your need to take up this mantle cut you off from people who care. I know there are people who care for you—the Bennet ladies, for example, and your cousin Mr. Darcy as well. Let them be there for you and, when necessary, seek out advice. When you have estates that need help, ask Mr. Darcy. He can help you there. You have problems figuring out the finances, ask someone for help. By the by, my cousin Mr. Gardiner has extensive experience and expertise in the realm of finance and investments. I am sure he would be willing to help," she said, offering him a small smile. "John Donne got it correct when he said, 'No man is an Island,' Colonel."

Theodore looked away for a moment and rubbed his eyebrow before responding. "I must admit that I have been, for lack of a better word, floundering. That is good advice. Thank you."

"Well, now that we have had our talk, let us join the girls. While I know they are becoming remarkable women, I sometimes think I will always see them as the little girls I met all those years ago. It happens that way when you do not always see what is in front of you because you only see what was in the past." Walking over to the Bennets, she smiled as the colonel fallowed her. Looking at this man, she had one of her strange intuitions, a strong feeling about him. He would be a very good husband to one of the Bennet girls once he found his way and was able to see what was right in front of him.

***

As Theodore approached Catherine with Lady Derby, she looked up and smiled mischievously. Eyes twinkling, she held out her bow to him. "Now it is your turn to practice."

"I thought I was here as an observer only?" Theodore managed to smile back at her, his lips curving into a gentle grin.

"No, that is how I got you here, but I have often wanted to see that you learn. Besides, the closer targets should make it easier for you. It is perfect for your first attempt." Taking the hand he held up in front of him in some form of defense, she placed her bow in it.

"Alright, I suppose I can go along with your plan. Though I will have you know I had some of the best aim in my regiment."

With an infectious grin, Lydia held out an arrow and gestured for him to step forward. "I would love to see your display."

Stepping forward as if his ability to shoot the arrow was automatic, he put the arrow in place as he had seen and pulled the string back. After a moment, he let go, expecting the arrow to shoot forward and embed itself in the target, only the arrow did not obey his silent command. It had fallen oddly at his side, eliciting a round of giggles from all the ladies present. "That is not what I expected to happen."

Catherine's lips twitched, as if she was trying hard not to burst into laughter at his expense. "Yes, well, you did not ask for advice, so we let you do what you thought was best. You were holding the arrow wrong. It was not notched correctly."

The next hour flew by with Catherine, Lydia, and Lady Derby teaching Theodore the basics of archery. Catherine smiled as one of his arrows finally made it to the target. "There you go. You hit the target."

"Yes, but it is nowhere near the center," Theodore complained. While he had been relatively good-natured about his learning curve, he couldn't shake his disappointment with the outcome.

"It took me months to hit the target. You are doing well," Lydia encouraged him.

Lady Derby approached the group. "I hate to ruin the fun, but your carriage has come, and I need to prepare for my calls later."

Looking around at the empty yard, Catherine's eyes grew round. "I am sorry we lingered so long. I do hope we have not disrupted your day."

"Oh, I had a marvelous time." Lady Derby smiled as Catherine and Lydia started to strengthen things up.

Going over to Lady Derby, Theodore bowed and said, "I would like to take the opportunity to thank you for having me, Lady Derby. I did not expect to learn so much while I was here."

"You are always welcome to come back. In fact, I will see about having you invited to one of our dinners. I think my husband would be more than happy to meet you." Walking with them through the house, she saw them off.

***

CATHERINE NOTICED THE TWINKLE in Theodore's eyes as he smiled, and it made her heart feel warm. He had offered to take them to Gunter's for ices before taking them back to Darcy House. "How are you liking yours, Lydia?" she asked.

Lydia had been sitting there, her face frozen in visible delight, with her eyes closed as if to better enjoy the flavor on her tongue. Opening her eyes, she blushed at being caught enjoying the treat. "I have to admit, this is really delicious," she said, taking another bite. "I have a weakness for ices, and you're aware of it. This time I tried bergamot. Did you get maple again?"

"Yes, it is my favorite, after all." Catherine took another bite. She enjoyed ices, but apparently not quite as much as her younger sister.

"I will have to remember how much you prefer ices if I need to bribe you in the future," Theodore spoke up from where he sat across from Catherine and Lydia.

They had taken their treats to the little park across the street and were eating it under the maple trees there. A gentle breeze danced through the leaves, creating a peaceful ambiance. It was a popular spot and while most came to see and be seen, other people were spread out, enjoying their own treats.

Catherine looked up and spotted Miss Selene Burgess and a gentleman that she did not know. She had almost forgotten how much she had enjoyed talking with her at the ball before the horrible accident that had taken Cedric's life. The young woman had seemed to be rather fond of Cedric and Catherine pondered this as she noticed Selene's lavender dress—a possible sign of mourning. Was it possible that she had been grieving Cedric's death in her own way? Catherine smiled as they connected eyes, happy when it appeared that she was coming over to greet them.

"Miss Catherine, it is a pleasure to see you here," Miss Selene called as she approached on the arm of a very tall gentleman who looked remarkably like her. He also had pitch black hair that seemed to curl in wild abandon, and deep blue eyes that seemed to see everything.

"Yes, I am so sorry that I forgot to reach out to you—" Catherine paused and looked over at Theodore. "I had meant to try to reach out to you, but, well..." She was worried about saying anything about why she had so distracted.

"I understand perfectly well." Selene smiled grimly. Everyone had heard about the accident that had taken the Earl of Matlock's life.

"Miss Selene, I do not think you know my little sister. Miss Selene Burgess, may I present my little sister, Miss Lydia Bennet? Lydia, my new friend Miss Selene Burgess."

"If we are introducing our younger siblings, may I introduce my little brother, Mr. Sebastian Burgess? Sebastian, my friends Miss Catherine Bennet and Miss Lydia Bennet, and this is Colonel Theodore Fitzwilliam, the Earl of Matlock."

***

Earl of Matlock. Those words caused a wave of grief and uncertainty every time Theodore heard them and he wasn't sure he would ever grow accustomed to it. He shifted his attention to Mr. Burgess as the young man spoke. "It is a pleasure to meet you all. My sister told me how very much she had enjoyed meeting you after the ball." The tall man's white, toothy smile was the first thing Theodore noticed as he bowed to them all.

Selene seemed to reach out towards Theodore, but then pulled her hand back. She waited for him to meet her eyes before speaking. "My lord, I had no way to reach out to you, but I wanted to offer my condolences. The world has lost a remarkable man. Although it may sound trite, the world seems less bright now that he's gone."

Even though he had already finished his ice, Theodore swallowed hard. He knew his brother had been developing feelings for the young woman, but it was nice to realize it had been reciprocal. "Yes, the world is darker without him in it. Thank you for your kind sentiments."

The silence was rather tense until Lydia spoke up. "So what flavor of ice did you choose, Mr. Burgess?"

"Oh, um, I am not fond of ices." Rubbing the back of his neck, he looked down at Lydia awkwardly.

"He only comes because he knows how much I enjoy them." Selene squeezed her brother's arm as she spoke. It was obvious they were quite close.

"Not like ices? Miss Selene, I am afraid there might be something seriously wrong with your brother." Lydia's playful jab at Mr. Burgess was a welcome distraction from the somber mood that had settled over the group. One by one, they began to laugh at her comment. Even Theodore smiled.

Chapter Seven

Theodore was humming happily when he returned home, causing him to pause momentarily as he went up the steps. How long had it been since he had hummed as he went about his day? It had been too long. The door opened automatically as he resumed his approach.

"Welcome home, my lord," the footman greeted.

"Thank you, Jones." Taking off his gloves, Theodore handed them to the footman.

"Theodore, you are home," was his mother's way of greeting from the landing halfway up the stairs. She had either been going up or coming down when his arrival caught her attention. "I had thought you would never return from carting those girls around. Really, I would have thought Darcy would know that you have much more important things to do with your time now that you are the earl."

Reluctant to let his mother's antics dampen his mood, he moved to the stairs, intent on heading to his room to prepare for receiving calls. Since his brother's death, he had tried to be present for the calls his mother would receive in condolence. "I enjoyed myself this morning, Mother. It was a lovely outing. We went to Gunter's for ices."

"I am glad you found the time to enjoy yourself. Frivolity like archery and Gunter's often is enjoyable, though your brother never seemed to have time for such things. He always worked so diligently, never one to indulge in senseless distractions." Worry etched his mother's face and her normally bold voice hesitated. "I had thought you were trying to follow in your brother's footsteps, but if you have decided against it, I understand. Not everyone is suited for the responsibilities he willingly assumed."

Theodore paused with his foot hovering over the stair in front of him. Had he really wasted his morning? No, he had been working hard for weeks. Spending time with the Bennets didn't mean he wasted the morning. Or did it? "I made a point of coming home in plenty of time to receive calls with you, Mother. I was just going upstairs to change."

A smile flashed on her face. "Oh, that is splendid. It really is a good time for you to be meeting with people who are actually important. In fact, we have been invited to an important dinner tomorrow night. All the right people will be there. I know we are both in mourning, but it is only a small friendly gathering, nothing so large as a ball or proper dinner."

Theodore knew that his mother was a very social woman, and he realized that it must be difficult for her to be cut off from her normal forms of entertainment. Perhaps this was why she was being so snappish. "I would be more than happy to escort you to the dinner tomorrow night. Who is hosting it?"

"Lord Talbot will host the dinner. He was a close friend of your brother and they worked on several projects together. I know he would like to get to know you as well."

"I will be happy to meet him, but if I do not dress now, I will not be able to receive calls with you." From four steps below, he craned his neck to meet his mother's gaze, the uncomfortable position reminding him of his childhood for some reason he could not place.

"Then I will let you go. It will take all the time you have for Barnes to get you ready." Shaking her head, she frowned.

"Is there something wrong, Mother?" Starting up the stairs again, he came even with his mother.

"No, not precisely. I know Barnes is a good batman, but he is no earl's valet. Your brother's valet is still in our employ. It might be beneficial for you to consider the need to use an *actual* valet." Looking at her son who was now taller than her, she saw something in his face that made her backpedal. Shaking her head, she smiled again. "It was merely a passing thought. Pay me no head. Your silly mother is merely wanting the best for you."

"I will be down shortly, Mother," Theodore assured her with a hard smile as he headed up the rest of the stairs. He did not quite understand his mother, but at least she seemed to be trying lately. He was going to do his best to help her through this hard time, even if they did not always get along.

Changing into the clothes that Barnes had set out for him, Theodore let out a sigh of frustration. Making and receiving rounds of calls was always a chore for him, despite its importance in London society. He would much rather be doing something of substance. His mind wandered as Barnes worked on his cravat. He couldn't help but think about his brother's friendship with this Lord Talbot. Was it possible his brother had close friends he was completely unaware of? He had often spent his time away from London. His brother, on the other hand, spent most of his time in the metropolis. Thinking about it made him miss Cedric more. He had spent so much time away from him when he did not have to, time he would never get back.

Looking in the mirror, Theodore squared his shoulders and yanked on his waistcoat. He had avoided his brother when he had avoided London. Maybe he could feel closer to him by following in his footsteps and upholding the things that Cedric had held dear.

His decision made, he nodded to himself in the mirror before turning to leave. He would not fall into the pattern of continued avoidance as he had before. Just because he found sipping tea in parlors while listening to gossip distasteful, he would not shy away from it. He had been raised to be a man of duty, and this was just a different form of duty. He would do what he had to represent his brother and follow where Cedric once led.

***

THEODORE QUICKLY FOUND HIS earlier resolve weakening. Despite feeling disgusted, he kept his lips sealed tightly, refusing to show any signs of discomfort. The evening was ceaseless, but he would not show his distaste for the men in the room around him. How could his brother have liked any of these people? They were all in a study of some sort, drinking port and talking mostly about their courtesans or mistresses or hounds.

How did people talk of nothing for so long? At least when they had spoken of horses for a moment, he had hoped things would turn in a better direction. But that had only led to talk of gambling and jokes, not the beautiful animals they apparently disdained.

"Have you seen the latest batch?" One of the gentlemen across from Theodore spoke directly to him, which had not happened much that night.

"Batch? I'm afraid I do not know what you are talking about." Theodore's response held a hint of frustration. The night had been a trial for him.

"The debutantes. This season has a few diamonds who have already been determined. There are several worth the chase, and maybe one or two worth catching." The man's grin was wide, and his eyes were glassy.

"I do not believe that is a subject we should discuss over port and cigars, if at all." Theodore's voice was hard. Looking at the man, he tried to remember his name, but could only recall that it started with a B. It was no matter; it was not as if he wanted to become friends with the fellow.

He knew how young bucks like the one across from him thought and talked. Not the sort of man Theodore wanted to spend his time with. Despite that, here he was stuck in a room with the man and his friends. Regardless of his inner criticisms, Theodore made a deliberate choice to carry himself with grace and politeness, even in the face of frustration. That said, he would not contribute to their inane behavior.

"The new Lord Matlock is not your type of chap, Bertrum. He is just as stuffy as his brother." This came from the man sitting next to Bertrum, though he did not appear as intoxicated.

"I had been told the people at this gathering knew my brother, yet this is the first any of you have spoken of him. I was uncertain if my information was correct." Theodore watched as everyone glanced furtively at one another.

"Your brother was a good man. We will miss him. When he came, he spent most of his time with the older generation speaking about various political issues. My father and Bertram's father are both at another gathering tonight." The man in the bottle-green jacket spoke up. "You have actually caught us on an unusual evening."

The silence was awkward until someone suggested they should return and rejoin the ladies. Upon their return, the ladies proceeded to fill the rest of the night with musical ballads. Theodore had to admit that he enjoyed listening to the music much more than he had enjoyed the port and talk with the gentlemen. None of the ladies who performed were half as good as Georgiana, Mary, or Catherine, but what could he expect?

***

"I ENJOYED LAST NIGHT. Mrs. Talbot is always having the best dinners. Her French chef is superb. I heard that several families were attempting to steal him from her, but none have succeeded yet." His mother stopped to take a bite of food from her plate. "It makes me wonder just how much they must be paying to keep him." Despite their late return the night before, she appeared energized this morning.

Theodore was not at all rested. His nights continued to be a struggle, and last night he had become preoccupied with the thought of his brother spending his time with men like that. Had Cedric really ignored their crass behavior, opting to speak with their fathers instead? Or had his brother not really gone to evenings like that? Or worse, did he go to evenings like the night before because being seen at the dinners hosted by the Talbots was so important to the society he was trying to impress? Theodore was having trouble wrapping his head around what his brother had been doing with his time. "I am happy that you enjoyed yourself, Mother. Though I would never trade Mrs. Goodwin for a million French chefs."

Lady Matlock beamed as if she had accomplished some impressive feat. "Thank you, you are a dear boy. I have managed an invitation to the dinner being held by Lord Hillson tomorrow night."

Another dinner so soon? Eyes widening, Theodore swallowed his food before speaking. "I had made plans with Darcy that evening. With the three ladies out for the season, I have been helping him keep an eye on things."

"You have too little confidence in Darcy. He is more than capable of watching those girls, or at least he should be. Besides, his wife will be there." His mother moved to spread some jam on her toast and took a small bite. "Such a daring woman as Mrs. Darcy would never let someone get away with something regarding her sisters."

"I know they are capable, however—"

His mother clapped her hands in joy, effectively cutting off the rest of his response. "Then it is settled! You will come with me to the dinner. I knew you would not want to make me look so foolish as to go back on my word. They are expecting you, you know."

Theodore sighed with the knowledge that his mother had him cornered. "I am going to the opera with them this evening. I suppose I can tell Darcy then that I cannot attend with him tomorrow."

"They are quite fond of the opera. I have never been fond of all the odd singing; however, it is a splendid place to be seen, especially as they have their own box," his mother mused. "Your brother was always such a slave to his schedule that he rarely had the opportunity to indulge in things like the opera."

Theodore paused at that comment, his fork in the middle of stabbing some of the delicious ham on his plate. He had gone to the opera with his brother often. Though he avoided town often whenever he was home, he had gone to clubs on occasion, but they spent most of their time together at the symphony and opera. There were even a few intellectual dinners. His memories of his brother seemed to differ greatly from the reality his mother was presenting. "I went to the opera several times with him this season before he died, Mother."

"He always enjoyed indulging you. Putting aside his responsibilities so that he could spend time with you and Darcy when you were in town was so very nice of him, wasn't it?" Offering a sweet smile, she took another bite of marmalade toast.

Theodore did not know what to say to his mother's remark. His brother never hinted at neglecting any responsibilities for him. The overwhelming feeling of love for his brother caused Theodore's heart to expand, yet the notion that Cedric would put aside his other commitments for their shared moments together was a heavy burden on him. "Cedric never let me know about any responsibilities that I was keeping him from."

"That was just like him. He was such a kind man, and you are becoming so like him. I am proud of how far you have come in such a short time. Being willing to take up the mantle of responsibility means a lot to me." She gave a tremulous smile before focusing on her meal.

***

LOOKING AROUND THE OPULENT room full of well-dressed people eager to be seen at the opera, Theodore rubbed his eyebrow. He wondered what percentage of the people present had actually come to enjoy the drama on stage. Like most intermissions at the opera or theater, the atmosphere was dominated by large and pretentious crowds, their presence impossible to ignore. Glancing back at Darcy and noting his darting gaze, Theodore frowned. His cousin still could not handle large crowds easily, and he felt even guiltier now for leaving Darcy to accompany his mother. "I am sorry that I will not be there tomorrow, Darcy." Moving further through the crowed they finally made it to the line for refreshments.

"I hate to see you doing so much that you do not enjoy," Darcy commented.

"I had not realized how much Cedric did until Mother informed me. Taking up his responsibilities has taken some getting used to, and I'm still trying to figure everything out."

"You have done an admirable job taking over Cedric's responsibilities. You took the time to reach out to all the stewards and are staying on top of issues as they arise. Your finances are in better order than most people's." Darcy shook his head, his eyebrows drawn together in a tight furrow. "I do not know what else there could be that you are worried about."

"I honestly cannot get used to all the gatherings. Mother explained to me that Cedric kept up a busy social life so that he could make the right connections for getting things passed in parliament." That was a long conversation he did not relish repeating. He simply did not understand why he must spend so much time with inane fools.

"You want to take Cedric's seat in parliament? I had no idea that was something you had wanted to do." Darcy squinted at Theodore. "Why has this not come up before now?"

"I have never wanted to take part in parliament, but how else can I continue Cedric's fight? Though I didn't spend enough time with him while he was alive, I'll honor his memory by working toward his goal." Theodore tried to smile as he spoke, but he knew he failed miserably. Swallowing hard, he tried to remain positive.

Darcy began to speak but was cut off as they reached the front of the line. They efficiently got their drinks and requested a footman to assist them in carrying everything back to the box. It did not take too long for them to return to the box where all the ladies were and passed out all the drinks.

"Did you enjoy the first half of the opera, Lydia?" This came from Mary, who sat next to her.

"I know it is wrong of me to admit, but I am not as skilled at Italian as I am in some of the other languages we learned. Despite that, I have been enjoying the energy and costumes. Now Georgiana," Lydia said with a grin, "I know enjoyed the music. I could see her fingers moving with the pieces."

Georgiana blushed at being caught. "I had not realized that I had been doing that. But the music is simply splendid."

"I wonder if the sheet music is available. Maybe we should look for it next time we go shopping, Georgiana," Mary said to Georgiana, who seemed to light up at the suggestion.

Theodore looked around the box, enjoying the soothing atmosphere. He knew that many, if not all, of the single men he had met at his mother's dinners would find an evening with so many unattached females a waste of their time. Was it a commentary on their narrow mindedness or the fact that most single young women had been trained to become nothing but vapid parrots? Regardless, Theodore found spending time with them all more than worth his time.

Darcy and Elizabeth were speaking softly in the corner, their love obvious for anyone with eyes to see. All the ladies were chatting, and Mrs. Ansley was watching them indulgently from where she sat. The topics that evening had covered music, dead languages, and, oddly enough, sheep. Elizabeth and Darcy were considering introducing a new breed of sheep at Pemberley. They had hopes it might create a healthier crossbreed with more luxurious wool. If only Theodore could spend all his evenings in such enjoyable pursuits.

"What do you think of the opera, Colonel?" Miss Catherine spoke up from where she stood at his elbow.

Theodore's eyes widened at her comment. He had not realized that she had approached him. Her pale blue dress was almost an ethereal gray in the dim lighting. The dress draped beautifully on her, accentuating her figure flawlessly. She was everything that was lovely, and it left him feeling confused. When did she stop looking like an awkward teenager and start looking like a poised woman? "I liked it better than some of the others I have seen. I do not care for the ones with battles scenes."

"I can imagine that having experienced battle yourself it is neither an accurate portrayal nor a comfortable reminder of your experiences." Miss Catherine's countenance reflected her concern.

"It is rather uncomfortable at times," Theodore agreed. It was not always easy to see the depictions of battle. Memories already haunted him. He did not need the blatant reminders.

She reached out and gently squeezed his arm, providing a comforting touch. "I understand that you have William to talk to, but if you ever need to share your experiences, I'm here to listen." Offering a small smile, she continued, "I am sure, however, that you wish to talk about lighter things tonight. Have you decided which of your estates you would like to visit first?"

Theodore briefly contemplated the fact that he could feel the warmth of Catherine's touch through his sleeve. Blinking, he stared at where her hand had briefly rested on his arm, before refocusing on what she had said. "There are so many. My brother rarely spent any significant time at his estates besides Matlock. I would like to see each of them. One thing Darcy said that I believe to be true is it is advisable to see the properties yourself. Even if I trust the stewards to send me complete reports on the conditions of the estates, it cannot replace seeing it with my own eyes."

Head tilted toward him, Miss Catherine's sea-green eyes glowed with interest. "I believe you are quite correct. There is also the fact that what you might find important may not be what your stewards deem worthy of mentioning."

"What do you mean?" Theodore knew that before they escaped their father's tyranny, the Bennet ladies had taken quite an interest in the management of Longbourn. He was, however, uncertain how involved each of the sisters were. Elizabeth had been quite the driving force and had taken on Pemberley with grace and determination. But was Miss Catherine just as involved?

"Well, for example, your steward may be focused on profits and the home farm or the state of the mansion's roof. I, on the other hand would want to know how the tenants are faring. I am much more concerned about their roofs than that of a large old building that is left empty most of the time."

Theodore took in what Catherine said with delight. So many of the people he had been meeting through his mother would never care for the situation of the tenant cottages. The consideration she showed for his dependents warmed his heart. "And that is exactly why I think I want to visit each of them. Though I think I would like to see the Scotland property the most because of the views. I have thought about traveling to each of them in turn depending on weather and how long it will take to get to each one." Theodore considered what it would be like to have Miss Catherine accompany him to offer her thoughts on the state of each property, but quickly dismissed the impossible notion. "The only way I can manage it without becoming overwhelmed, I think is by going about it in an orderly fashion."

Pressing her lips, Catherine tilted her head inquisitively. "How many estates are there?"

Theodore scratched the back of his head, a sheepish grin spreading across his face. "Five, I think."

"You think?" Catherine looked at him wide eyed.

"Well, it seems my brother had a habit of purchasing estates when people had the misfortune of going into debt and mismanaging them. After he acquired them, he tasked one of his under-stewards with upgrading their management, and they have all since become profitable. I have found evidence of five estates, but that does not mean it is not possible for me to find evidence of another somewhere at Matlock. My mother has been of no help in that regard."

"I have found that most of the young women I have met this season are similar. Only concerned with the fact that they can get the latest fashion and best lace, they care not where the money comes from to obtain it." A delicate roll of her eyes punctuated her level of disgust. Then, brightening, she grinned unabashedly. "I am looking forward to having you at the ball tomorrow. At least with you there, I will be able to have at least one intelligent conversation."

Biting his lip, Theodore managed to look abashed. "I will not be able to attend with you after all. My mother requested my attendance at dinner. Apparently, it is yet another dinner that I must attend if I am to uphold Cedric's goals. I am sure with your sisters and Georgiana there you will be able to have more than enough intelligent conversation."

Theodore watched as Catherine seemed to deflate, wilting before his very eyes. Her rapid blinking stood in stark contrast to how completely her face went slack. He had never anticipated her really caring one way or another if he was present.

Miss Catherine's response was cut off by the signal that the second act was starting, and she headed over to her seat with her sisters. The second half of the opera found Theodore distracted. The speed at which Miss Catherine lost her smile was so sudden and drastic that it stuck with him. She now seemed to wear a carefully crafted mask of neutrality. It was almost as if his presence at the ball was something that would have made her happy and he had deprived her of it. Did she enjoy their time together that much?

Chapter Eight

THE SPARKLE THE NIGHT once held was gone, and Catherine was afraid to admit why. Oh, the decorations were fine enough, though there were more flowers, candles, and mirrors than she would have preferred. Though compared to the opera the night before, it was all flat and frustrating. Without a dance with Theodore to look forward to, it was just another ball filled with more dancing and dull conversations. Any time she tried to delve into meaningful subjects like tenant welfare or philanthropy, she was met with puzzled expressions.

In a room full of happy dancing people, she felt lonely. Glancing around the ballroom, she had to remind herself to keep the smile on her face. Was this why so many of the debutantes she met seemed to lack any depth? Had they all lost their minds from boredom?

The idea crossed Catherine's mind that if she had only lace and officers in her head, it might have made an impression on her. Nonetheless, she believed she had more substance than that. Her mind was full of paint and stillroom recipes and the families at Pemberley that needed quilts. That was probably why all the talk of fashion made her want to scream.

"...and that is why we chose the other modiste, because really, who can shop somewhere with such a decided lack of quality?" The nasally voice of Miss Ranken finally finished the story.

Catherine looked around the circle of debutantes all dressed in a similar fashion and all seemingly enthralled in what she considered a meaningless conversation. For the life of her, she could not remember the short blonde's name. The best she could recall was that the woman was friends with Miss Mathilde, who was wearing a white dress with peach ribbons. Despite their friendships, however, the three young women all seemed to be vying for position in the group.

Miss Mathilde's friend nodded eagerly, causing the feathers on her turban to flutter. "It was a good choice, Miss Ranken. Mrs. Bell, if you can get in, is the very best."

When the conversation turned to the best shade of peach one should choose, Catherine could take the banality no longer. She couldn't muster any enthusiasm for apricot, peach, or salmon anymore and if they discussed one more color, she would scream. She spotted Elizabeth standing by the wall talking with Georgiana and saw a way out of her predicament. "Well, it has been lovely, but I see my sister signaling at me and I must go." With a quick curtsy, she walked gracefully away from the group.

Heading to her sisters, she became lost in thought. Was every ball destined to be so tedious? Or did Theodore's absence really change her night that much? Catherine was so consumed by her thoughts that she bumped into someone. "Oh, I am so sorry. I do not know where my mind was at."

"It was nothing—oh, Miss Catherine!" Miss Burgess smiled widely at Catherine as she recognized who had bumped into her.

"Miss Burgess, it is a pleasure to see you! Did you receive the note I sent you?" Catherine had enjoyed speaking with Selene and had invited her to tea the following week. She hoped the season wouldn't be so bad if she could make a friend.

"Yes, I did. I was going to send my response in the morning. Joining you for tea sounds like a delightful idea." Miss Burgess's eyes crinkled as she spoke and in one moment showed more genuine emotion than most people in the ballroom would exhibit all night. "How are you enjoying your evening?"

"I must admit I am finding the season less to my taste than I would have hoped. Though I have enjoyed the theater, and the opera last night was quite lovely." Though she managed not to frown, Catherine could not quite hide her distaste for the marriage mart events.

"Yes, after a while, it all becomes more of the same. I know how you feel. It is my third season, after all. Though at least being here for the season means we can attend the museum and the opera."

"I cannot imagine doing this year after year." Catherine kept her voice to a mere whisper. It would not do to insult the hostess or the Almack patroness who happened to be there that evening.

"No, you really can't." Miss Burgess maintained her smile, but her wide eyes conveyed she was as pleased as Catherine would be.

Catherine nearly burst out laughing at her expression and sentiments but contained her mirth. The rules of society said you never laughed like that in a ballroom. One may titter or possibly even giggle behind her fan quietly when no one was watching, but that was as far as you could go. "Oh, you poor dear, let me bring you over to my sisters so that we may commiserate with you."

"I would not have assumed that Miss Lydia was out already," Miss Burgess admitted, looking around as if trying to spot Catherine's youngest sister.

Shaking her head, Catherine linked arms with Miss Burgess. "She is not, but I have five sisters and three of them are here tonight."

"Oh my. I had a much older sister who passed a few years ago, and I've always wished for a sister closer to me in age, but *five*?"

This time, Catherine allowed a small laugh to escape. "Yes, I certainly have a surfeit of sisters. You may barrow one if you wish on occasion, as I have plenty to spare." With the way they were getting along so well, Catherine couldn't wait to introduce Miss Burgess to her sisters. She had a feeling that they would hit it off right away.

***

ARRANGING THE PILLOWS ON the settee for what was probably the fourth time, Catherine huffed in frustration. She was hardly ever this nervous, but Elizabeth had said she could preside over the tea as it was her friend they had invited. She wanted everything to be perfect. Gaining friends was hard for Catherine. For so long, she had tried to always blend into the background, letting others speak for her.

She had since found her voice, but that did not mean she was always ready to plunge forward, as some of her sisters did. Elizabeth and Lydia were both the sort to jump in feetfirst and hang the consequences. Catherine did not think she was born with such flair.

Catherine had resisted the urge to do a little dance when Miss Burgess agreed to come to tea. She would enjoy having someone who she could talk with at the balls and whatnot. She had her sisters, but it would be nice to have her own friend—someone to talk with without watching what she said so strictly or having to watch her back. Debutantes could be so catty.

"Everything will go splendidly; you do not have to worry so."

Catherine was startled by Mary's voice coming from the doorway behind her. Dropping the pillow in her hands, she swirled around to see Mary smiling kindly at her. "Only recently did I realize that I have always looked to you or Elizabeth or Jane or Mama to take the lead in social endeavors. But I have to do this on my own eventually, and I suppose now is the best time to start. Miss Burgess has earned my respect, and I want to make sure that I perform this task adequately." With a small smile, Catherine gathered the courage to voice her hope. "I feel that we have the potential to be friends."

***

MARY WATCHED CATHERINE INTERACT with Miss Burgess, who had given them all permission to call her by her given name, Selene. She wished she had seen Catherine's need for friends sooner. They had all been so relieved when Catherine had begun to come out of her shell after the whole debacle with Wickham. She had come a long way, but it had never occurred to her that Catherine rarely attempted to make friends. She spoke more often and interacted more freely when at gatherings, but she was never the one to start anything. Here she was hosting a tea and making friends. Mary was so proud of how far she had come.

"So, you have another sister who is not in London for the season?" Selene's kind voice flowed effortlessly, and she wore a warm smile as she addressed the ladies present.

Nodding, Lizzie responded. "Yes, Jane only recently left childbed, and is at her estate in the country."

Selene started to stir her tea contemplatively, as if judging whether to something. "I am glad she came through the ordeal well. So many do not make it through. We lost my older sister when she was brought to childbed too early."

"I know you mentioned losing your sister at the ball, but I did not want to force you to elaborate in such a setting." Catherine said, placing a comforting hand on Selene's shoulder. "Would you like to talk about it?

Eyes misty, Selene seemed to remember a not-so-distant pain. "It was not a very resent loss, but still only a few years ago. Her babe survived, so at least that is something. I have only had the opportunity to see her a handful of times, but she was a marvelous little thing."

"All babies find a way to be marvelous, though some struggle with it more than others." Lydia smiled widely as she spoke from her spot next to Mrs. Ansley. Though she was not out, she had been allowed to attend. At seventeen, she would be out the next season and would do better for the practice.

Her sisters well knew Lydia's love for babies, and they smiled at her comment. The last couple of years had been marked by a series of births in the family, which had left Lydia feeling thrilled beyond words. Mary looked at her youngest sister and couldn't help but think that Lydia's true contentment lay in being surrounded by babies. She would not put it past Lydia to marry a widower just because he had children she could love.

"In her last letter, Jane said things are going well and little Charlie is growing at a remarkable rate. While she is not fully back to her old self, she has every confidence in her complete recovery." Lizzie seemed to want to reassure those in the room that Jane was fine.

"Do you ladies mind sharing some of your treats?" That voice came from William as he peeked his head into the room. Walking over to his wife, his eyes softened as he gazed upon her lovingly.

Mary loved seeing the happiness that they still brought each other. She suspected her sisters felt the same for it meant the rest of them could hope for such love in their own unions.

"I am sure Catherine arranged for more than enough." Lizzie gazed up at her husband with just as much love. If Selene was not there, Mary knew she would have told him he could have the treats in exchange for a kiss.

"Is there enough for two?" The colonel's voice came from the doorway.

"Colonel Theodore, I did not know you would be visiting today. Please join us." Catherine stood to greet him and gestured him over to an empty chair near where she had been sitting. "Would you like tea?"

"If you do not mind us complicating your tea, a break would be nice. Going over ledgers has proven more taxing than marching through the mud on a summer campaign." The colonel sat, revealing his gratitude with a soft smile. "Hello Miss Burgess, you seem to be fitting in well with everyone. What do you think of the company of so many sisters?"

Mary let the conversation wash over her as she focused on the new development unfolding in front of her. As the conversation continued, both Catherine and the colonel continued to glance at one another. They attempted to be surreptitious, but if you watched them both, it became obvious. Smiling to herself, Mary decided she would not interfere, but instead wait and see if it developed further.

***

CATHERINE ROSE TO SERVE tea to the two gentlemen. Despite knowing how they both took their tea, she struggled to keep her hands steady as she prepared it. Seeing Theodore suddenly at the door had unnerved her. She had to clench her hands to get them under control. Handing William his cup, she moved on to making a cup for the colonel.

The act of handing him his tea almost scalded her. His touch was electric, sending a wave of heat through her body as she held the teacup steady. His hand enveloped her own when he took the teacup, and she had somehow felt it down to her core. Sitting down, she placed her hand over her heart, willing it to settle. Chastising herself for becoming distracted, she forced her mind to the conversation. She would think about her reaction at a later time, when she was alone. When Catherine could finally pay attention, Lizzie was speaking to Theodore.

"How do you find the ledgers? I know paperwork is not something you exactly enjoy. Was everything in order?" Speaking from where she was snuggled into William's side, Lizzie questioned Theodore. Catherine knew her sister was always delighted to have her husband with her, even though society did not fully approve of their constant need for touch.

With a wry smile, Theodore reached for a tiny scone. "I was just reviewing a few things with Darcy."

"I am surprised that Cedric did not have a man of business who handled things," Mary chimed in.

Theodore took a sip of his tea to wash down one of the scones before responding. "He had someone who handled business ventures who I have been in contact with, but it seems that he handled a lot of things himself."

"I can attest to how difficult it can be to take over things when you suddenly inherit, and Theodore has done remarkably well." William spoke fondly of his cousin's efforts, smiling at the man he had always been close friends with.

Catherine had been watching Theodore and noted how uncomfortable he seemed. Rubbing at his eyebrow, he stared down at his teacup, his lips curved downward instead of the usual easy smile he wore when conversing with the group. Was he embarrassed by the attention he was getting? Or perhaps he did not enjoy the reminder of his brother's death? Catherine felt the need to reach out to him, but instead decided it might be best to divert everyone's attention. "I am sure that you did not come in here to talk of business matters. I suggest a change of subject. There's talk of a new music repository being built on Bond Street. What are your thoughts?"

Theodore looked up when she changed the topic, and their eyes locked. Had he realized that she changed the topic for him? Would he be offended or grateful? Catherine gave him a fleeting smile and was relieved to see him smile in return. Blushing, she glanced away. It would be best if she was not spotted pining after him. What was she thinking?

Georgiana was always eager to discuss music and took up the topic change swiftly. "I am glad of any opportunity to peruse sheet music. I spend so much time practicing that I always enjoy obtaining new pieces."

"I wonder if the increased competition will affect the prices of the sheet music," Mary commented, looking at the practical side of things.

Not wanting to leave Selene out of the conversation, Catherine looked over at her once more. When she spotted her looking at Colonel Theodore, Catherine blinked twice in surprise. Was Selene fond of Theodore? It had never occurred to her that Selene might have feelings for him. Why did that possibility leave a strange ache in her chest? "Selene, do you enjoy playing an instrument? Would you be just as eager to have a new place to shop for sheet music?"

Wrinkling her nose, Selene shook her head in denial. "While I enjoy listening to the piano, I never could master it. I have attempted the harp but find myself not much better at it than the piano. That does not deprive me of enjoying the symphony and the opera. I attend both whenever I can convince my brother to take me."

"We must go together sometime. I hear they will do a new play in the next week or two. Do you have any plans to attend?"

The conversation continued to flow easily, calming her nerves, even though she thought she felt the colonel's eyes on her more than once. Overall, Catherine believed the tea with Selene to be a success, despite the weight of uncertainty that had settled in her stomach.

***

THE TINGLE IN HIS hand persisted, keeping Theodore's thoughts on his interaction with her despite having left the room and Miss Catherine behind some time before. She was a girl, and his cousin's sister-in-law. What was wrong with him? He couldn't possibly be considering Miss Catherine in a romantic manner.

He was certainly not looking at Miss Catherine as if she were an attractive woman who had drawn his attention. The fine tremor in his hand didn't escape his attention as he headed to Matlock House. Could his constant lack of sleep be causing this?

She had noted his discomfort and changed the subject. While he was grateful they no longer had to talk about estate matters, what affected him more was that somehow, she knew. While he loved Darcy like a brother, his commendation made him uncomfortable. She had realized that he was not comfortable and changed the subject. Was he really that transparent, or was it something else?

Their eyes had met, and that brief moment had made his heart thud uncomfortably. Her small smile filled him with reassurance, but then her blush filled him with heat. He was not so green that he did not know what he was feeling, but why was he so attracted to her? The changing of the seasons marked each new romantic endeavor for some, but that was not his style. He certainly was not like Bingley, who had spotted a new angel at every ball.

Refusing to admit what his heart whispered was true, Theodore rushed up the stairs to his townhouse. The door was swiftly opened as if by magic and he greeted the footman. Feeling the need for some exertion, he went to his room and looked for Barnes. What he needed was a trip to Gentlemen Jack's, to get his blood flowing and his mind moving in another direction.

***

THAT NIGHT, AS SHE lay in bed, Catherine stared at the ceiling trying to make sense of everything. The day had created a constant stream of questions that were swirling through her head. Well, mostly she questioned what had happened once Theodore had walked into the room. That was when what she could best describe as electricity had started. She had never felt anything like it before—the heat that surged through her when their hands met.

It was much more pleasant than the feeling that had followed—the hollow pain in her chest when she saw Selene looking at Theodore. Thinking about that had been her last clue. Her heart ached, and she knew it was a sign of the feelings she was developing for him.

It had taken a moment for her to admit it to herself, to even accept the possibility that she might be falling in love. The very notion that she might be losing her heart to Theodore had seemed ridiculous at first, but as she recalled each of their interactions, she realized with a sinking feeling that it might not be so impossible after all.

She tried to search her mind for the day, or the hour, that it had started. Love had already taken root before she had a chance to fully comprehend it. She had never dreamed that the beginnings of love would make her feel this way, or that it would destroy her so entirely.

She knew in her heart that her affection could never be reciprocated, and the realization was devastating. The contrast between the richness of his life and the emptiness of hers was stark. He had been places and seen things that would affect him for the rest of life. She was trapped in the world of debutantes, where every day was filled with dances, teas, and mind-numbing small talk. He would never see her as more than a girl.

What frightened her even more was the possibility of being caught in a hopeless case of puppy love. She would have to find a way to keep anyone from finding out. Her heart shuddered in her chest as she tried to find a way to lock her feelings down. The idea of seeing him again without giving away her emotions and making a fool of herself weighed heavily on her mind.

She would have to be polite and keep things light—nothing that would give her away. She could do it...maybe. If everything went according to plan, these sentiments would surely diminish as time passed, and then she could concentrate on surviving the season.

Chapter Nine

There was less of a spring in his step when he returned home than earlier in the day, but Theodore felt good for it. He was an active man, or had been for much of his life. Daily riding his horse or marching beside him took much more energy than sitting at a desk and reviewing papers and proposals. Slugging it out with other gentlemen was not something he did often, but he was grateful for the exercise. He was weary, but the exertion of it had helped settle him.

The same footman opened the door, and Theodore idly wondered how long the footman had to stand at attention by the door. He knew it was somewhat of a sought-after position, but he certainly could not just stand there for hours on end. Tucking the thought away to investigate at a later time, he trudged up the stairs to clean up. He was sweaty and would need to make himself presentable for whatever had been planned for the evening.

"Theodore, what has happened to you? You look like you've been dragged through a hedge backwards!"

Theodore looked up to spot his mother coming out of the sitting room. The tone of her voice caused him to wince, and he briefly wondered whether all mothers had the power to use that particular tone or if his was just a special case. "Good afternoon, Mother. I have been at Jack's and was just going up to clean up."

Coming closer, she looked him over like a general inspecting his troops. "I will never understand why gentlemen feel the need to bash one another about. Well, at least you have not bruised your face," she sighed. "We have been invited to dine with the Cabots this evening and I know you will try to look presentable. It's essential to represent the family well, and with several important figures present, it's even more crucial tonight."

Fighting the urge to squirm under her scrutiny, Theodore attempted to settle himself in for a conversation with his mother. He had not been this thoroughly inspected since he was a fresh recruit. While he had been happy enough that she was finally showing him interest, it was quite unsettling. She always seemed to have an explanation for why they had to attend yet another gathering. He could ignore her, he supposed, but he was at a loss as to what an earl's obligations were. She had a better understanding of how these things worked than he did. "I thought we attended the dinner you had been invited to a few nights ago."

Finally, turning away from him, his mother moved to rearrange a vase of flowers. Once she was satisfied with the arrangement, she turned back to him and smiled. "You have done *so* well upholding Cedric's position that we are being invited to even more dinners with more important families. It is vital to be seen attending all the right dinners if you are to have any hope of accomplishing even a fraction of what Cedric was attempting to do," his mother explained, studying his appearance once more. "Do not worry, they won't all be dinners. There will be several musical evenings."

Rubbing at the eyebrow that seemed to have developed a twitch behind it, Theodore considered his mother's plans. The use of the word *several* left him feeling uncertain, prompting him to question her. "Just how many dinners and musical events are we talking about?"

"Oh, I don't know, several a week? No more than four." His mother made a dismissive gesture with her hand. Then reaching into her reticule that hung at her wrist, she pulled out a folded slip of paper.

Running his hand through his hair, Theodore looked at the extensive list of events his mother wanted him to attend with her and sighed. "Mother, I do not quite understand why you are so insistent on all of these dinners with people I have nothing in common with."

"If only you had taken the time to understand your brother's methods for getting his bills passed, you would have a better understanding. Being successful in politics involves not only speaking in parliament but also socializing with the people and gaining their support." With a sniff, she turned away from him, and her shoulders slumped as she continued speaking listlessly. "It is what Cedric devoted his life to and you do not know, cannot comprehend. It is so sad that his legacy will be forgotten."

The thought of having to be social to gain the favor of those his mother wanted him to spend time with made Theodore slightly sick to his stomach. In talking to those people, he had learned that for the most part they were self-centered and unaware of the genuine problems in the world. Had Cedric truly spent his time with them trying to gain their votes? Moving forward, he placed his hand on her shoulder. "Mother, I will do whatever it takes to carry on Cedric's legacy of kindness and generosity. His memory will be cherished by both of us and all those who loved him dearly."

"Hearing you say that makes me so happy." His mother beamed at him.

Feeling compelled to at least commit some of his time to enjoyable pursuits, Theodore could not help but wonder about having time for himself. It seemed like his opportunities to just *be* were slipping away. "When will I have time to do anything for myself? I would like to spend time with people I enjoy talking to. Or possibly have an evening at home reading some of the books Darcy has suggested."

His mother recoiled as if he'd struck her. "Why you would do anything else I do not know. Do you know what most people would give to get into one of these dinners? And here you are being *invited*. Besides, a true gentleman does not need to read as excessively as your cousin Darcy does. *True* society doesn't hold such a dull hobby like reading in high regard."

"The books he has suggested I review are on estate management and crop rotation. Nothing frivolous, I assure you." Theodore was not going to say anything about the book he had been trying to finish called *L'Art de la Guerre*, or roughly translated into English, *The Art of War*.

"A true gentleman lets his stewards, and his people, do that kind of reading. You do not need to bother yourself with it. Learn to enjoy the good life you have access to now." His mother reached out to pat his shoulder, though the gesture left him feeling hollow.

Refusing to comment on the fact that her ideas continued to neglect his own hopes and desires, Theodore opted to point out that he was still standing there covered in sweat. Maybe that would get him a few moments of peace before he had to go to yet another one of these social events. "Mother, I really must get clean of all this sweat. If I am to be made presentable for your dinner tonight, I must see about bathing." Moving towards the stairs, Theodore slowly made his escape.

"Go freshen up, put on something refined, and maybe have your batman help you tie your cravat properly tonight. Wearing the same knot all the time will simply not do. If he does not know how, Timmins is still here and he can show him. Your brother always had the best cravat styles." His mother continued to call after him as he climbed the stairs. Theodore ran a hand down his face, dreading what was inevitably going to be a long night.

***

It was staring at him—a hare that someone had obviously worked very hard on. The creature's head and paws were still covered in soft, thick fur while the rest of its body had been reduced to a pile of carved meat. The creature's ears stood erect, as if sensing an impending danger, while its unblinking gaze remained fixed, leaving Theodore unsettled. It was disconcerting to say the least.

He liked rabbit. Truly, he did. He had eaten plenty of rabbit on campaign, but it never looked at him quite like this one did. Who wanted to eat like this? He had some boiled potatoes, which were quite good, but most everything else was far too complicated for his tastes. Pushing his plate back, he resigned himself to eating something more substantial once he got home.

He could not even settle into a pleasant conversation because he was seated between Lady Lavinia and Mrs. Meadowbrook. Someone might just be plotting his demise. Between the staring hare and the simpering ladies, his night could not get any worse. Theodore looked down the table at the prattling groups and wished he was nearly anywhere else.

"So, Lord Matlock, I was told that you fought in France before leaving the regulars." Lady Lavinia had taken a measly three bites and put her silverware down.

Theodore looked at her abandoned silverware for a moment before responding. Did she only plan on eating three bites, or did she also find the hare disturbing? "Yes, Lady Lavinia. I fought both in France and Spain before being wounded and coming home."

"I was always fond of the uniform of the regulars. I am sure you enjoyed wearing it." This came from Mrs. Meadowbrook.

What did one say to that sort of comment? Did these ladies know nothing of the horrors of war besides the fashion that went along with it? "The uniform served me well enough, keeping me warm and dry as a uniform should."

Mrs. Meadowbrook seemed to be put off by his response. Turning to the gentleman seated on her other side, she started conversing with him. Theodore was fine with that, as it left him only having to converse with Lady Lavinia. He desperately searched for a topic of conversation that wouldn't bore them both to tears. "Lady Lavinia, have you read anything of interest lately?"

"While I keep up with the latest fashion magazines, I rarely spend my time reading." She sniffed, as if turning her nose up at the thought of reading.

So she was not a reader. What else they could safely discuss? "What do you enjoy doing while in London?"

"All the correct things, I suppose. Going on calls. Shopping on Bond Street. Attending dinners hosted by the right people. Occasionally I visit Hyde Park. Oh, and attending balls is always important."

What did the girl mean by all the *correct* things? "And do you enjoy those activities?"

Lady Lavinia, face pinched and drawn, looked at him as if he was being cruel or confusing. Did she think he was trying to catch her out? He felt like there was a game at play yet he did not know all the rules. He much preferred more straightforward talk.

Lady Lavinia bit her lip for the smallest fraction of a moment, but then schooled her features into a serene expression. "I am afraid I do not quite understand you."

Though he had preferred that one second of truth to everything else he saw that evening, Theodore felt bad for making her uneasy. Trying to set her more at ease, he changed tactics. "I merely wondered which you enjoyed the most. You listed quite a few things."

"Well then, I suppose I do not have a favorite among them. What do you enjoy, my lord?" Lady Lavinia smiled when things seemed to get back on track.

"I enjoy spending time with my cousin Darcy and his family, and a well-executed play at the theater is something I truly enjoy." Theodore returned her smile, but noted the conversation was cumbersome at best.

"I love the theater, as well. What plays do you enjoy? The comedies or the dramas?"

Theodore studied her expression. It seemed to be schooled to perfection, but there was something about it that did not ring true. Was she hesitant to share her preferences because she was waiting to see what he liked? Why could no one answer truthfully? Instead they felt the need to follow some odd, unspoken script that seemed to proclaim what the ton liked was best.

"I enjoy comedies more than the dramas." Taking a small sip of wine to fortify himself, Theodore bit back a sigh. He had been right before—it was going to be a long night.

***

LEANING BACK INTO THE cushion of the carriage, Theodore closed his eyes while his mother prattled on their way back to Matlock House. "I am glad you enjoyed yourself, Mother. It looks like you have several friends in that group."

"Oh, there were several ladies that I have known for simply ages. It is always lovely to chat with old friends. What did you think of your dining companions? I do not know Mrs. Meadowbrook very well, but her husband died in a hunting accident not long after she was married to him. This is her first season since she came out of mourning. And Lady Lavinia, of course, is always lovely. Always correct and proper and so very pretty." The shushing sound of Lady Matlock's fan filled the darkness as Theodore mulled over her choice of words.

Why were people in his mother's set so focused on that word? *Correct* seemed to be a code word for acceptable to a chosen view. Shaking his head in the dark, Theodore tried to point out yet again why he was not fond of these gatherings. "They were nice enough, though I was happy when the dinner was over. Lady Lavinia, for example, was so afraid of saying the wrong thing that she refused to express any opinion on anything at all."

"You are too harsh on the girl. She possesses a faultless sense of decorum."

Sighing, Theodore looked out the window and realized they were closer to home than he had assumed. Hopefully, this night would soon be over. "I fault the fact that I could not have a genuine conversation with her. I would rather she have been original or say something unfashionable in her speech than parrot everything." It was all just so superficial, and it left him wanting something real. The experience made him compare the people to the meal, which prioritized aesthetics over taste, leaving him desiring a humble, homemade creation.

In the darkness of the carriage, he could barely make out his mother as she rolled her eyes. "Why would you want her to say the wrong thing? You gentlemen are so nonsensical sometimes. I say she has the best manners I have ever seen in a debutante in an age."

"I fear we will not agree on this, Mother." Not bothering to wait for the footman to bring down the steps, he jumped out of the carriage and away from his mother. Though as much as he wished to escape, he refused to be rude. He waited and offered his arm to escort her into the house. Once they were inside, he moved to the stairs and in the direction of his room, but could hear her footsteps echoing behind him and paused. Turning to her, he bowed in her direction. "Goodnight, Mother."

***

DESPITE THE LATENESS OF the hour, Theodore's mind refused to shut down and allow him to sleep. Barnes had brought him tea and a hardy snack at his request, so he sat at his window munching while he looked over the dark landscape of the city.

Yanking at his cravat haphazardly, he allowed his mind to wander. He could not help but draw comparisons between Miss Catherine and Lady Lavinia. His mother was of the opinion that Lady Lavinia was a remarkable debutante, and yet he could not like her. He wondered if she even knew her own mind or if her own thoughts had been entirely trained out of her. Though Lady Lavinia was known for her pleasing looks, he found her uninteresting and dull.

Miss Catherine, however, was not a popular sort of woman. In a world obsessed with blonde hair, blue eyes, and an angelic disposition, she was out of place with her brown hair and sea-green eyes. Theodore had noted that her eyes seemed to sparkle with a thousand secrets, and it was only now that he admitted those sorts of thoughts were decidedly more than friendly.

He had tried to ignore his reaction to Miss Catherine while at the dinner, but now that he was back home, he could not avoid the memory of her blush. It haunted him. Could he really be falling in love with her? And if so, what was he to do about? Did he want to pursue Miss Catherine? Could she ever grow to like him in return?

His mother was always slightly disparaging of the Bennet ladies, Darcy too, for that matter, but he could not care. He had seen the happiness that Darcy had found with Elizabeth and wanted that for himself. The kind of relationship he desired was not something most society women were capable of providing, and he was aware of that. Most society women had internalized the belief that love and close relationships were a frivolous pursuit for those who lacked ambition. Was it possible that he could find what he wanted with Miss Catherine?

What actions could he take to make sense of the feelings that were growing between him and Miss Catherine? His mind turned to tactics. One always did better with more information and not less. He would have to spend more time with her to get the answers that he sought.

It was a pleasant prospect, and he was able to finish preparing for bed with unusual enthusiasm. For once, he seemed to have something to truly look forward to. In his dreams, he and Miss Catherine laughed and talked for hours, and in what seemed like the first night in forever, he slept peacefully.

Chapter Ten

THE TIMING OF CATHERINE'S inhale was quite unfortunate. She had just taken a bite of breakfast when Theodore entered the room, and her startled gasp firmly lodged the bite of bread firmly in her throat. Her eyes began to water, and her face grew hot with panic as she realized she could not breathe.

A hand grabbed Catherine, and she could feel the strong thuds on her back as they tried to dislodge the bread. Things had started to turn hazy, and her knees gave out. She was vaguely aware of an arm slipping around her waist, and then a sudden forceful blow to her back forcing the food from her throat.

Air rushed into her lungs and she coughed painfully, nearly gagging as she struggled to breathe. Her cheeks were stained with tears as she fought to regain control of her breathing, each breath shaky and uneven. Her eyes clenched tight as she focused only on the life-giving oxygen slipping into her abused lungs. Eventually she realized that she was being supported, cradled really, against a large warm chest and there was a comforting murmur in her ear.

"That's right, take slow breaths." Theodore's voice was a mere whisper, more to be felt than heard.

Catherine blinked several times, her eyes still hazy as she struggled to regain her bearings. Across the room she could see Lydia, Mary, and Georgiana, each face etched with worry. Looking down, she found an arm wrapped firmly around her waist. She was being held by Theodore. One of his hands was caressing her hair, soothing her as she trembled. Was it the lack of air making her feel this way, or just him? Either way, the electric tingle was back and stronger than ever. It radiated from every place he touched her and refused to be ignored. He had saved her life and held her to his chest, whispering to her soothingly. How would she ever be able to act unaffected around him now?

The moment passed too quickly, leaving a sense of longing. He took a step back and gently led her to a nearby chair. Crouching down in front of her, he stared into her eyes, seeming to search for something in their depths. "Are you well?"

If only his look meant what she hoped it would. Catherine's heart ached with the desire to have his love, but she forced herself to move on. She was a young woman with little to no connection to high society and he was a mature man who had just become an earl. It was not possible he would ever see her that way. She knew her hopes were naive and unattainable. She felt her face burn with humiliation, and her heart lurched in her chest. What must he think? "I am so embarrassed. I do not know how that happened." Her voice was a mere whisper and sounded odd to her own ears.

"Just so long as you are well." Theodore's response sounded hoarse and strained.

Catherine hesitated on hearing his voice, but she could not think too much about it before Elizabeth materialized and physically pushed him out of her way. Theodore moved to the side and allowed Elizabeth to embrace her. Catherine collapsed gratefully into her sister. As much as she cherished her time with Theodore, it proved overwhelming. Breathing in Elizabeth's familiar sent, Catherine soaked in the comfort that her sister had always brought to her.

Leaning back, Elizabeth smoothed Catherine's hair away from her face. "I thought we had lost you, sweet girl. You are not allowed to scare me like that again."

"I will try my best. It not an experience I want to repeat." As she looked up, Catherine saw Mary's reassuring smile as she handed her a steaming cup of tea. Taking it with a trembling hand, she smiled gratefully at her older sister. "Thank you, Mary."

Elizabeth smiled at Mary in gratitude as well and then, standing, she kissed Catherine on the head and nodded to the teacup. "You drink that and take a moment to gather yourself." Turning to Theodore, she smiled tearfully. "Thank you for your swift action in saving my sister. I am sure you had not intended for such excitement when you came calling this morning. Is there something we can help you with?"

"It wasn't possible for me to do anything else." Catherine could feel Theodore's eyes on her as he responded to her sister. "I had simply thought to come and see what you ladies were doing this morning. I wanted to break free from my mother's plans, if only for a moment."

Lydia giggled from where she sat, but there was a slight edge of hysteria in it, a lingering effect of the morning's dramatic events. "I do not think that you will want to join us today. We are shopping."

Mary went to sit next to her, wrapping her arm around the younger girl that had obviously been affected by the stress of the morning. "I am sure you will be welcome to accompany us if you want. We may have difficulty finding a hat that complements your outfit, however."

"That is a risk I will have to take. I'll have to rely on the possibility of stopping at a teahouse, as finding a hat to match my cravat seems unlikely."

"I think we have a wonderful morning planned," Lydia said, smiling. "Especially if you buy the biscuits."

Catherine smiled at the merriment, but under that she dreaded what was to come. She was barely holding it together. Being this close to him and knowing how hopeless her feelings were left her feeling close to tears. Standing up, she squeezed Lizzie's hand. "I am going to go wash my face and see about freshening up a bit before we go."

Maybe she could look at it as if she was practicing how to live her life without him? As she walked up the stairs, she absentmindedly ran her fingers through her hair, pulling out the loose pins. Keeping her hands busy did not help the fact that she still felt the warmth of his embrace and the strength of his arms as he held her steady. How could she live the rest of her life without that incredible feeling and still find joy?

***

Pretending to shop for the perfect capote bonnet was not so very hard. She had spent many convivial hours shopping with her sisters in her nineteen years, so certain things were habitual. She could not have said what any of the bonnets looked like if asked five minutes later, but she reassured herself in thinking that no one could tell that she was discomposed.

Lydia came up to her with a length of ribbon in her hands and studied the bonnet she held. "I think that bonnet would really suit you. Are you going to get it?"

"I could not say," Catherine admitted. "I seem to be unable to decide." Actually looking at the hat in her hands, she did contemplate purchasing it. The brim was just the right angle and had a lovely green ribbon that would match her eyes, though it was too green to be considered peacock blue. It was an unusual find, but did she really need another bonnet? She had plenty of them at home. Did she even care?

Coming over, Colonel Theodore took the bonnet from her and looked at it, then back at Catherine. "I think that bonnet would look stunning on you. It matches your eyes perfectly. You should get it." Handing it back to her with a flourish, Theodore looked at her expectantly, one of his old grins back on his face.

"I think I will," she decided. She could not help but get it, not with him smiling at her like that. She held the bonnet with numb fingers and tried not to gaze too intently into his smiling face. How did he know that it would complement her eyes? Exactly how close was he looking at her?

Forcing herself to smile at Theodore, she tried to walk casually over to Elizabeth and Georgiana to show them the bonnet. He was entirely too charming for her own good.

***

THE TIMES WERE GONE when Catherine carried her own packages. Some days, she missed not being able to carry her own things. Ever since Elizabeth had married William, she had a footman who went with them on errands and carried packages. Today she would have been grateful to have her hands full of packages instead of wrapped around Theodore's arm. His very well-defined arm.

At least the depth of her bonnet's brim prevented her flush from being seen by him. She hoped so, at least. She would be mortified if it didn't. Elizabeth and Mary had gone into a bookshop as they always did, and now Catherine walked with Theodore, Lydia, and Georgiana, looking in the windows of the stores. There was not anything she wanted to buy, though she could have sworn that she had made a list yesterday.

A commotion up ahead drew her attention. Several young children were jeering at what appeared to be a fallen soldier whose crutch had either broken or had been kicked out from under him. The soldier gave a fleeting attempt to get up, only to fall once more, resulting in even more sneers and laughter. The way the soldier's shoulders slumped at the children's cruel words spoke of a pain that Catherine was all too familiar with.

Unable to watch the young soldier being abused any longer, Catherine made the snap decision to do something about it. Letting go of Theodore's arm, she rushed forward and confronted the boys. "Can you explain what's going on? What would your mothers say?" she demanded, crossing her arms. Turning to the soldier, she looked him over to see if he was injured from his fall.

"I am sorry for being a trouble, miss." The young, injured soldier hung his head, almost collapsing within himself. His weary demeanor belied his youthful features, making her wonder if he had experienced more than his fair share of hardships. The uniform that hung on his slight frame was faded and frayed at the edges.

"Being a kind person is no trouble at all. It is an honor and a duty to be kind to those around us, especially to those who can use our help the most," Catherine tried to reassure him.

While most of the boys had run when Catherine stepped forward, one remained. With his unruly mop of hair and bare feet, he appeared to be an urchin. His mismatched clothes no longer had any color they were so caked with grit and grime. He squirmed under Catherine's gaze, his face falling with what seemed like regret. "I did not kick your crutch, but I should not have laughed when you fell. I am sorry."

Catherine looked at the boy, who appeared to be around eight or nine. "What is your name?"

"Timmy, miss," scuffing his dirty foot on the ground in front of him, the boy looked down.

"Thank you for apologizing, Timmy." Catherine beamed at the boy, who nervously returned her smile. "Can you help me get Mr...."

"Jackson, miss," the soldier replied softly.

"Can you help me get Mr. Jackson to his feet?"

"Of course, miss."

They each took an arm and began helping him up. At one point they almost all went down in a heap, but Theodore stepped in to help, and together they got Mr. Jackson on his feet. Once he seemed to have his balance with Timmy's assistance, Catherine stooped down to retrieve his crutch. "Do you have somewhere to go, Mr. Jackson?"

Jackson nodded. "Yes, miss."

"Timmy, can you help him get there? I would hate to worry about him making it where he was going." Reaching into her reticule that hung on her wrist, Catherine took out her card and a small amount of money.

"I can do that," Timmy nodded proudly.

"If either of you are ever in need of employment, please make your way to Darcy House on Coventry Square. I am sure we can find something for you both." Pressing the card and coins into the soldier's hand, she closed his fingers around it when he looked like he would refuse.

Turning to Timmy, she held up a single coin. "I want to thank you for apologizing and being willing to help Mr. Jackson here. After you get where you are going, use this to treat yourself." Handing him the coin, she could not help but notice him lick his lips in anticipation for some treat or another. Like the soldier, he was on the thin side and could do with an extra meal. "Remember what I said. If you come to Darcy House, we would be more than happy to set you up with a situation. My brother-in-law mentioned they need help at the home farm back in Derbyshire, but I am sure that there are tasks here in London if you prefer the city."

"A real live farm?" Timmy's eyebrows rose into his messy bangs, his gray eyes wide. The look of awe on his face could not be missed.

"Yes, a real live farm." Catherine tried very hard not to laugh and possibly discourage the boy, but heard Theodore's soft chuckle behind her. What were the other options—a dead farm? It was a live farm indeed, and Catherine marveled at how children were always a delight.

"I will think on it, Miss. If I decide to go to this Darcy House, who shall I say sent me? You got our names, but we did not get yours. What is your name?"

"Oh, how very rude of me. I am Miss Catherine Bennet. It is a pleasure to meet you both." Offering a small curtsy, she smiled at them both.

Timmy attempted a bow before moving back to the soldier's side. "Let's go, old chap. Where's you staying at?"

Catherine smiled at them as they moved off into the bustling street. Chatting as they went. She turned back to Theodore, Georgiana, and Lydia, who were standing a few steps behind her. Flashing them a sheepish grin, she apologized. "Sorry for breaking off there. I simply cannot abide cruelty."

"Not at all. Those boys needed to be taken in hand." Lydia waved off her apology and turned to look back in the window they were in front of. "Besides, it gave me the opportunity to spot these delicious boots on display."

***

THEODORE HAD WATCHED CATHERINE'S interactions with the wounded soldier and the lad in utter bemusement. Unconsciously rubbing his leg, Theodore saw himself in the wounded soldier. If it were not for his family's money and Cedric procuring only the best for him, he would still be on crutches or forever crippled. He knew how people of society treated those who were less than perfect. Catherine was not the only one who had seen the soldier fall, but she was the only one who did something about it. The Bennet women were different from most people in society, he knew that. He knew they were kind, but watching Catherine move to the wounded soldier's aid had done something to his heart.

It felt as if his chest no longer had space for all the feelings that had suddenly appeared out of nowhere. Sifting through his emotions, he realized that if he was not yet in love, he was definitely falling. It was an odd thing to realize in the middle of a busy street with most of her family present. He only hoped he could act normally until he had time to properly think about everything.

***

CATHERINE NOTICED THAT THEODORE was rubbing his leg and narrowed her eyes in concern. Was his leg hurting from all the walking? She was going to say something, but then Theodore approached and once more offered his arm, which she happily took. "You realize that boy is probably a pickpocket?" he pointed out.

"Most likely, yes," she nodded. "The poor thing."

Theodore watched as the two so cast away by society walked away, then turned his attention to the people going about their business. The boy and soldier moved amongst the sea of people, gaining no attention or sympathy from anyone besides Catherine. "Most people would not take a moment to think about him or help either of them in any way."

"Most people are wrong. Like I said, kindness is an honor and a duty. Taking a moment out of my day to aid them both was not a bother. More than that, they will both benefit from it." Catherine moved with Theodore towards the display that Lydia was so fascinated with. When she realized he was not limping, she relaxed.

Looking up at him, she saw his contemplation. Her concern for him combined with her worries for Timmy and Mr. Jackson helped her push through her own uncomfortable emotions and converse with Theodore in a normal manner. "It is a crime, really, how society treats people like them. What choice does Timmy have? Becoming a pickpocket or going to a workhouse? Do you know how they treat people there? The way they treat orphans and people down on their luck is not charity; it is cruelty."

"I do not know specifics, but I have heard the conditions are harsh. At least they feed them." As Theodore looked down at Catherine, his eyebrows furrowed in interest.

"They feed them as little as possible so they survive, but not enough to thrive." Shaking her head in disgust, she continued, "The tasks they give them are not helping them gain skills to seek employment. It is merely busy work. Things like making and unmaking rope, and for that they get a bowl of gruel in the morning and a bowl of broth in the evening. People, and children especially, deserve to be helped in a better way."

His eyes widened as he took in the disturbing knowledge. "I know there are many things that need to be changed. One thing Cedric was attempting to put forward was some kind of act to aid the wounded soldiers. Currently, upon their return, they are left empty-handed, with no support, no place to stay, and the majority of them are unable to secure employment due to their injuries and the bias they face."

Catherine knew what she wanted to say, but wondered whether Theodore would react well to it. Turning, she looked at the display of shoes. Her eyes were drawn to the reflective surface of the window, where she could vaguely make out her and Theodore, their arms intertwined. There was something about the refection she saw there that gave her courage. "Though Cedric's project was admirable, there are other, more immediate ways that I choose to help. For example, I have heard of a landowner that helps teach wounded soldiers to read and write so they might find work as clerks and the like. You do not need all of your limbs or a strong back to do those tasks."

"That is an intriguing thought. Right now, I am so overwhelmed trying to learn how to fit into my brother's world that I do not think I could manage another project." Looking off into the distance, he rubbed at an eyebrow. "Maybe at a later time."

Catherine looked up at Theodore once more. She knew he thought he was doing the right thing by taking up his brother's crusade, only she hated seeing him so dragged down by the society he had been keeping of late. He was only just getting free of the blue devils he suffered from his brother's death. She did not want to see him enter yet another decline. "Just so as you don't overtask yourself trying to be someone you are not. I believe everyone can help in their own way, and your way does not necessarily have to be your brothers."

The sound of rustling packages announced the arrival of Elizabeth and Mary, who were accompanied by a dutiful footman. "Sorry to keep you waiting. The latest work from Byron had just arrived, and the shop was packed with eager readers."

Lydia turned back from admiring the shoes in the cobbler's window. "Did you purchase it?"

"No, though I like his works well enough. I was looking for something more along the lines of sheep husbandry. William and I have still not come to an agreement on what sheep to introduce to our current flock." Elizabeth was content and full of smiles as she spoke of the book.

Catherine knew that Elizabeth would not care that many society ladies would snub her for reading a book on animal husbandry.

She had always thirsted for knowledge and was eager to help the people who worked Pemberley land. "Were you satisfied with their selection?"

"While most of the books they had I had seen before, they had two I think might be helpful. I got them as well as a new book for Kiernan. I would like to give it to him when he is home from Eton next."

Theodore's head came up when he heard Elizabeth mention Kiernan. "How is the lad adjusting?"

The boy had endeared himself to all the Bennet ladies by offering to give them the brotherin' that he felt they were missing out on. Catherine knew that Theodore had become close to Kiernan as well when they all met. The child had been instrumental in helping to save Elizabeth and William from Wickham. In all the changes that had taken place afterwards, his family was invited to move to a favored position running the home farm at Pemberley. William had gone so far as to give Kiernan the chance to receive personalized instruction and eventually attend Eton.

"Despite not belonging to society, his intelligence and integrity have allowed him to form friendships and create his own circle. There will always be bullies and negative people, but I think despite that, he is thriving." Elizabeth grinned as they began moving towards where they were to meet the carriage.

Nodding his head, Theodore smiled at Elizabeth. "That is good to hear. He's such a remarkable little scamp that I can't help but feel he'll accomplish great things." Arriving at the carriage, he began helping the ladies climb in. "Are we done for the day?"

"Of course not!" Lydia jerked her hand back from Theodore's attempt to help her into the convenience. She looked at Theodore as if he had lost his mind.

"Oh?" Theodore looked at Lydia, eyebrows furrowed in confusion.

"We must end the morning by making a stop at a tearoom. Don't you remember? You are buying the biscuits." Tilting her head, Lydia's smiling blue eyes dared him to say otherwise. Then, accepting his assistance, she bounced into the carriage and sat between Mary and Elizabeth.

"Of course. How could I have forgotten?" Theodore's bold laugh burst forth and, jumping into the carriage, he cried. "To the tea shop!"

Chapter Eleven

THEODORE SAT SIPPING HIS tea and allowing the girlish chatter to flow around him. There had been so much going on that he had little time to contemplate the scare he had that morning. His first sight of Catherine sitting there chatting with her sisters and Georgiana had been quickly marred when she started choking. Though she was fine now, those moments when he knew she was unable to breathe seemed to last an eternity. His heart raced, still just thinking of how close he had come to losing her.

One thing was for certain: the question of how deep his emotions were had been answered. This wasn't a casual inclination; it was an intense, emotionally charged longing. He realized his racing heart and cold terror were directly related to how much he loved her. Even now he found himself repeatedly glancing her way, as if to reassure himself that she was alive and well.

He was glad he had decided to come visit this morning. Not only was there the possibility that Miss Catherine could have died without his aid, but he had also learned what he needed to know. Though he had always enjoyed his time with all the Bennet ladies, he was realizing how much he thoroughly enjoyed conversing with Miss Catherine.

He had wanted to aid her when she first rushed off at the sight of the commotion, but Lydia had held him back, telling him to watch. She had reminded him that Miss Catherine had come a long way, and it was good to see her courage rising to the occasion. She would not want anything to hamper it.

Theodore was glad he had stood back. She had been a sight to behold, helping both the soldier and the boy and doing it without any condescension, treating them both with respect and kindness. He was certain that both the soldier and young lad would be better for the interaction. Her kindness alone had soothed something in him that was still injured from his time in the military.

A sudden giggle from Georgiana alerted him to the fact that he had missed something while he was lost in thought. "I am sorry, I was not attending. What did I miss?"

Georgiana smiled at his discomposure but filled him in on his lapse. "Do not worry, we were only talking about what kind of biscuits we preferred. It appears that we all made different selections for the most part. But you did not respond when asked about your preference."

"Oh, that was rather rude of me. I must admit, I had my mind on other matters." Theodore tugged slightly at his cravat and averted his gaze, but not before catching what appeared to be a blush on Catherine's cheeks.

Mary, who sat next to him on his left, patted his hand reassuringly. "No harm done. Here, we will start again. I just love the lemon biscuits they have here. What is your favorite, Colonel Theodore?"

"I think I prefer the less sweet items, though this chocolate biscuit is quite good. I find the slight bitterness to be quite enjoyable."

Theodore resisted the temptation to let his mind wander again and directed his full attention to the conversation. He had ruminated enough for the morning.

Theodore waited until the others had gotten into a side conversation about the merits of some type of a new hat before turning to Miss Catherine, who sat on his right. "I realize this is your first season, Miss Catherine, and you haven't been in London very much before now, but have you found yourself enjoying it? What do you enjoy doing while in London?" He knew it might not be nice, but he was wondering what she would say and how it would compare to Lady Lavinia's vapid response from the night before.

"Though I most certainly prefer living in the country to the city, there are things I have found I was rather not fond of. I was at the menagerie they had, but I found it rather sad to see the beautiful animals all in cages, and I must admit we go to the museum rather more than I would like." Pausing, she smiled broadly before continuing. "The museum is something that Lizzie and William absolutely love, so we go rather frequently. Recently I have spent my time observing them instead of the exhibits. I rather enjoy watching them debate about whatever they are viewing. The love they have for each other is something special, something to be envied and sought after even."

"Indeed, it is something for the record books, or better yet, the poets," Theodore agreed wholeheartedly. He desperately longed for the kind of love that Darcy had and believed that searching for it was worth the effort. Knowing he wasn't the only one on such a quest was heartening. The mere idea of Miss Catherine wanting it too stirred something inside him. "I am sure there are things you enjoy doing beyond watching Elizabeth and Darcy argue."

Miss Catherine gave a slow grin. "My time in London does have its advantages. I am not the music lover that Georgiana, Mary, or even Lizzie is, but I enjoy the theater and symphony. Though, I wish that all the other attendees were less concerned with seeing and being seen. It can be quite distracting, all their gawping. All my masters are here and the lessons I receive are quite enjoyable. I know my painting has improved greatly as well as my work with pastels."

It was most certainly a different answer from what he had heard from Lady Lavinia. Miss Catherine had something so much more real about her. She disregarded societal norms on acceptable conversation and boldly expressed her opinions, irrespective of popular views on the matter. "I am glad that you have found things that you like while in London. The country's slower pace of life and connection to nature make it more appealing to me than the fast-paced and artificial environment of the city. Would you believe I know people who stay here year-round? But I do not think I could do it."

Miss Catherine shook her head disapprovingly. "Nor I. I truly doubt I will be able to maintain my equanimity for the whole of the season. The marriage mart events are rather less enjoyable than I would have hoped."

Theodore found it interesting that neither of them were truly happy at the season's social events. Though he would like to wash his hands of the whole thing, he knew he did not have that option.

"The thought that I will have to be active in the season regularly, and possibly the little season as well, has been rather daunting."

"I had heard it mentioned that you were considering taking your brother's seat in parliament. I did not know you were fond of debates and putting forth legislation and the like." Miss Catherine's eyebrows had drawn together, making the cutest little crease on her forehead.

As distracted as he was falling in love with the crease between Miss Catherine's eyebrows, Theodore still managed to respond. "I never would have considered it if not for Cedric's death, but I feel the need to be true to what he worked for in helping people."

Miss Catherine paused and looked at him sharply for a moment before smiling softly. "Helping people is an admirable goal, and I hope you find a way to do it while being true to yourself. There are as many ways to help people as there are grains of sand on the seashore."

Theodore hesitated and would have questioned her statement if Elizabeth had not drawn his attention. She had taken the opportunity to remind them all that the proprietor would most likely want their table back, and they had dawdled over their tea long enough. The clatter of dishes and chairs as they left the teashop drowned out the possibility of Theodore resuming their conversation. Perhaps it was for the best.

***

THE FIRST THING HE heard when he returned home was, "Where have you been all day?"

Handing his outer things to the footman at the door, Theodore turned to spot his mother standing as she was prone to on the stairs. He was starting to think she had sentinels to alert her when he was walking down the street so she could pounce on him as soon as he walked through the door. Was this the only way she would greet him now that he was an earl? He managed to keep his expression neutral, even though he felt like grimacing and rolling his eyes. He faced her directly. "I was out. You did not have any dinners planned for us to attend this morning, did you?"

Huffing in exasperation, his mother looked down at him as she had when he was a child. "Don't be obtuse! I would hope that you would keep me informed of your social engagements. I know you are trying to cultivate the right image I would hate for you to undo that unthinkingly. Being seen with the wrong people can cause more harm than you understand at this point."

Looking up at his mother, he became distracted by the fact that she always seemed to confront him while she had the advantage of height. It was a sound military strategy, though he did not appreciate it being used against him. Climbing the stairs so they could speak at less of an angle, he responded to her claim. "Mother, you are being unreasonable. I know Cedric never kept you informed of his every movement. You certainly do not tell me who you are meeting for tea."

"Cedric was aware of the unwritten rules of society, while you are still trying to figure out the intricacies of it all. I know you expressed a desire to follow in your brother's footsteps. I just do not want to see you disappointed." His mother pressed her hand to her lips, her face contorted with emotion.

"Do not worry, Mother. It takes a lot to disappoint me. Besides, I was accompanying all the ladies from Darcy House on a shopping trip. Perfectly respectable, perfectly amiable, and I had a very enjoyable morning. In fact, I had a very interesting conversation with Miss Catherine."

"Is that right?"

Theodore smiled at his mother. He knew she had said she wanted them to grow closer now that it was just the two of them. She was quite prickly, but he hoped they could put forth the effort to bridge the gap. "Yes, she is a remarkable woman. I have enjoyed coming to know her better this season. I want to wash up a bit from the grime of outdoors, but why don't we sit down and have some tea? We can talk about our days."

His mother remained motionless for a second, her smile appearing to be frozen in place, before she shook her head. "No, I do not want to bother you. I know you complain you do not have enough time to yourself, and we do not have any dinner plans. Why don't you relax, and I will see that the cook sends you a tray and some tea." Turning, his mother hurried down the stairs.

He stared after her for a moment, wondering if he should follow her, but he did not know what he would say. Turning back, he continued up the stairs and into his room. Perhaps he would finally have the time to finish the next section of *The Art of War*.

***

THEODORE SAT IN HIS chair, staring at the words on the page. He was normally a dab hand at reading French, but his mind could not seem to focus on the words. They danced and flitted before his eyes, almost mocking his efforts to read and better himself. He knew his mind was wandering, unable to focus on reading, as it was preoccupied with thoughts of Miss Catherine and the delightful morning they had spent together.

There had been something about her instant movement to aid the wounded soldier. As the soldier moved away, Theodore noticed his limp was so pronounced that he was unable to walk without heavily relying on his crutch. That could have been Theodore. Probably would have been him if not for his batman and his family's money that provided a clean environment and medical care.

Theodore knew one of the reasons Cedric had been fighting to put forth benefits for wounded soldiers was his own injury. Cedric had seen what the war had done to him and wanted to help others who likewise suffered. It was a wonderful cause, and Theodore could not help but want to support his brother's noble efforts. Yet Miss Catherine had been very insistent that he did not lose himself in the attempt.

Was that a possibility? Was he at risk of losing who he was by trying to see to his brother's work? The task he had taken up, fulfilling his brother's aspirations, was not a bad one. He had been lost before his brother had died and with his death, Theodore saw a purpose that he could take up. Having something to work towards was something he needed. He was tired of wandering aimlessly through life.

In a fit of frustration, he huffed and threw himself out of his chair, causing it to scrape against the floor. He was getting nowhere, trying to ponder if he was losing himself by trying to take on his brother's legacy. It was possible he was losing himself to the effort. He would normally never put up with all the dinners and social events his mother was suggesting. While he was doing it with the thought that it was for his brother, enough of those kinds of actions and he would not be able to recognize himself. Pacing around the room, Theodore debated what he owed to his brother. His brother did anything he could to help him. Shouldn't he return the favor? Somehow, the idea was less appealing than it once was.

After a fruitless period of pacing, Theodore surrendered to the fact that he wouldn't be deciphering the issue that day. Instead of getting stuck in the quagmire of his confusing circumstances, Theodore shifted his focus to something more promising. Miss Catherine was something much better to contemplate. Now that he knew that he truly had feelings for her, what was he going to do about it?

He resolved to court her, and hopefully she would eventually come to reciprocate his feelings. He would also need to speak with Darcy and let him know of the development. Theodore could only hope that his feelings for Darcy's sister-in-law wouldn't cause too much trouble.

Chapter Twelve

How had she gotten to this point? Catherine was never opposed to a walk through Hyde Park. That was not why she was so discomposed. Being stuck in the city did not feel as confining if you could visit nature, and she enjoyed nature. Walking through Hyde Park was always lovely if you could ignore all the people trying to be seen. She had planned on avoiding Theodore for a while to get over her feelings for him, or at least be able to hide them better. Yet here she walked through the park with Colonel Theodore, Lydia, Mr., and Miss Burgess, and she wondered how she had gotten herself into this situation.

The morning had been normal, and she had plans to continue her work on her latest painting. She had been working on the project sporadically, but with renewed determination, she planned to make progress. As it was a gift for Theodore, she wanted to get it just right. She had spoken with her painting master about a problem she was having with the light and shadow. With his guidance, she was hopeful about creating the scene exactly as she had envisioned it. Despite all her plans, Catherine was not up to her elbows in paint and smudges. She was dressed in her latest walking dress and her new capote bonnet walking on the arm of Selene's brother, Sebastian.

It had started when Lydia had bustled into her room and demanded that she change. Lydia insisted she wanted to go for a walk and Catherine *had* to go with her, there was no choice in the matter. She was quickly dressed and ushered downstairs only to find Theodore waiting to accompany them. Seeing him smile at her from the foot of the stairs had sent her heart thudding in her chest. She still had not recovered even when they ran into Selene and her brother at the entrance to the park.

So distracted by how quickly her plans for the morning had changed, she had not been up to conversation. Lydia, being the sweetheart she was, had taken control of the conversation and was regaling Mr. Burgess with stories about young Artie. Up ahead, she saw Miss Burgess on Theodore's arm, and she hated the feeling of resentment it gave her. She was not a resentful person. Selene was a lovely woman, and he deserved lovely. She was also older and most likely more to his taste. No matter what she told herself, however, she could not shake the jealous feeling she felt watching Theodore with Selene.

***

SELENE SUPPRESSED A CHUCKLE as she watched Lord Matlock beside her. It was obvious to anyone with eyes that he had developed quite the pash for Miss Catherine. She pondered for a moment, briefly considering the merits of ignoring the situation, but ultimately decided that wouldn't be any fun. "So, Lord Matlock, just how long have you had feelings for Miss Catherine?"

The man beside her stopped in his tracks and looked down at her, shock evident in his wide-eyed expression. It was only a moment before his shoulders slumped and he looked away from her. "Is it as obvious as that?"

Tugging slightly on his arm to get him to continue walking, she smiled at his consternation. Selene's inner matchmaker immediately sprang into action as she began to plot how to help her new friends. "I am sure being a relative outsider helped me detect it. People who are close to someone tend to stick with preconceived assumptions about a situation, whereas newcomers can sometimes see simply what is. But the question remains: how long have you had feelings for her?"

Lord Matlock's brow furrowed as he stared off into the trees, appearing to be deep in contemplation. Glancing back down at Selene, he stated simply, "It has been a recent development."

"I would like to see my friend happy and, as far as I can tell, you are a good man. Your brother certainly was." Selene knew he would not necessarily be disposed to come clean about his feelings to her, but maybe if she offered to help? "With your permission, I would be inclined to offer my assistance. But if I am to do anything, I will need information. How goes the quest to win her fair heart?"

His words spilled out slowly and deliberately as he recounted some of his tale. "Darcy and I spoke this morning, and although he was surprised, he did not object. He is so completely happy with his wife Elizabeth that he wants everyone else to have their own chance at finding bliss." Laughing, he stopped momentarily, as if remembering something from the encounter. "He even arranged things so that we could spend some time together this morning in the park. Though

I had hoped to have her on my arm, not your brother's. No offense intended."

Selene had to stifle her laughter. She was having the best morning, a pleasant walk, and even a new love to help along. How splendid. "None taken. Rest easy, for my brother has no designs on Miss Catherine. His attentions lie elsewhere I think."

"That is good to hear." He said the right thing, but his voice had a hint of irritation, hinting at his lingering discontentment.

Selene looked behind her to check on the group following them. She was not surprised to note that though Miss Catherine was on his arm, it was Lydia he was smiling at and chatting with. He had always had a pash for energetic blondes, and further inspection showed something even more interesting. It revealed that it was possible Miss Catherine was quite blind to Lord Matlock's affections. Probably due to the fact that she was working so hard to hide her own. How interesting indeed. "Do you believe that Miss Catherine shares your feelings?" she questioned.

An exasperated huff came from Lord Matlock. "That is why I wanted to spend the morning with her so that I could find out."

"And by some stroke of fate, you happened upon us, derailing your plans as Miss Lydia invited us to tag along on your escapade," Selene tsked, offering a mischievous smile as she solidified her plan in her mind.

***

JUST WHY WAS SELENE laughing so? It was simply not fair. Catherine didn't want to be consumed by jealousy, but she couldn't help the way she felt. She told herself it had to stop; she had to get over her feelings or she would spend the rest of her life in a jealous huff.

"Oh, look at the lovely little benches. Let us all sit down and watch the water," Selene announced from the front of the group.

"Yes, let's," Lydia agreed and hurried her pace to the water. "Do you suppose there are fish in the stream? Maybe if there are, I could bring Artie with his nurse to show him. His surprise at anything new is just darling."

"Anything is possible," Mr. Burgess responded while leading Catherine to one of the benches, only he did not sit down next to her. His sister did. "Thank you for allowing me to walk with you, Miss Catherine."

"It was a pleasure, thank you." Smiling as best she could, Catherine thanked him as she knew she should. With a bow, he followed after Lydia, who was looking into the water. Watching him walk away, Catherine couldn't help but feel envious of how easily he connected with her sister. She was confident there was nothing there, but should something develop, there would be no impediments. Unlike her own emotional entanglements, which were proving to be quite imposable.

"I am sure that you would have enjoyed the walk more had you been on Lord Matlock's arm." Selene's voice was a mere murmur as she spoke from her spot next to Catherine on the bench.

Though spoken softly, Selene's words were quite jarring to Catherine. Catherine's gaze landed on the woman with pretty, raven hair, and tried to smile happily. "You both made a very pretty couple. I think you will make a wonderful match if things work out that way. I can assure you he is the best of men." Catherine was determined to conquer this petty jealousy. She would rise above it, even if it killed her.

Despite what Catherine hoped was encouragement, Selene's eyes widened, and she responded with a sudden rush of words. "Oh, do not hurt yourself by saying such things. I fear you will break if you try to smile any harder. I am simply trying to help you. Please do not think that I am interested in your gentleman."

A furious blush crept up Catherine's cheeks. Had she been that obvious to everyone? "I am sure I do not know what you mean. I have no gentleman to call my own. If you are under the misconception that you need to step aside on my account, that perhaps I have a prior claim, it is not so."

Shaking her head, Selene reached over and took Catherine's white knuckled hand in her own and squeezed it. "Don't try to be a martyr; it won't do any good. Trying to give him to me won't benefit either of you, since he likes you in return."

Catherine looked into the woman's cerulean eyes in wonder. What had she just said? She opened her mouth to question Selene but found she could not come up with the words she wished to speak.

Closing her mouth after having said nothing, she bit her lip in silent contemplation, her mind a whirl. Theodore liked her in return? She had already convinced herself that it was not possible, but here Selene was telling her it was the truth. Was it possible that her foolish love was not so foolish after all? Trying once more, she looked at Selene, her voice almost desperate. "How can you know his feelings on the matter?"

"Well, for one thing, if you were to look up you would see him watching you with concern. I strongly believe that he can perceive your distress at the moment." Looking up, Selene appeared to observe the man they spoke of more closely. Catherine could tell from her snicker and raised eyebrow that she had a clear opinion on the matter. "I would also guess that right now he is contemplating the best way to come over and see to your wellbeing."

A furtive glance in his direction did reveal that Theodore was concerned. The mere thought that he might be concerned about her sent a wave of goosebumps up her arms and down her back, creating an almost irresistible urge to shiver. Clamping down on the hand that held her own for support, Catherine whispered, "I have been trying for some time to conceal my feelings. With this possibility before me, I find I do not know what to do."

"Do? I suppose there are several things that you might do. You could play as if you do not know and watch him follow you around like a puppy until he gains the courage to let you know of his feelings on his own. Or, if you are very brave, as I suspect you are, I say you should confront him about it." Selene smiled at Catherine, squeezing her hand again in support before casting a glance over her shoulder.

"And perhaps you can confront him about it sooner than expected. He is coming this way."

***

LIZZIE SAT ON THE floor next to her beloved husband. They were taking advantage of the free time they had managed to wrangle and were spending it with Artie. His little hands clapped as his father stacked the blocks for him. Resting her head against Darcy's shoulder, she sighed in happiness.

Leaning down, Darcy kissed her forehead before asking. "So do you think our Kitty will lead him on a merry chase?"

"I suppose it is possible, but my sister does not strike me as the type to force a man to chase after her. We both know she has developed a regard for him, though I suspect she thinks she has succeeded at hiding it. How would you like to have him for a brother as well as a cousin?"

Artie reached out and knocked over the stack of blocks and then giggled in glee as they all tumbled down. "Good job, little man." Darcy reached out to ruffle their son's hair. He seemed to think for a moment before looking at his wife with a smile. "I am already close to my cousin, but I would love getting closer. I know I can never be a replacement for Cedric, but I think it would be nice for him to have a brother to rely on again. He already fits in so well with our family. Ever since he worked with me to help free you all from Mr. Bennet, he has been warmly embraced by all, especially your mother.

"Bock! Bock!" Waving his hands wildly, Artie picked up a block from where he sat and showed it proudly to his parents. Artie's wide green eyes and curly dark hair marked him easily as their child if their love for him had not.

"Yes, my love, you knocked down the blocks. Do you want your papa to stack them up again?" Lizzie took the block and held it out to her husband. She flushed when he took the block from her and kissed her wrist before stacking the block with its friends. "I would love to see them both happy the way we have found happiness. Who would have thought that my little sister would become a countess?"

Leaning down, Darcy nuzzled Lizzie's temple. "Everyone deserves to find such happiness, my love. Especially your sisters. It would bring me great joy to see them all in loving matches."

Watching Artie start rubbing his eyes, Elizabeth drew him to her. She recognized the look as only a mother could. Her son would very soon be asleep. She was slightly sad that their time together was over now that he needed a nap, though she got an idea looking down at his sleepy face. "Do you know what I would love to see?"

"What would you love to see?" Darcy stood and then leaned down to help his young wife up off the floor while she held their tired son in her arms.

The nurse came up to them, and Lizzie handed over her sleepy son, taking a moment to kiss his curly crown before letting go. With a playful grin, she tugged her husband into the hallway. "I would love to see Artie get a little sister."

"It took us nearly a year before we managed Artie." Darcy tried but failed to maintain a doubtful demeanor. His uncontrollable grin, complete with dimples, gave away his true thoughts. "I am not opposed to attempting that endeavor, but what if we have another son? Will you be disappointed?"

"Not at all. We can always keep trying." She headed towards their room. Walking down the hall together, she felt his fingers intertwine with hers, and it brought a smile to her face. Sharing a room was not common among couples of the ton, but they had always done things differently. Lizzie laughed as they made it to the room they shared and pulled him in after her. "I won't complain."

***

"Miss Catherine, are you well?" Theodore's voice was laced with worry as he spoke.

The sound of Theodore's voice coming from right behind her sent another wave of goosebumps down Catherine's arms, and this time she did shiver. Turning, she looked at him. She knew she was blushing, but there was nothing she could do about it. "I am well, though I would not mind continuing on the walk we were taking."

"I would be more than happy to oblige you." Offering his arm, he smiled when she took it.

Catherine noticed that Mr. Burgess had taken both Selene's and Lydia's arms and was walking with them as well. The change in the pairings left her feeling nothing but happiness. She much preferred walking with Theodore. Despite trying to maintain propriety, Catherine relished the sensation of holding his arm. The goosebumps had come back, or had they never left? Trying to distract herself, Catherine watched the trees blowing in the slight breeze of the spring morning. "It is a lovely day to be out for a walk. I always enjoy watching the trees in the breeze. I have attempted to paint it, but never have gotten it quite right."

Looking around, Theodore appeared to take note of the breeze moving things about. Looking back at Catherine, he seemed concerned. "It is lovely, but I would hate for you to catch a chill."

"Oh?" Catherine replied, caught off guard by how his protective tone seemed to kindle something within her. If she was allowed to feel these amazing things about him instead of trying to ignore them, she might get carried away.

To prevent the breeze from reaching Catherine, he moved his larger body in a protective stance. "I noticed you shiver earlier. Are you feeling cold? Do you want to return to Darcy House?"

Unable to keep a smile off her lips, Catherine nervously licked them before speaking. "I am enjoying my time with you. Maybe we can take the longer path back?"

"Of course." Turning, Theodore took the path that would lead them in a larger loop before returning to Darcy House.

How did one tell the love of their life just how much they meant to them? Was there an easy way to express such a thing? Or did one always have to endure feeling like they were going to vomit a kaleidoscope of butterflies in order to confess their feelings? "I have something to confess."

"That sounds rather foreboding. What could you have done that could merit such concern?" Theodore pulled Catherine closer to him, and she felt her body relax in his embrace.

Catherine resisted the urge to lay her head against his shoulder. She briefly wished they were back at Pemberley where no one would have batted an eye had she done so. "Not so much something I have done, but there's a secret I'm anxious to tell you, and I'm afraid of your reaction."

Theodore paused as if to assess her, his eyes full of worry as he leaned in. "I'm here for you, and I'll always be a safe place for you to share anything," he said kindly.

Glancing back, Catherine noted that the others were out of earshot and were distracted looking at something. It was most likely Selene's doing. The wonderful girl really was a darling friend. Realizing this was her chance, Catherine took it.

"IthinkIloveyouandIamhopingyoucanreturnmyregard." Gasping for breath after saying everything in a rush, Catherine closed her eyes. Face aflame, Catherine felt like they would be surrounded by those butterflies at any moment. She knew she had spoken so fast that it was nearly impossible he understood her, but she did not think she could say it again. Peeking up at him, she hoped with everything in her that he would not make her repeat herself.

With his eyebrows drawn together, Theodore looked to Catherine as if he was trying to do long division in his head, or possibly translate Portuguese. "Are you saying that you have feelings for me? Romantic feelings?"

Chapter Thirteen

It took Theodore a moment to catch up with Miss Catherine's fast-paced delivery. His brow furrowed as he tried to take in the depth of what she meant by her rushed words. So many questions hurried through his mind. She loved him? And was asking if he could return her regard? Could he actually be so lucky? Was it going to be that easy? He expected to have to work hard to gain her affection, but she was saying she already loved him. "Are you saying that you have feelings for me? Romantic feelings?"

"Yes," Miss Catherine whispered.

Miss Catherine's face was fiery with a blush so dark he began to wonder if it was entirely healthy. "Well, that certainly makes it simpler. Here I had thought it would take ages to turn you to my way of thinking."

Miss Catherine's head shot up, and she looked at him directly, her eyes searching. "Are you saying that you are able to return my regard?"

"Most heartily." Rubbing the back of his neck, he looked up at the sky and then back at the woman who had caught his heart. "I have this strange sensation that Artemis has favored me, without requiring me to undertake any of her trials." Theodore glanced away from her surprised countenance to notice that their standing still on the path was gaining attention. Pulling her along with him, they began to move along the path once more. "I must admit I had not expected you returning my affection. I did not know you already felt favorably towards me."

"I had thought, that is to say," Catherine bit her lip, her eyes never leaving his face as she struggled to express her thoughts. "I had feared that you could never return my feelings and have been trying to hide my own." Miss Catherine turned her gaze from Theodore, but her grip on his arm grew stronger.

Theodore was astounded to learn she had been hiding her feelings from him. "Why would you think yourself unable to gain my affections?" Looking down at her, he wished that society did not require woman to wear such all-encompassing hats. He longed for a glimpse of her hair playing in the wind. Instead, all he saw was the top of her rather fetching bonnet. The comforting thought occurred to him that he could invite her to stroll somewhere private like Pemberley or Matlock. Far from the prying gazes of old biddies who disapproved of something as simple as an uncovered head. That was if, of course, things proceeded as he hoped they would. Maybe at some point in the future he could ask her to forget her hat.

Tilting her head, Miss Catherine looked up at him from under the brim of her bonnet. "For one thing, I am younger than you are, and I had thought you would prefer a more mature partner in life. It is why when you were walking with Selene, I had thought you would prefer someone more like her."

Nodding his head in understanding, Theodore was able to see why she might feel that way. Though he was anxious to reassure her. "While there are ten years that separate us, I do not feel you are in any way immature. We have talked many times, and I have found our conversations of so much more substance than most people I speak with. You have more ability to discuss subjects that matter than most of the men I come across at all the dinners my mother has been making me attend. You should hear some of the mind-numbing drivel that they spout." Theodore's heart swelled with joy as he saw the slow smile of relief on her face. "In all truth, I believe you are so much wiser to the world and its suffering than many of the people I encounter, and that means a lot to me. I, on the other hand, thought you would think me too old and battle worn."

Catherine managed to bump into him playfully with her shoulder. "Men differ from women. While men become more distinguished, woman merely go on the shelf. I have seen debutantes engaged to men twenty years their senior or more. There was a girl Jane met during her London season that was engaged to a man her grandfather's age. Society seems to find age unremarkable as long as the gentleman is the older of the two. What is the ten years between us to me?"

Appreciating all of their plain talk, he was relieved to realize that most of the impediments he had seen for them were melting away. With the issue of age out of the way, Theodore's next concern was about his persistent nightmares. He did not want a marriage like most of those in the ton. His desire was to have a similar happiness to what his cousin had with his wife—one bedroom, not two. His nightmares, though improved, were still there, and he wanted her to know what she could be getting herself into. "I feel I must warn you that my time in battle has marked me more than can be seen. My sleep is often disturbed by nightmares."

"You forget then that my sisters and I fought our own battles, while not the same sort you fought against Napoleon. I have my own scars and, yes, nightmares. We shall simply have to be there for one another." Catherine patted his hand where it rested on her own on his arm. "Perhaps they will fade with time. We will have years to help them do so."

Feeling the bottom drop out of his stomach at her words, Theodore paused a moment to allow his world to realign. She was willing to stand beside him and help him through his trials, making it seem like the most natural thing in the world. How had he managed to be blessed with the love of the woman standing next to him? "When I began this walk, I did not know the direction things would head in. It seems as if we have gone from both suffering from unrequited love to looking at our lives together years from now."

Miss Catherine's giggle was soft but effective in showing her the joy of the moment. "Yes, that does seem rather fast, but we both seem to be of a mind."

"Miss Catherine, would you do me the honor of entering into a formal courtship with me?" Theodore was somewhat certain she would accept, yet he still felt a flicker of doubt as he held his breath in anticipation. It had briefly crossed his mind to propose, but he decided it would be better to take things slower.

"It would be my pleasure, Colonel Theodore."

Theodore was happy to see that her blush had moved to a healthier glow than before, and her smile had him catching his breath. He had always thought she was a lovely girl, and then felt she was a beautiful woman. Now, with the love that he saw in her eyes, she took his breath away. Swallowing convulsively, he decided he no longer wanted her to call him colonel. "I would have you call me Theodore whenever possible. Would you mind if I called you Kitty?" Theodore wondered if she would be okay with such a term of endearment.

"Not at all, though…" Catherine blushed, looking up at him as she got a mischievous twinkle in her eyes. "I think I will always prefer Artemis when you are especially happy. I hope you will not mind me sometimes calling you Theo, though Theodore most of the time."

He had no idea how much she had liked it when he called her Artemis. The idea of calling her something special when he was especially happy filled him with a sense of warmth. "I suppose we should let our families know of our decision. Is your Uncle Gardiner in town still? I will need to speak to him about permission to court you."

"Yes, with my father out of the picture, he is the one in charge of us unmarried ladies."

"Then I will have a meeting with him as soon as may be." Theodore's mind instantly went to all the things he needed to do to proceed properly. He was not going to let this joy slip through his fingers. Too much sadness and stress had pervaded his life as of late to throw away what could be the best thing that ever happened to him.

***

Sneaking had become part of Timmy's life. You snuck to avoid the bullies. You snuck to slip by the toffs when they ignored you on the street. He knew better than to cross paths with the men who wanted him to steal and went out of his way to dodge them. Most of all, you avoided old Maggie who ran the flash-house.

When Miss Catherine had paid attention to him, he was shocked. She was not like any toff he had met before. She actually looked at him, saw him for who he was, and as if she was really concerned about him, had offered to help him. She did not just toss him money as she walked by. No one had looked at him to see him since he lost his mother.

He was using his hard-won skill to check out the toff lady's house. He knew some pretended to be kind but were more rotten than ancient Sally's old vegetables. Spending his days running errands for the grocers and vendors, he managed to barely scrape by, but sleeping on the street was never fun and the thought of a farm was appealing. He didn't think he had ever had a lung full of fresh air in his whole ill-begotten life.

So he was slinking around the street near Darcy House. One could learn a lot by being quiet and watching. He had already figured out that the house two doors down had a master who drank to excess and bothered the maids. So far, the people at Darcy House seemed kind. The servants all seemed well dressed and well fed, and he hadn't seen any crying maids on the back stoop.

He would not show himself quite yet. He was not about to get stranded out in the county with some bad uns. After his mother died, he was on his own, tossed out on the street with nothing but the clothes on his back. There had been one or two people he had met that offered to take him in, but eventually they showed their true colors.

They first had taught him to pick pockets and separate people from their money, but when he had balked at some of the methods he was thoroughly beaten. He left that *home* as soon as he was able to escape. The second time he had been taken in, he had promised to help an old washer woman. Only she liked to get drunk, and when she was drunk, she got violent. He did not stay there long either. After that, he managed to stay on his own and had learned enough to get by. Since he had already managed to avoid old Maggie for such a long time, he figured he might as well bide his time and ensure that he wasn't throwing himself into the fire.

***

THEODORE PRACTICALLY FLOATED ACROSS the square to Matlock House. Everyone had been ecstatic when they were informed that he was courting Kitty. Darcy had seemed ecstatic that he had found such happiness. The room was filled with the sound of laughter and hugs as the well-wishing continued and refreshments were brought out. Now he was returning home to see if he could find his mother to let her know.

When the door opened for him, he smiled at the footman standing there and handed him his hat and gloves. "Good day, Jones. I hope your day is treating you well so far?"

"Yes sir, thank you," Jones replied with a smile.

With the memory of his intended question just out of reach, Theodore waved his hand in frustration. "How is um...I want to say Sarah? Sally? Barnes told me you are recently engaged."

Jones's face lit up at the mention of his betrothed. "Sally, sir, and she is well. I want to thank you for allowing her to come serve as a maid here."

"I was happy to arrange it. It sounded like her previous situation was not at all beneficial. I was glad Barnes alerted me to the issue. Let me know if you need any time off for the wedding." Nodding at Jones's smart bow, Theodore went up the stairs to find Barnes and ask where his mother might be.

"Colonel, it is good to see you in such a happy mood," Barnes remarked as Theodore came into his room.

Theodore felt a rush of pleasure, and his face broke into an uncontrollable smile. If he kept the smile up, he thought his cheeks would ache by nightfall. He had no desire to stop, though. Looking over to Barnes, his grin still evident, he exclaimed, "Congratulate me! Miss Catherine has agreed to an official courtship. I had expected it to take some time to convince her, but it turned out she had been grappling with her own feelings for me all along."

"Congratulations Colonel! I had suspected something was different of late. Do you have any plans for future developments?"

Barnes looked expectantly at Theodore, a wide grin stretching across his face.

Barnes's hopeful expression encouraged Theodore to continue talking with his old friend. "Everyone in the Darcy household was beaming with joy when we revealed our news. I still need to speak with my mother. Despite my return, I have not caught a glimpse of her yet. I also need to see Mr. Gardiner to make it official. Miss Catherine may be staying with Darcy this season, but her Uncle Gardener is the one who I must speak with."

"I am truly happy for you, sir. From all I can see and what I hear via the servants, she is a remarkable woman who is quite capable of helping you to take on any number of estates and responsibilities." Barnes had finished with putting the clothes away and turned to go but stopped at the door. "I think your mother is in the downstairs parlor."

"Thank you. I really must tell her. She is constantly worrying about the family line dying out. I hope that she would be happy for that reason at least. Optimistically, perhaps she will stop throwing young, marriageable girls at me." Theodore tugged at his waistcoat and squared his shoulders. "Wish me luck, Barnes."

"Good luck, sir." Barnes gave a small bow of his head.

Theodore walked out of his room with a purpose-filled stride. Theodore was so caught up in his joy and desire to speak with his mother that he missed Barnes saying, "I believe you are going to need it."

***

"MOTHER, I FOUND YOU," Theodore greeted as he walked into the parlor. His mother was sitting in one of the chairs reading one of the more recent fashion magazines.

"Were you looking for me, dear?" His mother asked, glancing up from the dress design she was perusing.

"I want you to know that I have entered into a formal courtship with Miss Catherine Bennet." Theodore could feel his smile stretching across his face and looked at his mother with expectation. He knew she had been pushing him towards debutantes like Lady Lavinia, but that was never going to happen.

"Oh." Lady Matlock put down the magazine and turned to her son with a carefully blank face. "I am sure her family is thrilled with this development."

Theodore looked at his mother, careful to analyze her expression and posture. Her blank face left him wondering what emotions she was trying to conceal. "That was a very carefully worded non-statement, Mother. You do not seem very enthusiastic."

Pausing as if to find the right words, his mother seemed to hesitate, but then said, "While I can tell you are rather pleased about the match, I will admit to reservations."

"Reservations?" Theodore's elation began to fade as a sense of unease set in. His mother had always believed in the importance of bloodlines and marrying for money, but he had never shared her views. Or at least he hadn't after he had seen the wonder of a true loving marriage in Darcy and Elizabeth. He mused about whether she would raise any objections to him and Catherine being together. It seemed like that might be a strong possibility.

"I know that you have *feelings* about the matter," Lady Matlock continued after taking a moment, her mask slipping only slightly when she wrinkled her nose. "I think Miss Catherine is a sweet girl, and her sisters are everything that is fine. However, the role of Countess of Matlock requires a certain set of abilities, and I'm not sure she has them."

Sitting down on the chair across from his mother, he leaned forward, eager to sway her opinion. "I doubt you have a full understanding of her, Mother. You don't truly know her. Would you believe that I think that she is more suited to be a countess than I am to be earl? Not only does she understand estate management, she also knows how to implement practices that benefit the tenants."

"Yes, I am sure she does, what with Mrs. Darcy's fascination with helping her husband with his duties. But that is not what I was speaking of. I am worried about the social aspects of the role. The burden of being a countess means being adept at navigating the complex social circles that come with the title."

Theodore's mind raced as he struggled to find the right words to convince his mother of Catherine's abilities. She had overcome so much, but he knew his mother would care little for most of his arguments. "She has never had any problems with interacting in society, Mother." Grimacing, Theodore recognized the inadequacy of his response, not to mention the untruth of the matter. Theodore knew all too well the challenges that Catherine faced when dealing with animosity. She had made tremendous strides in her ability to handle adversity.

"You struggle with the requirements yourself and you were born to it. She was not. I fear she will crumble under the strain." A pained smile graced her face as she looked up into his eyes. "Do not think I am demeaning the girl. Like I said, she is very sweet. She will make a very good wife for someone. Just not *you*."

"She makes me happy, Mother. Is that not enough? For your son to be happy?" He knew there were parents who didn't care about their children's happiness, but he had hoped his mother was not one of them. She was not that heartless. Or was she?

"I would love for you to be happy, my son. What you must understand is that the ton is a hotbed of gossip and backstabbing, especially when it comes to an earl's choice of wife. I just worry. It's in a mother's nature to worry, and I am no exception. Gossip will come out of the woodwork for whoever you choose, and I worry she will not be able to handle it." Her hand was soft as she reached out and grasped his own, offering a silent show of support. "I know you would hate to be the cause of Miss Catherine's suffering. I will pray that your Catherine will be able to handle any challenges that come her way."

"That is all I ask. Once you get to know her, you will see just how remarkable she is." Theodore's smile returned in full force as he held tightly onto his mother's hand. In the back of his mind, a nagging worry lingered about his mother's dissatisfaction with the match, but he didn't want to let it consume him. He was happy, and he wanted to remain so. He would not borrow worry. Should she turn nasty, he would act, but not before.

"Yes, I am sure." A smile spread across Lady Matlock's face as she looked at her son. Her smile, he noted, however broad, didn't quite reach her eyes.

Chapter Fourteen

CATHERINE PACED AROUND THE room. How was it possible for her to be so ecstatic and terrified at the same time? On the one hand, the thought of Theodore's smile and the happy glint in his eye sent shivers down her spine. She couldn't help but daydream about their future together, envisioning lazy afternoons spent in his company and little blue-eyed children playing at their feet. On the other hand, the thought of being a countess made her want to cast up her accounts.

Though she had agreed to a courtship and possibly more with Theodore, it had dawned on her that morning that being with him meant more than just being with the man she loved. It meant becoming a countess the moment she said her vows. She was the daughter of a country squire. A very inept country squire at that. How could she become a countess?

Panic began to rise, and she could not help but walk quicker while she paced. Would she have to change in order to fit the mold of a countess? If she stayed true to herself, would she shame Theodore by not conforming to society's standards? She would never willingly embarrass him, but she could not let herself fall back into the shadows she once existed in. Knowing that biting her lip would only worsen her anxiety, she dug her nails into her palms to distract herself.

"Catherine, dear, whatever is the matter?" Lady Derby entered her sitting room, worry clear on her face as she approached. Sitting on the settee, she patted the cushion next to her, "Come sit with me and we will chat while we wait for tea."

"Thank you for granting me the opportunity to call unexpectedly, Lady Derby." With a heavy sigh, Catherine sank onto the cushion beside her, feeling the softness give way under her weight. "I fear I have gotten myself into a bit of a bumblebroth."

Lady Derby's wise eyes seemed to pinpoint the cause of Catherine's frazzled state. "Could this have anything to do with the gentleman you attempted to teach archery not too long ago?"

Catherine blushed and dropped her face into her hands, hoping to hide her embarrassment and gather her thoughts before confessing. Taking a deep breath, she peeked up at Lady Derby over the edge of her fingers. "I love him but...I have no idea what to do. How does one go from being simply herself to becoming something as grand as a countess?"

Lady Derby's kind smile bloomed into a full grin. "Ahh, you have developed feelings for Lord Matlock, and he possibly has feelings for you in return?"

"We are courting, or we will be once we receive Uncle Gardiner's permission." Despite her unease, Catherine's lips turned up into a wobbly smile.

"And only now that things are progressing as you want it to, you are realizing that he is an earl." Lady Derby smiled, her eyes going hazy for a moment before she looked back at Catherine. "I actually remember the moment I realized the same when I accepted Lord Derby. He was a viscount at the time, so I knew he was titled, but I had not thought much of it. Until I did. Then I became completely overwhelmed."

Hearing that Lady Darby experienced similar worries brought Catherine some comfort. "I was so happy, but then it dawned on me that he is now an earl and I would become his countess. While I have been filled with sympathy for him as he struggles to adjust to his new position, I never pictured myself taking on similar responsibilities." Noting that she had been twisting handfuls of her dress with her anxious hands, she began to search in her reticule for something to occupy them. Taking a handkerchief out, she began to twist it in her hands instead. It would not do to ruin her dress simply because she was out of sorts. "There is nothing particularly remarkable about me. As a debutante, it's a constant challenge for me to navigate morning calls without making any verbal missteps."

Lady Derby's response was marked by a smile that held traces of both experience and compassion. "I may be a countess, but it does not make me especially remarkable. I simply have more people that I am trying to care for. Yes, there are people that make a big to do of a title, but it is only a big to do if you make it one." She looked directly into Catherine's eyes and softly asked, "What is your greatest concern?"

Taking a moment, Catherine composed her thoughts and aligned her concerns into a cogent order. "I understand how to run an estate and make sure the tenants are taken care of. It is the people of the ton that worry me. I am not one of those ladies who is overly concerned with fashion or being seen by the right people. I most certainly am not at all like the current Lady Matlock."

"I believe that Lord Matlock's mother is the sort who likes to put on a grand display of her status of being a countess. You do not have to model yourself after her." She paused for a moment, grimacing in distaste. "Frankly, I would not at all suggest you model yourself after the current lady Matlock. She is known for her desire to show up her supposed friends, while I am known for my charity projects. You can be known for whatever you want."

Catherine's eyes widened slightly, her mind sifting through thoughts in a flurry. Hadn't she just told Theodore that he did not have to conform to being the kind of earl his mother wanted? It would seem that the same would hold true for her. They could be unique together.

Sinking into her chair, Catherine felt a wave of relief as she smiled at the encouraging news. "That is so very reassuring. I know Theodore has been trying so hard trying to walk in his brother's shoes. Theodore has not told me, but I know he is miserable going to all the dinners his mother tells him he is required to attend to uphold Cedric's legacy. I just want him to be able to be himself." Catherine's voice held a touch of vulnerability as she shared her sincere desire for Theodore's happiness. "I cannot understand why he has allowed her to take over so much of his life. He was a colonel in charge of troops in battle and yet he is allowing his mother to make him miserable."

Reaching out, Lady Derby clasped Catherine's trembling hand. "The weight of grief can make you lose sight of who you are after the loss of a loved one. People often struggle with expectations, both ones they think their loved ones have and ones they have for themselves."

With a pensive nod, Catherine confessed, "I have been struggling to find a way to help him."

Lady Derby's wistful eyes were supportive as she mustered a short-lived ghost of a smile. "Just being there for him is all you can truly do. He must find his own way back to himself. Have faith that he can manage it. I believe he is a good man and can find his way in time."

"I am glad to hear it," Catherine whispered softly, her words filled with gratitude. "It is a struggle to watch him go through this, but I will have faith that with more time and my love, he can set his own course." She looked up as a smartly dressed maid entered the room with the tea tray. Smiling, she noted all the delicious treats on display. She had been in such a tizzy that she had not eaten anything but toast and tea this morning, and Lady Derby's cook was a dab hand at pastries.

Without wasting any time, Catherine was promptly presented with a cup of tea, its steam rising enticingly. She happily selected a delectable pastry filled with the fragrant combination of apple and spices. Their conversation became less about reassurance, and more about things that would help Catherine as she stepped into the role of countess. As they talked, Catherine's worries seemed to disappear as fast as her pastry did.

***

Timmy finally found the courage to approach the side stoop that morning. When he had noticed the scullery maid and cook scrubbing vegetables in the morning sun, he decided to approach. He had scoped things out enough to give a small trust a try.

Taking off his cap, he approached the two chatting ladies. "Good morning. I was wondering if I might help you with your work this morning. Maybe, can I get a bite to eat in return?"

The older woman stopped what she was doing and looked him over before smiling warmly at him. Reaching over, she picked up a small bucket of potatoes in water. "You come sit over here and scrub these up good and I will make it worth your while."

"Thank you, missus." Going over to her, he took the bucket and the scrub brush she handed him and sat where she indicated. He reached into the water and started at his tasks. As jobs went, it was not too hard and sitting in the yard was nice. Soon enough the women started chatted again, ignoring, or seeming to forget his presence.

"Did you hear that Sally is no longer a maid at Derwent House?" the younger woman asked while she worked.

Not bothering to look up from her task, the other woman replied, "So she finally did leave that place? I do not care how much they pay, it is not worth the roaming hands of that son. Did she get a better position?"

"Yes, well, to hear the talk. Lord Matlock, from across the square, found out that Sally was in a tight spot and offered her a position as an upstairs maid."

"Good for Sally. She's a hard worker." The older of the two women nodded firmly, and Timmy noted that her smile radiated warmth and kindness.

"Apparently their footman Jones is engaged to the girl and when Lord Matlock found out how he worried for her, he made it so they could be in the same household. Lord Matlock is just like his cousin, Mr. Darcy. Neither of them will abide someone mistreating their servants." Despite her work, the younger woman's face displayed a quiet pride, a reflection of her devotion to the family she served.

"Our Miss Catherine is right smart catching that gentleman. He is not like some of those other lords."

"He is a good man, despite his title."

"That he is."

Timmy let their conversation slide over him, afraid to move too much or they might realize he was still there. He was relieved to hear that the people he had started to consider trusting were a good lot. You could tell a lot about a person by paying attention to their servants. Both ladies seemed happy and hard-working, but not in a resentful way. They also were kind women. Women he would not mind working alongside.

He kept to his task of scrubbing the potatoes with the brush, but soon enough, he was done and did not want to overstay his welcome. "I finished." Picking up the bucket, he brought it over to the older of the two ladies for inspection.

Her head came up to look at him with a smile. "That was quick, and you were as quiet as a mouse sitting there working. I was likely to forget you were there. This is a good morning's work. You stay here a moment, and I will get you your reward." She turned back into the house with the bucket and was gone for a few minutes.

Eventually she returned, but not with the scrape of stale bread he assumed he would receive. She held in her hands a paper-wrapped package and a warm pastry. He could see the steam rising off the top, twisting into the cool morning air. "That is too much. I only scrubbed some potatoes," he stammered. Feeling flustered and overwhelmed, Timmy put his hands behind him, almost afraid to take the gifts. Because they were gifts to him—the likes of him never got good food fresh from the oven.

"The Darcys are good people, every one of them. They would never begrudge a hard worker a reward." While the maid studied him, his stomach took the opportunity to growl loudly. "Tell you what, look at it as an incentive. On Tuesday we do the washing and I would be appreciative if I had some extra help. Maybe you will come back to help me if you know how good the cooks' food is."

Nodding eagerly, Timmy gave a little bow and said, "Thank you, missus!" before taking the offered package and pastry.

Once he felt far enough away, he ducked down an alley and looked over his earnings. Not wanting it to get cold, he devoured the pastry in quick order. He relished the delicate, fluffy texture of the treat, savoring the way it seemed to dissolve on his tongue, and reveled in the bursts of sweet berry preserve. There were other flavors besides the berry, but he could not place them. All he could say was that they were perfect, evoking memories of his childhood home and the loving presence of his mother, who would fill their house with the aroma of her baking. Slowly savoring his treat, he had to blink rapidly to fight the unwanted tears that threatened to fall.

Swallowing the last bite, he wiped the crumbs from his face and turned to the package. Inside he found what appeared to be two sausage rolls, a hunk of cheese, and a handful of cherries. He could eat for *days*. Clutching the package lovingly to his chest, he planned on how he could keep it safe. He would say this—for the Darcys, they may be wealthy toffs, but their people were generous. He would definitely be returning to help with the wash.

***

"Catherine, I know that Theodore's mother invited you over for tea, but I would like to come along with you. I would like to remind Lady Matlock that there is solidarity with the Bennet sisters. Even when we marry and lose the Bennet name, we remain sisters." As they looked through the morning's correspondence, Elizabeth's voice carried a mix of curiosity and trepidation from her spot next to Catherine.

As she placed the invitation on the table, Catherine couldn't shake the threatening feeling that emanated from its elegant wording and expensive paper. "It seems as if you are as wary of her as I am." Elizabeth had offered to help her go through the invitations that had started coming when people found out that Catherine was courting the Earl of Matlock. They were discussing each one over tea.

Trying to understand the nuances of acceptance and refusal seemed a daunting and perplexing endeavor. She could not attend every gathering that she was invited to. Their overlapping times prevented that, even if she kept the busiest of schedules, which Catherine refused to do. She needed time to herself, as well as her charity work and archery practice.

"Yes, well, William and I have both been concerned about how controlling she has been of Theodore's social schedule. I would hate to fall back into bad habits, but I cannot like that woman." Elizabeth stirred her tea with agitation.

"I do not think that this is a case where presumed pride and disdain is actually shyness and anxiety. Coming to understand William deeper left you with an amazing love and now the most darling little son." Catherine's grim smile was directed at Elizabeth when she added, "Though I am uncertain of the potential outcome of my attempts to be friendly with Lady Matlock. The only possibility that comes to mind is heart palpitations."

"Yes, well, I am coming with you," Elizabeth responded, putting down her cup of tea and embracing her younger sister. Giving her a last little squeeze, she asked, "Now would you rather go to the musical evening held by the Kensington family, or the intellectual dinner held by Mr. and Mrs. Ambrose?"

***

"MRS. DARCY, I HAD not expected you when I invited your sister, Miss Catherine. I may not have enough biscuits." Handing a cup of tea to the woman who had come into her home uninvited, Lady Matlock kept only the thinnest veneer of civility. Mrs. Darcy's unexpected arrival was just another example of how the Bennet chits never conformed to societal expectations. Lady Matlock had hoped to use the tea to intimidate the girl her imbecilic son had fallen for.

Mrs. Darcy took the provided teacup with a brilliant smile, somehow unintimidated by the cold welcome. "Oh, I am not one to overindulge in biscuits. I am sure you will be fine. After all, you have so many years acting as hostess. I am sure you know that the first rule is to always be prepared for unexpected visitors."

How dare that country upstart from *nowhere* refuse to back down? Refusing to relinquish her authority, Lady Matlock redirected her attention to Miss Catherine. The girl's silent resilience was incredibly annoying. She was a naive young lady and Lady Matlock was certain her inexperience would make her susceptible to influence. Nothing else would do. "Miss Catherine, it is a pleasure to see you. You look rather well in that dress."

"Thank you, Lady Matlock. It is a favorite of mine." The girl's face lit up with a smile before taking a delicate sip of her tea.

"It really says something about your beauty that you can pull off a dress from an inferior modiste." Lady Matlock watched as the barb took hold, eager to watch its effects. It was not an especially cruel shot, a glancing blow, so to say, but it would tell her more about the girl's mettle.

There was a subtle widening of Miss Catherine's eyes, followed by a smile that caught Lady Matlock off guard. "Oh, it is simply a matter of knowing what flatters me and not allowing myself to be exploited by a modiste who values her name and marked up fabric over genuine style."

Lady Matlock fought the urge to gape like an idiot at Miss Catherine's comment. It was only her years of experience in managing her position in London's gossip mill that she could maintain her composure. How could a girl with practically no experience in the ton parry a barb with such skill? She had not yet decided on what to say next when Mrs. Darcy opened her mouth.

"Of all my sisters, Catherine has the best eye for color and form. She has helped us tremendously when choosing our wardrobes." Elizabeth smiled at Lady Matlock from beside her sister on the settee. Taking a sip of the tea provided, she grinned before saying. "This tea blend is a simply splendid combination of flavors. I compliment you on finding it."

Before Lady Matlock could respond, Miss Catherine smiled at her and leaned forward almost eagerly. "I want to thank you for inviting me to tea. Though we have known each other for some years, we have never been very close. It was nice of you to reach out so that we can come to a better understanding of one another. My sister Lydia made this bouquet for you from her small garden." Miss Catherine practically beamed as she handed Lady Matlock a little nosegay.

Looking down at the flowers in dismay, Lady Matlock attempted to regain control of the situation. How were they managing to handle her so well? With all the courtesy necessary, they had kept her from saying what she wanted to. "I felt that it was the thing to do, considering all the time my son is insisting on spending in your company." Deciding on another barb she bit out, "Lord Matlock could spend his time gaining supporters in the ton and yet he is spending time with you."

Miss Catherine took a serene sip of tea, seemingly unmoved. "I am so happy that you recognize just how much your son loves me. Please understand just how deeply I love him in return. I will do everything within my power to see him truly happy, no matter the obstacle."

"Yes, my son has used that word quite a lot. In my day, it was considered vulgar to bring up emotions and topics like *love*." Lady Matlock wondered how a girl of nineteen from the country could maintain her composure and attempt to take control of their meeting. Shouldn't she have caved before now? "*Love* is not something people of the higher circles concern themselves with. I understand that people with your ascendants may become fixated on such things, but it is not my choice to have my son dragged down to your level." *To hell with civility*, Lady Matlock thought as she felt her composure quickly unraveling.

"Surely, as a mother, you love your son." With a pause, Mrs. Darcy's eyebrow arched inquisitively, silently questioning. "Your only remaining son, I might add. Or are you insinuating that you feel no love or dedication towards your own son?"

Sitting up straight, Lady Matlock eyed her niece-in-law and the girl her son was falling under the spell of. They remained unimpressed and undaunted by her countess title and her authority in the ton. "I assure you I feel all that is *proper*."

"I am sure that you do." Miss Catherine put her teacup down on its saucer. "I do thank you for the kind invitation to tea. It has been reassuring to know just where you stand on my relationship with your son. I know you are a busy woman, and we shall not keep you from your plans. My sister and I must get back home and see to our own plans."

Panic threatened to rise as Lady Matlock realized her opportunity to disparage the girl was quickly unraveling. "Well, if you feel that you must leave. Until the Covington Ball, stay safe, and I look forward to seeing you. It will be interesting to see what a stir your courting my son will make. Bear in mind, the ton can be thorny, so it's wise to approach your dealings with prudence. Gossip has a way of unearthing secrets, and it can be merciless in its delivery." Pausing, she put down her teacup and stood before standing and brushing out her skirt. As she smiled at Miss Catherine, her stare remained frigid, silently communicating her disdain. "I would hate for the love you seem to share with my son to be tested so soon in your relationship."

Moving to the door, the sisters gathered their outer things and prepared to leave. "Do remember to put the flowers my sister sent in to water. She put a lot of thought into the selection of each bloom," Miss Catherine reminded her as they started out the door.

"Of course,," Lady Matlock replied with a smile that fell as soon as the door closed behind them. She promptly removed herself to her own private sitting room.

How had it gone so wrong? Miss Catherine had never impressed her much. She had always seemed quiet and unassuming when they had met in the past. She had hoped that even if she could not convince her son to abandon the chit, that she would be able to run roughshod over the girl and still get her way. Why did her son have to fall for someone with a backbone? It would ruin all her plans.

They were not conforming to the roles she wished them to fill. It was becoming clear to her that this would be a tougher challenge than she had initially thought. She could find solace in the fact that the other pieces of her plan were falling into place swiftly, leading towards the conclusion she had set in motion. The Bennet chit may be laughing and confident of her position now, but Lady Matlock would be the one laughing at the Covington Ball.

***

ELIZABETH WAITED UNTIL THEY were far enough away from Matlock House to not be overheard when she asked, "Just what did Lydia put in that bouquet?"

"You know our dear sister so well," Catherine replied with a mischievous grin. "Let's see, there was a hydrangea for boastful vanity. I am assuming she was implying it was a trait of Lady Matlock, not me. Orange lily for hatred, and yellow carnation for disdain. I also saw some tansies, which I think means a threat of war. I presume Lydia is saying she senses the lady's conceited vanity and sees through her facade to her true self. It is also possible that Lydia is threatening to declare war on Lady Matlock if she treats me with disdain or hatred." Looking at Elizabeth, Catherine burst into peals of laughter before leaning up against her sister who linked arms with her as they walked. "I love my sisters," she declared.

"Ah, Lydia is such a dear, and so fond of floriography. Who knew that when she got her hands on that little French book, she would immerse herself in its pages, discovering a newfound passion for the language of flowers," Elizabeth said happily as they approached their home. Once they had entered Darcy House and made it up the stairs, Elizabeth turned to her sister and asked, "How does it make you feel to have Lady Matlock as an enemy?"

"Well, I think it helps to know that she would have treated any girl her son chose who was unwilling to comply with her dominance the same. I am sure she has a very biddable debutante chosen for him. I have heard Theodore speak of a Lady Lavinia before." Catherine sat down and made herself comfortable in her favorite chair in Elizabeth's sitting room. "On the other hand, I am not overly fond of having another person like our father to deal with."

"I do not want that for you either. It is enough to deal with one horribly controlling person in a lifetime. I am lucky, I suppose, that both of William's parents had passed before we met. I am uncertain they would have approved of me. Sometimes, when I hear about how they mistreated him, I feel a burning desire to give them a piece of my mind. Maybe they are the lucky ones." Elizabeth sat down next to Catherine and took her shoes off, tucking her feet under herself as she sat. "You know you have our whole family behind you, no matter what you do or what your struggles are. Is Theodore worth the frustration and annoyance of constantly dealing with his mother's overbearing personality?"

Catherine shot her sister a look of disbelief. "Of course he is," she answered before leaning back in her chair, staring off into the room. "You know she must be up to something. The real question is what is his mother plotting?"

Chapter Fifteen

URGING HIS HORSE FORWARD, Theodore headed back towards Mayfair. He was glad that things had gone well in his conversation with Mr. Gardiner. He had gone into the meeting with the man as nervous as a green recruit facing the brigadier general after a prank gone horribly wrong. Even though he had met Catherine's uncle once or twice before and Theodore had been impressed with his joviality, he still feared the man's opinion of his suit. Despite his initial worries, the meeting had gone better than Theodore could have expected. The man's only concern was whether Theodore would be able to protect Catherine from the cruelties of high society. When Theodore had replied that he would always protect Catherine with everything that he was, for it was impossible for him to do anything else, it had cemented things. He was officially courting Miss Catherine. How remarkable was that?

He had long thought he would never marry; he had not wanted some poor woman left at home or following the drum. Then after he left the regulars, he had thought the likelihood of finding a love like Darcy's was impossible, but somehow the stars were aligning on his behalf. His face lit up with an uncontrollable grin he couldn't suppress.

On his way back to his home, he tried to come up with an idea of what he could do to charm Catherine. He wanted to pamper her with the things that brought her joy as they courted, but he had never courted a lady before. What did ladies enjoy doing while courting? What would Catherine specifically enjoy?

He would ask Darcy, but he was unsure if his cousin would have any better ideas. Darcy had courted and become engaged in the country while defeating a series of villains. Their courting activities were limited to strolling through the garden and engaging in intellectual pursuits like debates and chess matches. Theodore did not feel that he and Catherine were the sort to engage in esoteric debates. He would have to find some other method of courting his lady.

He would plan to maybe walk with her at the fashionable hour in Hyde Park. Or they could go to Gunter's for ices. His mind consumed with ideas, he only realized the apple peddler's cart was in his path at the last moment, swerving to avoid disaster. Realizing he had to get his mind out of the clouds, he focused on making it back to Catherine in one piece.

***

"So how are thing proceeding with your charitable foundation, Lizzie?" Lydia inquired.

The whole family and Mrs. Ansley was gathered in a rough circle for tea. Of course, Elizabeth and Darcy sat together on a settee. He was happy to follow their precedent by sitting next to Catherine on the other settee.

Handing Mrs. Ansley her teacup, Elizabeth answered her sister with a look of pride. "It is going rather well. We have gained enough funds to provide the school children with a trip to the seaside."

"What kind of school are you supporting?" Theodore had known that Elizabeth was active in a charity or two, but he could never seem to get them straight.

"I am supporting a school for children in the city who have lost their families. It gives them a safe place to live that enables them to learn to read and write and gain a trade and apprenticeships."

"It is nice that you will be taking them to the seaside. Please let me know if you need assistance in anything. I can help corral them and carry baskets, or even provide more financial support," Theodore responded, happy to try to help where he could. Tea with Catherine and the Darcy household was always a pleasure. The conversation was intriguing and the pressure to conform was absent. They were actively contemplating strategies to offer genuine help to people.

This was so much better than simply discussing it as an abstract concept, as so many people at his mother's dinners did. He had often heard people acknowledging the need to help the less fortunate, but never once had anyone ever followed through the least bit. Helping people was not just for show, it meant something, and it was like a breath of fresh air to be with like-minded people.

"I will let you know once we have more of the plan in place. So many of them have had such sad beginnings. I wanted to create a joyful experience for them to cherish," Elizabeth said, a smile spreading across her face. "With the way their little faces light up when shown the least bit of affection and consideration, it is no wonder I have become so attached to them all."

Leaning forward in her seat, Georgiana directed her attention to her cousin. "So Theodore, are you going to put an announcement in the papers about courting Catherine?"

He turned to Catherine, his lips curling into a warm smile, before shifting his gaze back to Georgianna. "I would love for everyone to know about my interest in Catherine, but I do not know the rules on doing those things. Catherine, do you have a preference?"

Catherine blushed under his scrutiny, but after clearing her throat replied, "Truly, I do not mind waiting for an engagement to be in the paper. Lizzie, your at home is tomorrow. Perhaps we may let it be known to our friends then that we have entered a courtship." Pausing for a moment, she stirred her tea. "By the time of the Covington Ball, everyone should know that we are in a relationship. Or at least the people we care to know. You will be attending the Covington Ball, won't you?"

"My mother already told me that we shall be attending that ball. We are finally far enough into our morning that we can began to attend some of the livelier events for the season without raising any eyebrows." Sensing Catherine's hesitation when he mentioned his mother's plans, Theodore hurried to try to reassure her. "I am sure that my mother will see that I am perfectly capable of directing my own schedule. Either way, I will be insisting that I spend my time with you."

"Colonel, I really must say that it seems odd to me that your mother is directing your schedule so very much. You directed troops in battle. Surely you can figure out how to schedule your own entertainments." With a small clatter, Lydia set her teacup down and fixed a narrowed gaze on him. "As much as I like you, I do not know if I appreciate you allowing your mother to dictate who you see. Aren't you capable of doing that for yourself? Shouldn't the only woman allowed to make those kinds of suggestions now be my sister?"

Theodore paused, contemplating what Lydia said. He appreciated how close Catherine was to all her sisters and that they would be willing to stand up for her when they thought she needed the support. Looking at the others in the room, he realized that none of them seemed to disagree with her statement. His mother's directives grated on him, but he yielded to them, trusting her expertise on the duties of an earl. It seemed that the people he was closest to were growing discontented with his constant compliance to her directives.

Theodore's energy waned as he slouched in his seat, but his smile remained genuine as he glanced at the instigator of his thoughts. "Lydia, thank you for making me think about that. My constant worry about fulfilling my responsibilities as an earl and preserving Cedric's legacy has resulted in an overbearing influence from my mother." He shifted his body, his eyes scanning the room's occupants, before finally resting on Catherine sitting beside him. "Despite my reservations, I have allowed her to control my actions. I apologize for not doing anything about it before now."

"You are forgiven as long as you remember to make time for me," Catherine teased with a smile and reached out to pick up a chocolate biscuit from her plate and placed it on his. "We are courting, and I wish to spend as much time with you as possible. It is not every day that a lady gets courted by the man who holds her heart." Catherine picked up her tea and took a drink, her eyes sparkling above the cup.

Theodore grinned from ear to ear. Catherine had clearly realized that he had polished all off his cookies, prompting her to offer him his favorite treat. Theodore looked at the woman who held his heart in return and just knew he had to spend more time with her. "What are your plans between now and the Covington Ball? I hope there is something we can enjoy together."

Tapping her chin for a moment, Catherine replied, "Gunter's is always a favorite of mine, or we could practice archery?"

Theodore gently took her hand, bringing it to his lips for a tender kiss. He then placed his free hand over his heart with a touch of theatrical flair. "Artemis my goddess, I am at your service. Name the day and I will be there."

Lydia giggled before asking, "Can I be the chaperone? You know how much I love ices."

***

WALKING WITH CATHERINE ON his arm was not something which was entirely new, but it had become magical with the establishment of their relationship. They were following Lydia as she happily looked in shop windows and occasionally turned back to chat with them. Lambert, Catherine's maid, had come as well for propriety's sake and she trailed discreetly behind them. At the end of the street was Gunter's, where they would enjoy the delights that the tea shop provided. Until they reached it, there was plenty of enjoyment to be had walking down the street and gazing into the windows.

Of course, they were gazing at each other as much or more than they were looking at the items in the windows. Looking down at his love, Theodore once again bemoaned the current dictates that ladies wear bonnets. He would much rather see Catherine's glorious hair than the top of her stylish bonnet. "Would you be at all scandalized if I told you that I live for the day when we can walk arm in arm while you go without your bonnet? Maybe at one of my country estates or even Pemberley."

"I do believe I should be offended. I will have you know that my bonnet is the utmost in style and fashion." Tilting her head so that she could look up at him from under the brim of her hat, she gave him a teasing smile. "If I were a different woman, I would complain that my delicate feminine sensibilities were offended by you wanting to view me without a bonnet. However, I think it is something we could arrange."

If Theodore was entranced by the grin Catherine gave him, he was lost when she giggled at his expression. "Right, and how soon do you think we can abandon London? Have we endured enough of the season?"

Playfully smacking his arm, Catherine looked back down the street. "With Mr. Goulding here for part of the season, I would hate to pull Mary away from the opportunity to develop something with him."

Placing his free hand to his chest, he jested, "The sacrifice I make for my love for you and your sisters."

"You know you love us, and you would be thrilled to see Mary well settled. I am very certain she loves him. You of all people cannot deny them the opportunity for love."

Patting the arm that held his own in agreement, Theodore smiled, appreciating the connection they shared. "They have been dancing around one another for some time. What do you suppose is the hesitation?"

Theodore watched as Catherine absentmindedly rubbed the side of her nose, seemingly lost in thought. Then, after a moment, she responded with certainty in her voice. "As a second son, Mr. Goulding often felt overlooked and underestimated. I believe he is only a few months older than Mary. He is in his last year of education at Oxford. If I had to guess, he is afraid of proposing with no prospects to offer her."

"I can commiserate with the man. It is difficult as a second son. Our society causes us to shift for ourselves so much of the time." The young man had not seemed to be destined for the church or the military, and Theodore wondered what his prospects were.

"According to Mary, he has a sharp mind and a strong fascination with the art of designing and constructing buildings. I have also noticed that he can hold his own in conversations about estate management and crop rotation when speaking with Lizzie and William."

Theodore's mind moved to how he might help this Mr. Goulding. He had met him a few times and he seemed very nice, but he had never had any in-depth conversations with him. If they were truly in love, Theodore would not wish for them to be kept apart merely because of the man's position as a second son in a world where birth order determined status. "What sorts of buildings?"

"Mary stated that he was most interested in making homes that were effective for families. Apparently, the family manor of the Gouldings is old and a mishmash of odd add-ons and its layout is inconvenient for the family and staff. It is hard to heat effectively in the winter, and dampness is a problem. All of that is to say he started wondering at a young age how he could effectively change things to the benefit of all."

Lydia came back and gently tugged Catherine towards the alluring store she had set her eyes on. "Kitty, come look at the lovely trinkets that they have in this window."

Theodore hurried with the sisters so that he would not lose the benefit of having Catherine on his arm. The window had a display of various bits and bobs, jewelry, and trinkets. He noticed how excited Lydia was pointing out the different little things that she liked. "If you like this that much, Miss Lydia, why don't we go inside?"

"Wonderful suggestion, Colonel," Lydia smiled, all but vibrating with excitement.

Going to the door, he released Catherine so that he could open the door for the sisters and the faithful Lambert who trailed behind. The ladies seemed to flit around the store of odds and ends in some sort of odd order that only females understood. Watching them with an indulgent smile, he was happy to let them wander. He looked down at the display next to him and saw a display of penknives. One of them instantly caught his fancy.

"I see you have found one of my more gentlemanly displays." The proprietor nodded to the glass case that showed his wares.

"Yes, would you mind if I take a look at that knife there?" There was no hesitation as Theodore's finger singled out the one he instantly favored. It was bronze, not steel like most of the others, and there was a green stone that was inlaid in the handle. While beautiful, it was the arrow design it sported that piqued his interest the most.

"Marvelous choice, sir. This is a nice little penknife and though it is bronze, it has an impressively sharp edge," the man explained as he opened the case to take out the knife. Laying it on a piece of velvet, he also put a sheath next to it. It was slightly longer than the average penknife, coming to close to three inches. "It comes with a charming leather sheath to protect the user from the edge when not in use. The handle, if I may say so, is a work of art. The arrow design showcases the exquisite combination of green dragon skin agate and meticulously crafted bronze. It is slightly more expensive than some of the others, but still a good purchase."

"It is worth whatever you are asking. Unfortunately, I don't have much on me right now, but could you please send the bill to the Earl of Matlock?" Handing the man his card, Theodore looked up and spotted Catherine and Lydia looking at something across the store. Catherine looked up and smiled at him from across the room before turning back to what her sister was saying. "Can you make it look presentable for a gift?"

Following Theodore's adoring gaze, the older man grinned. "Ah, yes, I can certainly do so. It's not often you come across a lady who can truly appreciate the intricacies of a blade like this," he observed. Exchanging a knowing wink, he reached down to retrieve a velvet bag and deftly concealed the knife within its soft confines. "The ladies love things in cute little bags. This should do nicely."

Theodore accepted the small package from the proprietor and a sense of anticipation built within him. He gingerly slid it into the pocket of his greatcoat, feeling its weight against his chest. "Thank you."

The elderly proprietor's face lit up with a warm smile as he looked at Theodore. "If you will forgive my presumption, my wife and I have been together for some thirty years and it all started with a look like that. May you have as much happiness as my Martha and I have."

"I plan to." Giving the man a salute, Theodore moved back to Catherine's side, already wondering how he might present the gift to her.

***

CATHERINE LOOKED UP AT Theodore, a smile on her face. He had been so amicable about taking her to the candy store, then without hesitation he had purchased the pound of chocolate drops she asked for. When he asked if she wanted one, she shook her head and the poor dear had looked perplexed. Now they stood in front of a nondescript building near Cheapside.

She could see he was confused but was willing to leave him in the dark a while longer if it meant she got to surprise him. As she entered the small garden, she could already hear the distant sounds of play, growing louder with each step she took towards the refined building. Grinning, she waited for the squealing. It did not take long.

Soon they were surrounded by a gaggle of children, their little voices all vying for her attention.

"Miss Catherine!"

"It is not Thursday, Miss Catherine. Why did you come today?"

"Who is with you Miss Catherine? He is so tall!"

Catherine leaned down and hugged them all in turn. They eventually noticed Lydia and Lambert and went to them for hugs as well. Catherine spotted the dorm mother in charge of the group and smiled. "Hello, Mrs. Cleaver. How are you and the children doing today?

The woman was of middling age and with such a cheerful disposition, her smile was infectious. "We are all fine, miss. We have just been taking advantage of the nice weather to let the children expend some energy. I see you have brought a visitor."

Blushing at the knowing look in Mrs. Cleaver's eyes, Catherine replied, "Yes, this is Lord Matlock. He is Mr. Darcy's cousin."

While several of the children had split off to talk with Lydia a few had stayed, including a little girl who was staring silently at Theodore with her thumb in her mouth. Kneeling so he was more on her level, he offered her a smile. "Hello, my name is Theodore. What is your name?"

Taking her thumb out of her mouth she whispered, "Sara."

"Well, it is nice to meet you, Sara. Do you like it here?"

The girl nodded, a smile spreading across her face. "It is clean and warm, and the food is really good. Though they are making me learn my letters, I do not really mind."

Chuckling, Theodore smiled up at Catherine before continuing his conversation with Sara. "They made me learn my letters when I was your age too, but I enjoyed it eventually. You probably will too."

She watched Theodore speak with little Sara for a moment before turning back to speak with Mrs. Cleaver. "I brought some treats for all of the children, and I thought while I was at it, I could show Lord Matlock around a bit."

"That is so nice of you. I will make sure all the children get some."

Catherine reached out and gave the older woman a hug. "Make sure you and the other dorm mothers and teachers get some too." Noticing that Sara was still talking with Theodore she asked, "Sara, I was hoping to show Lord Matlock around the school. Would you be willing to guide us?"

"Yes!" Reaching out, Sara took Theodore's hand and began walking towards the building. "I know where everything is! Would you like to meet Mrs. Smith? She cooks the food."

Eventually they made it up to the top floor of the school and Catherine explained, "Some girls learn to take care of the smaller children on the lower floors, but this is where we practice with the girls on household chores. They can also learn how to serve tea or work on ladies' dresses. Most girls, when they are old enough, can find a position as a maid or even as a nurse to small children." Inside the room, a few older girls were working on mending fancy dresses with some of the older women.

"What about the boys?" Theodore asked, still holding Sara's little hand.

Catherine continued walking around the set up that resembled the inside of any typical well-to-do house. "When a lady visits the school, she brings her lady's maid to help with the girls and her carriage is brought around back where the boys learn about the horses and how to work with the tack. They learn how to be grooms or sometimes footmen. I have known William to send over his valet to work with some of the older boys."

"It is all remarkable, much better than the alternative for most orphaned children in London." Looking down at the little girl next to him, he smiled softly.

"Yes, though Elizabeth is looking into something similar to be set up in Derbyshire, or at least in the country. Children are in need everywhere." With a proud smile, Catherine turned back down the stairs knowing it was time they head back to Darcy House soon.

***

"WAIT A MOMENT BEFORE you go up." Theodore took hold of Catherine's arm, detaining her for a moment before she went up the stairs. The time he had spent with Catherine had been amazing, but he had to bring her back home so she could get ready to attend a function that evening. Between meeting all the children at the charity school and just basking in Catherine's presence, it had been a great day.

Smiling up at him, Catherine tilted her head. "Of course. Did you need me for something?"

"I must go to one of my mother's dinners this evening, but I want you to know that wherever I am, I am thinking about you. And on that note," reaching into his greatcoat, he pulled out the velvet package and handed it to her, "I want to present this to you so that you will have something to think of me by when I am not there."

Taking it with wide eyes, Catherine held it delicately in her hands. Working the small knot open with one of her delicate fingers, she peeked in the small pouch. Pouring the small blade onto her open palm, Catherine gasped. "Oh, my." She dropped the pouch and started tracing the intricate design with her finger. "It is marvelous."

"I know it is not always appropriate to carry around your quiver, but that doesn't mean you are not always Artemis. I thought you might enjoy having an arrow that you could carry around with you."

"It is absolutely beautiful." Catherine's teary response was full of awe. "Thank you."

Theodore was glad his efforts had been so rewarded. Catherine's expression was reward enough and would buoy his spirits through the dinner he had promised his mother he would attend. He knew he would have to curtail some of his mother's promises if he was going to enjoy his time in London with Catherine.

***

THEODORE FOUND HIMSELF WONDERING about his mother's lack of interesting friends. Could the influence of these superficial people explain why he had always found his mother slightly cold and detached? If she had tried to fit into this world all her life, it was no wonder that she expressed so little of what she felt. If that was the case, he found it all the more reason to pity her. It was no way to live.

Theodore restrained a sigh as he attempted to pay attention to his dining partner talk about lace. Looking around the room, he saw most everyone talking and eating and having what appeared to be a pleasing evening, but he could not enjoy it.

"I know she thought she could get it by me, but I know when someone uses Brussels lace and when someone substitutes it with something inferior. So obviously I will not be giving her another opportunity to earn my business," Lady Lavinia fumed.

How had he once again ended up seated next to Lady Lavinia? He had told his mother that he did not favor her as a dinner partner. Unlike previous occasions, she wasn't paralyzed with fear of her own shadow and freely voiced her opinion, albeit about lace. "I am sure that was quite the experience."

What else could he say? The conversation was about *lace*. He had a strong wish to attend at least a couple of dinners with Catherine. At least then he would be able to spend some time in an enjoyable conversation.

His mother assured him she would let her friends know he was courting Catherine so that they could add her along with the Darcys to the invitations. She did, however, also remind him that it was up to the hostess on whether she wanted them to attend, and he couldn't help but wonder if it was an intentional slight or an oversight. Was there a polite way to ask the hostess why she did not invite Catherine? If so, he could not think of one.

"Will you be attending the Covington Ball next week?" Lady Lavinia asked before taking a small bite of the food on her plate.

"Yes, I am looking forward to it. It will be the first ball I will attend since I started courting Miss Catherine Bennet."

"Oh?" With a severe upward glance, she regarded him in complete surprise. "I had not heard that you were courting anyone."

"Yes, I am delighted to be courting Miss Catherine Bennet. I am surprised my mother did not convey it to you. You seem so close to her." Across the table, he could see his mother engaged in conversation with her dinner companion, pointedly ignoring any attempts at eye contact from him.

"Well, perhaps she thought that you are only *courting* the girl. It is not like you are engaged. In our circles, engagements are more recognized." Lady Lavinia took another bite and then turned to talk to her other dinner partner.

Theodore looked down at his plate and grudgingly took a bite. The food in his bowl was more art than sustenance. The soup had odd pieces of toasted bread floating in it in the shape of hearts and stars. The meat had been forced into congealed cubes that floated along with the bread. What was wrong with a good well-roasted chicken breast? He had little hope for the next several courses. If they brought out another one of those tormented hares, he did not know what he would do.

As a soldier, he was used to eating what was put before him and not complaining, but he decided that he would certainly turn down another dinner invitation from this house. Instead of his present surroundings, he daydreamed about being at home, indulging in the scrumptious meal prepared by Mrs. Goodwin. Even Darcy's cook was better than whoever this family employed.

More and more, he realized that he would have to have a conversation with his mother about what dinners he would be attending. Even after his previous conversation with Lydia, he had hesitated, not wanting to upset his mother. Waiting for the right time was obviously not working. He had been leaning too heavily on her decisions for what social gatherings he needed to attend for too long. Now that he had recovered somewhat from the loss of Cedric, he felt he could make some of these decisions on his own. Though he obviously could not have that conversation tonight.

Chapter Sixteen

As Catherine looked in the mirror, she could not help but wonder if Theodore would like her hair. Lambert had tried a new style and though Catherine liked it, she was anxious to see his reaction. Lambert looked at her with a hopeful expression and Catherine offered her a reassuring smile. It was not Lambert's fault that she was so nervous. "It is simply lovely. Thank you for your hard work."

Lambert beamed, "Thank you, miss. You will take his breath away if my guess is right."

"Oh, I do hope so." Pressing her hands to her cheeks to cool them from her growing blush, she began to think the ball would be something she might actually really enjoy. She would be able to spend time talking with Theodore and she could have two dances with him without setting the ton's tongues wagging. It would be a night to remember.

Lydia came bouncing into the room with little Artie on her hip. "Oh, you do look lovely! Doesn't Kitty look lovely Artie?"

Eyes alight, he nodded with a big grin. "Vuvleee!"

Catherine smiled at the pair though she avoided Artie's hands as he tried to reach out for her to hold him. As much as she loved him, she was certain he would muss her dress. Leaning over carefully she kissed his cheek. "Thank you, Artie. Do you think Theodore will think I look pretty?"

"Very pity!" He nodded before rubbing his eye with a small fist.

"There you have the stunning endorsement of a man with good taste." Cuddling her nephew to her as he began to yawn, Lydia smiled at her older sister. "Mary and Georgiana are almost done, and I am sure that Elizabeth is well on her way to being finished as long as William was able to keep from helping her."

Both sisters burst out laughing at their joke. Everyone knew how much Elizabeth and William loved each other. If they didn't, they were completely blind. It was the kind of love they had both been searching for and that Catherine was certain she had found.

"Just think, next season I will be out and you will be married. It is a rather good thing, or we would not all be able to fit into the Darcy carriage." Lydia started dancing in place, twirling slowly with Artie. "I cannot wait to be out; I will dance all night and have the most fun."

Shaking her head at her sister's antics, Catherine said, "If you enjoy the balls then I will be happy for you. As for me being married, I am not even engaged yet. Who knows? Mary could be a wife before I am."

"That is very nearly impossible. I have seen the way Theodore looks at you and Mr. Goulding has not even asked to court me," Mary said as she entered the room, a sad smile on her face despite how beautiful she looked.

Reaching out Lydia gave Mary a careful hug. "Don't you worry, Mary. Once Mr. Goulding graduates from Oxford he will ask you, I am sure of it!" Returning her attention to Catherine, Lydia winked and added, "I am sure it is nearly time to leave; you go have fun! Theodore will take one look at you and propose on the spot. If he doesn't, well, he will just have to deal with me."

***

THE CEILING OF THE room was adorned with elegant drapes of deep purple and navy-blue fabric, creating a regal atmosphere. Mirrors attached to the ceiling reflected the candlelight, adding a touch of enchantment, and the whole look evoked the sensation of dancing under a canopy of twinkling stars. It was the most beautifully decorated ball she had ever attended and yet she was lost to the charm of it.

Despite its beauty, the ball was not going as she had expected. As she came into the main ballroom, she noticed the whispers and glances from the people around her, making her feel self-conscious. Mary was certain there was fresh gossip afoot and cautioned her that whatever it was would pass. She reminded Catherine that they would take care of whatever it was, as they always did. Like a family. She bowed to her older sister's wisdom and attempted to ignore the gossip. The people's actions were all just futile attempts to assert dominance over one another. Many spread lies when they could not find truth, especially if it put them in a good light. Catherine could not wait until they had been in town long enough so that they could leave for the country.

Though she was not overly fond of the posturing present at balls, she normally liked to dance. Her last partner had been quite clumsy though and had torn her skirt in his bumbling attempt to dance the country reel. She found a quiet corner in the retiring room and began stitching up the small rip in her skirt with the help of a kind maid. Not long after, a group of ladies came in chattering. Their gossip was filled with tantalizing insinuations, none of which had any basis in truth. They had not seen Catherine in the corner and so they spoke of her at their leisure.

Though Catherine was not surprised as she had suspected the new gossip was about her, the knowledge of someone spreading lies—and hearing those lies—about her was a painful reality she couldn't ignore.

"I knew those Bennet girls were no good. Did you know their mother married mere months after she was widowed?" Catherine frowned as she struggled to try and place the voice. She did not take kindly to people being cruel to her family.

"Really? I am not surprised. I heard it said at calls today that Miss Catherine was seen trying to pull Lord Deerhurst out on the balcony at one of the balls earlier in the season. When her attempts failed, she lashed out by flinging a glass of wine."

Catherine could see how someone who was vindictive could twist things to come up with that. Someone out there was working extra hard to ruin her reputation in the eyes of society. She continued to listen, deciding it was better to be aware of the issues before she went back out to the ball.

The first voice continued, "I find the whole courtship with Lord Matlock to be rather havey-cavey. He could reach so high; I know for a fact that his mother was close to announcing his betrothal to Lady Lavinia. Why would he choose to align himself with a nobody whose appearance is forgettable at best?"

Blinking back tears, Catherine bit her lip. While she had always known she was not as beautiful as her sister Jane, it had been a long time since Catherine had considered herself a nobody. Their talk was starting to remind her of her father and his belittling ways. Before she was able to overcome that blow, the next one was quick on its heels.

"She appears meek enough in a crowd, but she must have some well-practiced arts and allurements to have snagged the new earl so quickly. Though one must wonder if there is a reason that she is so desperate to marry."

Arts and allurements indeed! Catherine wanted to pretend like it did not affect her, but the thought that people who knew her might believe such lies hurt. Once her skirt was done, Catherine thanked the maid and offered her a few coins before turning to confront the gossipers.

Though they appeared to startle at her sudden appearance, only the youngest girl who was close to Catherine's age had the decency to look ashamed of her behavior. "You may say of me what you wish, but I would request that you not disparage Lord Matlock. He is all that is honorable and would never behave in any manner that would be unacceptable. His request to court me is a great honor and I would not wish for him to be pilloried for his devotion to me." Before they had the chance to response, she left the room with her head held high, refusing to cower under the weight of their lies.

Catherine had only just reached the ballroom when she noticed she was being intercepted by someone she would rather not see again. Eyes narrowing, she recognized Viscount Deerhurst's slimy grin as he approached and suppressed a shudder. She was determined she would not shrink before him as she had the first time.

"Miss Catherine, I would like to put our differences behind us and have come to request a set." Smiling, he executed the perfect bow and reached for her dance card.

Moving her card out of the way, she refused to let him claim a dance. Catherine knew it might impact the gossip if they danced, but she could not be sure whether it would be positive or negative. Regardless of its impact, she refused to comply with his disgraceful behavior. "Although I appreciate your willingness to resolve our differences, dancing with you is not something I'm inclined to do."

It was clear Deerhurst tried to hide his reaction with a smile, but his facade of joviality cracked when his eyes drew together with a menacing glint. "If you refuse me, you will have to sit out the dances that have yet to be claimed. Do not be missish."

"Although I would prefer to be polite and cordial with everyone, I find that I cannot grant you your wish. You presume too much if you think I would grant you a dance." Drawing herself up, Catherine stood her ground. "I have not forgotten your actions the last time you asked to partner me for a set. I would hate to waste another perfectly good glass of punch."

"The Earl of Matlock is out of your league, and you are naive to think otherwise. I might have granted you my condescension before, but I know how to act now. You will regret treating me in such a manner." The viscount stood tall with his shoulders squared, his muscles taut beneath his finely tailored attire. Though he was handsome, there was something unsettling about his twisted smirk and the way his eyes flashed, revealing the darkness within.

Catherine stood firm, tilting her head defiantly as she gave a curt curtsy. "And yet I am satisfied with my choices. I am pleased not having you as my dance partner." Turning away, she left him and sought out one of her sisters, or possibly Selene.

She scanned the room and spotted Mary speaking with Mr. Goulding. She made her way over to them, trying to ignore the cuts as she walked through the crowd.

***

"WHAT HAVE YOU HEARD?" Mary asked Mr. Goulding hoping to find out why everyone had been whispering about her sister. She had enjoyed watching her sister blossom and conquer her fears and was determined not to let a group of mean-spirited women break Catherine's newfound confidence.

Mr. Goulding quickly regarded their surroundings, as if making sure his voice would not carry to anyone who would use the information against the Bennet sisters. "Your younger sister's reputation is being tarnished by rumors that she is literally throwing herself at Viscount Deerhurst and Lord Matlock."

"How dare they say that about Kitty? She would *never*." Mary snapped her mouth shut rather than let her anger get away from her. Closing her eyes, she took a quick breath and blew it out through pursed lips. "She has come so far. I cannot let this hurt her."

Reaching out to Mary, Mr. Goulding took her hand and gave it a gentle squeeze. "We won't let her get hurt," he whispered.

Mary stood motionless for a moment, savoring the fact that Mr. Goulding supported her and her family so completely. She looked to see if she could spot Elizabeth and William where they sat. "I am sure Elizabeth knows something is going on by now. We will have to come up with a plan to fight these lies." Turning back to Mr. Goulding, she smiled at him and squeezed his hand in return. "Thank you for your support. It means a great deal to me and my family."

"It is my pleasure to be of service." He bowed with a smile and Mary couldn't help the blush that crept up on her cheeks.

***

MAKING IT TO HER sister, Catherine reached out to take her hand and whispered, "I have just come from the retiring room. Mary, have you heard what they are saying?"

"Yes, dear, it is outrageous. We will devise a strategy to negate these accusations. It is probably someone who is jealous of your splendid match." Pulling Catherine closer, Mary gave her a quick hug.

As she pulled away from her sister's embrace, Catherine noticed Mr. Goulding standing nearby. "I am so sorry for ignoring you, Mr.

Goulding. It is good to see you this evening. Have you come to ask for a dance from my lovely sister?"

"Yes, I have made sure to reserve her supper set. I would also like to ask you for one of your sets, if you would be so kind as to grant a dance."

"Oh, I would love to, only I just refused a set with Mr. Deerhurst. With what he attempted the last time I danced with him, I was not about to repeat the experience." Catherine's voice was laced with a subtle growl, but she quickly offered a warm smile for her sister's suitor. "So, regretfully, I cannot accept any further requests for dance partners."

"Whatever did he do last time?" Mary's eyebrows drew together, and her eyes turned sharp.

Catherine's mind wandered back to that fateful night. It felt like so long ago. "He attempted to pull me outside after I refused his invitation to cool off with him on the balcony. He would not take no for an answer." Shrugging her shoulders, Catherine smiled wickedly. "Faced with no other option, I tipped a glass of red punch on him. His cravat was probably ruined, but I was able to break free from his grip."

Mary's face transitioned from horror to outrage. "How did I never hear of this?"

"It was the night that Cedric passed and with everything going on..." Shrugging her shoulders, she continued, "I never brought it up."

"I know you ladies are going off to find your family, but if I may, I have a thought." Mr. Goulding offered a wide grin to both sisters. "It is possible that I asked Miss Mary if you had a dance available and *she* granted me one of your dances after dinner. That would not break the rules."

Catherine couldn't help but return his grin and was grateful her sister had found such a clever potential match. "You are correct. I look forward to our set later in the evening, Mr. Goulding." Catherine and her sister both curtsied and moved on to where Elizabeth and Darcy sat. Mrs. Ansley sat with them, her eyes on the dancers, presumably making sure all was well with Georgiana on the dance floor.

As they approached, Catherine noticed her sister's controlled expression and could tell she was thinking hard. Elizabeth had always been so witty, and Catherine suspected she was fighting the impulse to go across the room and find a way to insult the women responsible for spreading lies. "I see you have heard the gossip."

"Yes, well, I have always known that the ton was full of catty idiots but still, sometimes I just do not know how we ever spend any time here." Elizabeth snapped her fan closed in a huff.

Reaching over, William patted Elizabeth's hand. "The museums, dear, think of the museums."

"Well yes, I am rather fond of those." Looking up at her sisters, Elizabeth's expression turned fierce. "We will find a way to combat the latest stupidity. Do not worry overmuch if you can help it."

"I will try, Lizzie." Catherine looked around the room and tried to spot Theodore. Things would not be as bad as they were if he were by her side. He had said he would be coming that evening and she hoped that nothing had gone wrong.

While she waited for Theodore to show, Catherine observed as William led Lizzie to the dance floor. She knew he had never grown accustomed to the hustle and bustle of crowds, even after all this time. Yet there he was, twirling around the dance floor with her sister. Catherine was aware he would much rather be at home enjoying a good book and yet he was at the ball because he wanted to support her, Georgiana, and Mary. She could tell he was putting in a lot of effort to make the situation comfortable for her and her sisters, despite his own discomfort. At least he was not without some benefit. Whenever he had the chance, he would join Elizabeth for a dance, losing himself in the moment. He had told her once that dancing with Lizzie had entirely changed his view of the pastime. According to him, when his wife was in his arms, the rest of the world faded into the background. Watching them dance made her think that despite what was going on with the gossip, she and Theodore had every reasonable chance to be just as happy.

"I am surprised you are willing to show your head with all the talk of your behavior of late. It really is rather disgraceful." Miss Eliss's abrupt comment came from nowhere.

Turning her gaze to the spiteful woman, Catherine sighed. She had always doubted the friendship the woman had espoused. "I did not see you there, Miss Eliss."

"Just what do you have to say for yourself, Miss Catherine?" The way Miss Eliss held her head high and pursed her lips made it clear she felt superior.

"There is nothing I wish to say to you. It is not worth it. Why waste my energy when I know you will not have the decency to respect what I say?" Ignoring the girl in front of her, Catherine returned her attention to the couples twirling and dancing with elegance on the dance floor.

Miss Eliss took another step forward, causing Catherine to instinctively take a step back to maintain her distance. Miss Eliss's sneer twisted her face into an expression of pure malice and was not flattering in the least. "Decency? *You* speak of decency. I heard you became so enraged at Lord Deerhurst when he would not go on the balcony with you that you spilled punch on him on *purpose*. What exactly did you want to do with him on the balcony?"

If Catherine was not so angry, she would have been concerned that the girl's expression of disgust would become permanent. How dare this woman attempt to hurt her in such a way? She had done nothing to her and yet she was trying to pull Catherine down with her cruelty. She had spent enough of her life cowering from such a person it was not going to continue. "I have told you I will not dignify your accusations with a response. It is apparent that you have never been a true friend to me. You cannot wish to spend any more time in my presence. Goodbye." The intensity of her anger took Catherine by surprise, and she found herself wiping at her wet cheeks. She had never been so angry that she had cried before. The combination of bewilderment and annoyance was overwhelming. Catherine sensed a presence directly behind her and assumed it was either Mary or Mrs. Ansley. She was grateful she was not alone in this struggle.

"Well!" Miss Eliss exclaimed in a huff.

"Do go away, Miss Eliss. I will not have you persecuting the woman I love."

Catherine looked up with a smile at the voice that had joined the fray. "Theodore."

"I am sorry that I am so late, Kitty." Leaning in closer than was strictly proper, he wiped at the tears that hovered on her lashes with his thumb before pressing a loving kiss against her cheek. His eyes searched hers with concern as he said, "I had intended on getting here earlier. There was a mix up with my carriage and when it started raining, it snarled traffic. Then there was a line to be dropped off and while I thought of walking the last bit, I did not want to arrive looking like a drowned rat."

"It is no matter. I am glad you are here now," Catherine smiled up at him. It had looked like rain earlier and on top of everything else going on, Catherine had worried he might have been in an accident. Shuddering at her dark thoughts, she chose to focus on how happy she was that he had arrived.

Mrs. Ansley coughed at that very moment, causing everyone to look her way. As she dropped the remaining bit of biscuit in her hand, her hands immediately went to her throat. Miss Catherine rushed to her side and started rubbing the woman's back. "Are you well, Mrs. Ansley?"

Rasping roughly, she said, "I am sorry, I only swallowed wrong." Blinking rapidly to clear her watering eyes, Mrs. Ansley tried to clear her throat only to start coughing again.

"Why don't I go get you and Mrs. Ansley some refreshments?" Theodore suggested.

"I'm fine. I—" Another cough disrupted her statement that she was indeed not fine.

"That would be lovely. Thank you, Theodore." Catherine smiled as she continued to try and help Mrs. Ansley.

Reaching out, Theodore took Catherine's hand and bowing over it, kissed her knuckles. "I will return shortly."

Only moments after Theodore left, Lady Matlock approached, her lavender gown elegant despite its nod to her mourning. The pleasant smile on her face seemed to lose its luster as she looked at Catherine. "Oh, Miss Catherine, I have heard the rumors and I wanted to come and lend you my support. People love to talk, my dear, and your aspirations to catch an earl is a topic that will never fail to spark conversation."

Catherine fought the urge to roll her eyes at the woman and her factitious show support. She took the older woman's hand in her own and gave it a gentle squeeze as she forced a smile onto her face. "It is so kind of you to come and lend your support, though I feel I must inform you that you are mistaken. I am not trying to *catch* an earl. Frankly I already have an earl, and I would love your son no matter his position and responsibilities. To me, it matters not if he is an earl or a soldier. It is his inner qualities that make me love him so deeply."

"You have some very original sentiments, Miss Catherine." Lady Matlock's face had lost all traces of her former smile.

Lady Matlock appeared to tense slightly when Catherine had mentioned love and it was obvious the woman did not support the idea of such affection in a marriage. Catherine had never been very close to Lady Matlock and was slightly intimidated by the possibility of the woman being mother-in-law. This did not prevent her from noting the way her speech of support rang false. Catherine fought the urge to call the woman out of her false comfort. She knew, however, that she did not want to make more of an enemy out of her by being rude while on display in the middle of the ballroom. "Yes, I believe some hold my sentiments to be unusual. Thank you for your support, Lady Matlock." Catherine curtsied without looking away or backing down.

Lady Matlock's eyes had just narrowed when Theodore returned with some lemonade for Mrs. Ansley. "Hello, Mother. Are you enjoying the ball?"

Smiling broadly, Lady Matlock replied, "Yes, it is lovely, despite the gossip circulating."

"Gossip?" Theodore glanced from his mother to Catherine with concern in his eyes.

With a tsk, Lady Matlock shook her head. "Yes, I did warn you that gossip was probable."

"Yes, I know, Mother. I also know you have been part of society for longer than I have been alive, so I am sure you can help things along." Catherine noticed that though Theodore smiled, his eyes had grown hard. "If you let everyone know how much you support our match, who can say anything? You are the Countess of Matlock after all."

"Well," Lady Matlock replied with a tight smile, "I suppose I should circulate the room then." She left their group and crossed the ballroom without so much as another glance.

They were quiet for a moment before Theodore smiled at Catherine. "So, were you able to save any dances with me?"

"Be glad I penciled your name in for the supper set before Lord Deerhurst accosted me." Catherine wrinkled her nose at the memory.

Stepping closer, Theodore practically growled, "He *what*?"

"He wanted to dance with me, and I refused him. He was rather displeased, but we were close enough to others that he could do nothing about it." Patting his arm, Catherine was glad when she could feel the muscles under her hand unclench. "Because I turned him down, I cannot dance with any additional gentlemen, so my dance card is rather empty. Would you like to sit with Mrs. Ansley and chat until the supper set?"

"Try and keep me away." A slight chuckle escaped his lips as he pulled a chair out for her.

Giggling as she sat, she looked deeply into his eyes, happy to be with him after all the earlier unpleasantness. "I would never even want to try." Catherine knew the night would be hard, but she would hold her head up against the gossip and suspicion and was grateful to have Theodore at her side.

***

THEODORE LOOKED AROUND THE ballroom from where he hovered on the edge, in the shadows. Catherine was ensconced with her family. Their defenses were up, and their heads were held high in defiance of the gossip making its way around the room. He was glad she was protected while he was away from her.

The things he had heard that night made him wish he was less civilized. He had been on his way back from using the facilities when one of the gentlemen that he had met at one of the endless dinner parties approached him. The man, whose name he could not recall, asked, "So between gentlemen, how did she convince you to court her? I will admit that Miss Catherine seems meek and even timid in company, and I never gave her a second thought, but I am wondering if I misjudged."

Nostrils flaring, Theodore had struggled to keep his tone relatively level. "What are you implying?"

Taking a long slug of whatever was in his flask, the man continued, "She must have done something that made courting her worth your while. Everyone is speculating about it. She does not have an impressive dowry, her connections are meager, and though pretty enough, she is not especially well-endowed. She must have some amazing skills, right?" With a lopsided grin, he seemed to wait for Theodore to confirm his suspicions.

Theodore's blood boiled so fast that he was dizzy. Glaring fiercely, he took a step closer to the man who clearly did not recognize the danger he was in. He wanted to pound the man into a bloody pulp but refrained. Instead, he threw his arm around the man's shoulders and drew him in close, his whisper deadly. "I know you know I am an earl, but did you know I am also a colonel from the regulars? I survived a great many battlefields by whatever means I had to. I could end you in a moment if I chose to, even without my weapon, but I will not. Do you know why?"

The man's inebriated gaze sharpened, and the whites of his blue eyes grew large. Shaking his head, he whispered, "No, why?"

"Because you are going to tell everyone that I am courting Miss Catherine because I love her. You are also going to tell them that Colonel Theodore Fitzwilliam, the current Earl of Matlock, protects those he loves. I will use all the means at my disposal to make sure she is safe, happy, and loved. If anyone ever disrespects her as you just did and I find out about it, I will know how to act." Shoving the man away from him, Theodore stalked away.

Now he was trying to calm down before he approached Catherine, but it proved to be rather difficult. The tears he had seen on her lashes when he had finally arrived had destroyed him. Though she put on a brave face, he knew that she did not cry easily. Those tears were his fault. It felt as if he was the reason people were talking about Catherine. If he was still just a retired, wounded soldier the gossips never would have cared who she was courting.

From where he stood, Theodore could see that Catherine was still being talked about by the way the other ladies watched her and laughed behind their fans. While his previous threat may have put a stop to the rakes and men who might insult her, he had no power over the matrons that seemed to be cutting her. Whatever his mother was saying to support Catherine did not seem to be helping much at all. Was there anything he could do to fix things?

Dread, cold and heavy, rooted him to the spot. He loved her too much to let her suffer this way. He had to come up with a solution, but he had no idea how to proceed.

Chapter Seventeen

It had been a mostly sleepless night for Catherine, but it was a new day, and the fact that she was on her way to see Theodore brought a smile to her face. After the ball, she hoped they could talk to come up with a strategy to fight all the nasty rumors. She had a few ideas already but was sure he could contribute more.

Walking to Matlock House did not take very long. Catherine looked over to her maid, Lambert, who was accompanying her, and noticed the woman's smile was unusually bright. Catherine suspected that Barnes and Lambert were developing quite the friendship, and possibly more. Catherine wondered how sweet it would be if her lady's maid and Theodore's batman developed their own relationship.

As she neared the front door, it swung open, and the friendly butler led her toward one of the grand sitting rooms on the first floor. Barnes stood in the hallway just outside the sitting room while Lambert settled into a chair just inside the doorway. Between the two of them, propriety would be more than covered.

Catherine smiled at Barnes as she usually did, but her smile wavered when she saw the concern etched on his face as she walked into the room. Her mind raced as her steps shortened. Granted, the night before had been a horrible mess, but that did not change anything, not to her.

She had a good cry when she had gotten home, but her conversation with Mary had strengthened her resolve. Remembering her conversation with Lady Derby had also helped her to realize that she and Theodore could work together to solve their problems. She didn't subscribe to the idea that love fixed everything, but she did believe it gave you the strength to endure and overcome.

Entering the room, she noted Theodore sitting in a chair by the empty fireplace. He seemed so unlike himself that she froze where she stood. "I received your note, Theodore. What is it you wanted to discuss?"

Looking up when she spoke, he gestured at the chair next to his own. "Come in and sit down. We need to talk."

"Your entire demeanor is worrisome. Has something horrible occurred?" Moving over to Theodore, Catherine sat down and reached a hand out to him. He looked nearly distraught. There was definitely something wrong and her instinct was to offer him comfort.

Theodore's hand enveloped hers for a moment, squeezing it tightly before letting it go and returning it to her lap. "I know what we wanted, but I fear it is not possible."

"I do not understand." Catherine felt the bottom drop out of her stomach. "What are you saying?"

Theodore gazed deeply into Catherine's eyes. The blue of his eyes was accentuated by the dark circles underneath, giving him a tired appearance. "Last night, I saw the pain on your face when they cut you. I care about you too much to be the one to bring that kind of pain into your life. The title of earl comes with a never-ending stream of demands and expectations that I'll have to endure. It is like a creeping miasma and it is working its way into all aspects of my life. I do not want you to be miserable along with me."

"Do you think me that weak that I cannot bear a few ill-aimed arrows flung at me by simpering termagants?" Shaking her head, Catherine got to what she saw as the root of the matter. "I still do not see why you insist you have to submit to this title in the way you believe. I know you believe you must emulate your brother in this, but there is more than one type of earl. You do not have to stick to his methods," she insisted, recalling Lady Derby's advice. "You say that you must find a way to help people, but his methods are not the only ones. There are other ways to help people with what you have been given. I have faith that you can find a way that will not make you miserable. You are your own man, or at least you were before your mother got her hooks in you."

"Do you expect me to forgo my responsibilities and give up on what my brother worked so hard for? Even though I want to pursue a different path than my mother's wishes, I recognize her efforts to offer guidance and support." Catherine saw the struggle on Theodores face, the agony in his eyes. She could perceive the conflict in him between what he wanted and what he thought he should do. "She is the last surviving close relative I have. I know you want to marry me, but your hopes are surpassing what is realistic."

Drawing back as if she had been slapped, Catherine's voice lost any remnants of warmth. "You are not allowed to sully my love for you with your presumptions and fears. Do you think for one moment that I would commit myself to a man who questioned my judgment, as you apparently do? While you may have fought the Corsican tyrant, I have lived under the reign of my own tyrant. I will not do so again."

Shaking his head, Theodore stood and began pacing through the room. "You have to understand. I cannot allow you to suffer because of me. It is simply not possible for us to be together."

Rising from her chair, Catherine planted her feet and confronted him. "I am not under my father's thumb any longer. I am not a child. I am a nineteen-year-old woman. You cannot compel me to do anything. You cannot force me to understand your foolishness. Yes, I was caught off guard by their cruelty and yes, it affected me, but I will not cower before them. I am no longer the girl that I once was. Why can you not see that it is only you who makes me suffer by choosing to follow this course?"

Clutching at the fabric of his shirt over his heart, Theodore seemed to struggle with how to respond. "The very notion that you might suffer because of me shatters me. I can commit myself to a life of dealing with the snobbery of society, but I cannot do it to you."

"So what if I am cut? Do you truly think I am so fragile as to be swayed by gossip? If you do, you think lees of me than I had hoped."

Catherine watched him as he agonized, her heart breaking as he made his choice.

"If you and I married, there would be balls, and dinners, and events. We would find ourselves regularly interacting with society. After last night, watching them cut you, degrade you...I cannot do it." By the end of his speech, Theodore's voice had faded to a whisper.

"I never would have thought that I was the strong one in this relationship. I know you hesitate to act against your mother, that you feel she is all the family you have left and that all she does is in your best interests. She speaks of your brother's memory and of what he represented." Taking a step forward, she reached out only to withdraw her empty hand just as quickly. "You loved your brother, and you want to do right by him, but this is not the way. I have been subjected to such controlling venom before, so I can recognize what is at its core. Your mother is trying to control you and make herself feel larger. My sisters and I fought for our autonomy in any way we could. You, on the other hand, are willingly surrendering to your mother's control. You are committing yourself to perdition of your own free will. It is sad, really." Going back to her chair, she picked up her reticule.

"You do not understand." Theodore collapsed into a chair across the room. He rubbed his face vigorously, digging his fingers into the crevices of his skin.

"Oh, but I do. Since you no longer want me to be part of your life, I will leave." Catherine turned away from the man she loved. Trembling with the surfeit of emotions that ran through her, only stopping once she reached the open doorway. Taking a breath, she held it as she did when she practiced archery. She steadied her heart for what was to come.

Without turning back to look at him, she spoke, hoping that her voice would have some resonance and that she could force some sense into his obviously malfunctioning brain. "I wonder what your brother would have wanted for you. Would he want this life for you? The one your mother says is right? Or would he have been proud of you for choosing your own path, finding your own happiness?"

With a signal to Lambert, who now stood at the ready, she took one last look at him before walking out of the room, wondering if he would ever understand how much she loved him.

Chapter Eighteen

"I WONDER WHAT YOUR brother would have wanted for you. Would he want this life for you? The one your mother says is right? Or would have he been proud of you for choosing your own path, finding your own happiness?" And with that, she walked away, leaving Theodore alone. He watched her go, feeling hollow and empty. Her parting words ran through his mind as he sat in the chair, staring into space.

Seeing her anger and hearing her counterarguments made him doubt himself. He had been so sure about his decision, had agonized all night about it. It had all made sense when he decided that they could not marry after all. She would be better off without him. She could find another man who would not draw censure to her. Without the weight of the gossips' disapproving grumbling, she could finally unleash her true brilliance.

He had known there would be pain and possibly anger, but Catherine's arguments had power and logic. Was it possible that she saw things more clearly than he did? Was it possible that his mother had ulterior motives?

Could he do good in a different way? Was it really possible? He contemplated whether there were other means to contribute to the greater good. He had taken his mother's word that Cedric's way—*her* way—was how people got things done. He had taken her knowledge on the matter because she had spent so many years as a countess, but was it possible that she did not know any better? Theodore let his head collapse to the back of his chair, weary from the emotional struggle and lack of sleep.

What hit him the hardest was when Catherine asked about his what his brother would think. She had accidentally stumbled on what his brother had told him to do. He had been broken and bleeding, and yet somehow Cedric had managed to tell him to find his own happiness. Theodore realized then that his efforts to overcome the events of that night caused him to neglect the importance of his brother's statement.

So his brother had wanted him to find happiness, but how could he do that while also upholding Cedric's legacy? No matter how he seemed to look at it, he could not seem to find a clear path. Most of all, he realized that if he did not have Catherine in his life, there could be no happiness.

***

BARNES HAD NEVER SEEN the colonel so despondent. He had spent a significant portion of his military career serving alongside him. He had patched up many of the colonel's wounds after numerous battles and had even helped get him home after he had been injured at Badajoz. When the colonel had been forced to sell out, Barnes had stayed with him and left the military as well. Even then, when all that the colonel knew had been taken away, he had never been this miserable.

Barnes was never one to enjoy the pomp that came with titles and high society. He knew that some servants enjoyed the prestige that came with serving a well-to-do family, but he was not one of them. As he looked at the colonel, he could sense the turmoil that had disrupted his life after his brother's death.

Deciding that he needed to offer him at least some tea, Barnes went down to the kitchen to gather what he needed. Entering the room that was often busy no matter the time of day, he found the cook comforting one of the younger maids. "Is anything amiss, Mrs. Goodwin?"

Mrs. Goodwin looked up from setting a cup of tea in front of the crying maid. "While Lady Matlock is kind enough to the servants, her friends are often not. Lady Matlock is talking with one of her friends in her sitting room. Poor Sally let one of the teacups clatter when she was serving the tea and Lady Talbot yelled at her. The woman shoved the teacup back at her, sloshing the tea on Sally. "

Barnes noticed that Sally had a compress on her arm. Apparently the girl had been burned. He was glad that for the most part, the family he worked for did not act in such a manor. Though he knew the colonel would not have stood for such an action, his mother was another story. Barnes could not abide the woman, but it was not his place to say anything.

Sally put down the teacup with a rattle and looked up at them. "I am not usually so clumsy, but when I heard them talking so badly about Miss Catherine, I was surprised."

Barnes fixated on the statement, and he couldn't shake the feeling of its immense importance. "What were they discussing regarding Miss Catherine?"

"Something about the gossip. How a plan was working? I am not sure exactly what they meant. They were right nasty, though."

"Is she still here?" Barnes looked at Mrs. Goodwin expectantly, as if everything was resting on her answer.

"Yes, she normally stays at least an hour when she comes. They are close friends, those two," Mrs. Goodwin responded with her eyebrows raised, clearly curious.

"Mrs. Goodwin, we will need tea in the colonel's sitting room in about half an hour." Turning, he hurried out of the room and rushed back to the colonel. Finding him still slumped in the chair on the main floor, he rushed up to him in a manner that he normally never would.

***

THEODORE LOOKED UP WHEN Barnes rushed in, almost frenzied. He couldn't explain why, but his military instincts were telling him that something was about to happen. "What is wrong?"

"Colonel, we must hurry. Follow me. I believe there is something you must hear."

Theodore's heart raced as he jumped up from his chair. Despite his previous weary demeanor, he felt a rush of energy. He trusted Barnes, and he knew he would only act this way if it was something serious. Without question, he followed him out of the room and into a series of back hallways the servants used. When it seemed that they were getting close, Barnes signaled for silence. Moving with the utmost care, he saw Barnes open the door with a deft hand, leaving it ajar to allow them to listen to the conversation.

A feminine voice made its way to his ears through the slight opening where the door was agape. "The latest campaign against the girl has been so successful, the next one can only do better."

"Did you see her expression? It was priceless. When her former friend cut her, I could not be happier." That was his mother. While he was aware she had a catty streak, the thought that she took pleasure in others' pain made Theodore shudder. Who was she talking about?

"You did very well, looking surprised at the gossip swirling around the room. Your half-hearted attempt to comfort Miss Catherine was perfectly done. No one could have guessed that you were the engineer of it all."

The unknown feminine voice was back, and he still could not place it, though he no longer cared. They were talking about Catherine! Theodore's fingers itched to fling open the door and confront his mother and her nasty friend. Barnes, however, seemed to notice his inclination and shook his head before placing his hand on Theodore's shoulder in a restraining manner.

"Of course I had to maintain my shock and surprise, otherwise my son might suspect me and my plans." His mother's voice floated through the door, along with her chuckle.

"By the by, how are those plans going?"

"I have him pretty well convinced that I know more than he on how he should spend his time. Once we have the encroaching mushroom out of the way, I will convince him that Lady Lavinia is the only suitable bride. My reign in society is all but cemented."

"My youngest sister is the best option—so timid and trained to stay silent and out of the way."

The sound of Theodore's racing heart roared in his ears, silencing everything else. He was consumed by anger, his body tense and ready for action. The temptation to burst into the room where his mother plotted was strong, but he yielded to Barnes's insistence and allowed himself to be led back through the labyrinthine hallways. Eventually, Theodore realized he was back in his sitting room and Barnes was setting a cup of tea in front of him.

Looking up at Barne's grim continuance, Theodore finally managed to form words. "How did you know that was taking place?"

Barnes fiddled with the tea set on the table nearby for a moment, as if hesitant to explain. "I had gone down to the kitchen and the young maid Sally, Jones's fiancée, was being seen to for a burn. It seems that Lady Talbot was upset at her for letting the teacup rattle and she sloshed the hot tea on her in retaliation. When I asked for more details, Sally revealed that she was shocked and saddened by the hurtful things being said about Miss Catherine. I knew you needed to hear what they were saying about her."

Theodore scrubbed at his face and let out a low growl of frustration. "How could I have been so foolish? I knew my mother was selfish, but I believed her when she spoke about growing closer together after Cedric died."

"She saw that you were vulnerable in your grief and used it to her advantage." Barnes spoke with a glower, clearly making no effort to hide his dislike for Lady Matlock.

"You heard what I said to Catherine, and what she said to me. I have made the biggest mistake of my life." Theodore wanted to bang his head against the wall but refrained from doing so for it would only damage the plaster.

Barnes stood silently, his eyes fixed on Theodore, and stroked his chin. "You have the ability to set things to rights. Miss Catherine is not a vindictive woman. I am sure she will forgive you with time, and maybe some appropriate groveling."

"I do not begin to know how to set things to rights with Miss Catherine," Theodore admitted with a sigh, still trying to process what he just learned. "My life has been derailed to such an extent by my mother that it will take a Herculean effort to get back on track."

"May I suggest, then, that you seek the advice of those who might know more than you on the matter? It is not as if you do not have people within your sphere that can help you."

Feeling like smacking himself in the head, Theodore could not help but remember all the times people had recently offered their aid. "Going to others for advice is a sound strategy. In fact, I was told to do so by a countess recently." Standing, Theodore moved to his desk with purpose. "I have several letters to write. Barnes, can you find out where the Derbys will be the next several days? Maybe I can arrange to speak with them at a ball or obtain an invitation to dinner."

"Yes sir, I will work on getting you that intelligence," Barnes replied before quickly leaving the room.

Arranging several sheets of paper on the table before him, Theodore first wrote a few missives that would arrange meetings the next day. Setting them to the side for Barnes to see to, he began contemplating how he was going to word the letter he was going to send. He had a significant amount of respect for the former Mrs. Bennet, now Mrs. Hawkins. He really could not fathom why he had not contacted her before now about his regard for her daughter. Now things were, of course, much more complicated. He recognized she deserved to hear from him and was eager to receive her input on the unfortunate situation he found himself in.

Once his letter was complete, he leaned back in his chair and contemplated his plan. His time away from the military had not dulled his understanding of military tactics in the slightest. If you knew neither yourself nor your enemy, you would succumb in every battle. He had certainly proved the adage from *The Art of War* true. While he had appreciated the message, he had not taken it to heart until that moment. It was no wonder he had felt so lost since he had taken on the role of earl—he had lost track of who he was and what he wanted. What was worse was that he had lost track of what Cedric wanted. With his dying breath, Cedric had told him to find his happiness. How had he forgotten that?

His mother's manipulations had helped him lose his way. He realized now that he had never really known his mother and therefore had lost every skirmish with her up until that point. He had not even known he had entered a battlefield. In this case, knowledge really was power.

Now that he had come to realize his error and his adversary, he could not help but plan for his success in a way that was familiar. He knew himself better today than he had since he came home injured. He also knew who his mother was and what she wanted. It was time that he put his knowledge to use and come up with an offensive against his mother and her tyranny. Surely she would be easier to overthrow than Napoleon.

***

THEODORE WAS GLAD HIS mother had not arranged for them to attend a dinner or ball that evening. It would give him the opportunity to confront his mother in a setting that he chose. The rules of the house would be changing. His mother would soon find that she was no longer in control of him or Matlock House.

Sitting at the head of the table, Theodore watched his mother. He knew she would begin her attack soon. Now that he had analyzed her pattern of behavior, he was ready.

Smiling at her plate, Lady Matlock cut a small slice of something and brought it to her mouth before regarding him. "I do hope that Miss Catherine has recovered some today. Sadly, she is just not cut out for society's slings and arrows." Her smile from earlier had faded, replaced with a furrowed brow and delicate frown.

Unfazed, Theodore watched his mother with care while continuing to eat his own meal. She had a remarkable talent for deceiving others. Now that he was looking for it, he could see the truth behind her pretty words. "You would be surprised how good she is with arrows."

"That is exactly what I mean. No woman of true society would admit to such an uncouth hobby." His mother wrinkled her nose as if a foul odor had offended her delicate sensibilities. "It is not her fault. Her mother did her best, I am sure, but growing up in a family of tradespeople meant she was not raised in the gentry. She did not understand the high standards we have and thus could not pass on those standards."

"I will be sure to warn Lady Derby then. She must not know of you and your friend's disapproval of her and her hobbies." Theodore winced as his mother's knife scraped against her plate, creating a discordant screech. Suppressing a smile at her reaction, he continued. "It was her influence that brought the Bennet ladies their love of archery."

"I was unaware that you knew the earl and his wife." Taking a small bite, his mother could not hide her slight pallor.

"Yes, Miss Catherine introduced me to Lady Derby. She is their aunt's cousin. Lovely woman, I must say. She seemed very fond of Miss Catherine and her sisters." Pausing to take a bite of his food and chew it contemplatively, Theodore continued his line of conversation, eager to bring his mother down a peg. Normally, he wouldn't have been so cruel, but his mother's actions changed everything. "I am eager to meet her husband. She has invited me to a family dinner later this week."

"Oh, I do hope that it won't conflict with the plans I have already made for us." His mother's eyes narrowed as her face contorted into a deep frown.

Now it was time for his counterattack. Theodore smiled blandly at his mother before he began. "I am sure that whatever plans you made for yourself will not be a problem, as I was the only one invited." Pausing, he took a sip of his deep red wine. "I heard that you were visiting with Lady Talbot this afternoon. Did it go well?"

"Of course,," she replied, her enigmatic smile quickly returning. "Visiting with her is always a pleasure. She has a wonderful disposition."

"It is such a pity that you will not be able to have her here again." Theodore cut into his meat and took a bite while keeping his eyes on his mother, waiting for her reaction. He was not disappointed.

His mother sputtered inelegantly and then seemed to choke. Taking a sip of her wine, she cleared her throat before replying. "Don't be daft. She is over regularly. We are the best of friends. What could prevent her from visiting?"

"I learned that she burnt one of our maids this afternoon by sloshing hot tea on her on purpose. It is my duty to ensure that those we have taken responsibility for are not ill-used in any way. I have let the butler and footmen know that she is to be turned away if she comes again." Carefully looking his mother straight in the eye, he threw down the gauntlet. "I will not have cruel people in my house."

Her eyes widened momentarily before she smoothed her features. "You would ban my friend on mere servant talk?"

Taking another bite, Theodore chewed, unrushed by his mother's exasperated expression. Swallowing, he responded. "The girl's skin was red and blistered, Mother. This is not merely gossip or supposition."

Waving her hand as if to negate his statement, his mother pushed forward. "Accidents happen all the time, dear. If she was, in fact, burned, someone should have told me. I will see to it. We do not need to do something as foolish as banning my closest friend from the house."

"It was not an accident, and frankly, I do not trust you to see to it as you were in the room when it happened. You are liable to let the maid go instead of acting as the mistress of the house should." He maintained a composed demeanor, seemingly undisturbed by her mounting frustration. Instead, he continued to focus on his meal and the clink of cutlery that resonated in the air.

With her meal clearly forgotten, Lady Matlock began to argue in earnest. "I am the mistress of this house. I am the one who oversees the staff. What could you mean by trying to step into my place?"

"I mean to take control of my life and the people in my household." Theodore's stare was hard. It was the one he had used on raw recruits that had tested his patience. Despite his initial belief that it had no place in his current situation outside of the military, he found it curiously fitting with his mother.

A nervous titter escaped his mother as she played with her napkin. "Why would you think you don't have control over your own life?"

"Because, mother, I now realize that you have cunningly orchestrated every aspect of my life, molding it to suit your own desires and ambitions. Your actions were never for my benefit, but rather to further your own agenda. The realization of this betrayal cuts deep, for I trusted you implicitly, never suspecting the ulterior motives hidden beneath your facade of motherly love." As Theodore's voice filled with emotion, it began to grow gruff and husky. Not having completed his speech, he took a moment to clear his throat before plunging forward.

"To my utmost regret, I now understand that your intentions were not limited to controlling my every move. You sought to tarnish the reputation of Miss Catherine, a woman who deserved none of the ill-treatment you inflicted upon her. Your relentless attempts to smear her good name have only become evident to me now, as I have finally broken free from your manipulative grasp."

Leaning forward, his mother looked as if she wanted to interrupt him. Theodore's glare proved to be so fierce that she snapped her mouth shut. His mother looking as if she had been slapped as she slumped back into her chair allowing him to continue.

"I am burdened with guilt and regret for my lack of insight. I failed to protect Miss Catherine as I should have, allowing your machinations to go unchecked. My naivety and blind trust in you have caused irreparable damage to her reputation and her well-being. I can only hope that she can find it in her heart to forgive me for my failures."

Finally speaking up, Lady Matlock argued, "You saw me trying to comfort the girl. How could you believe such lies? How could you take sides against me? I am your *mother*." She brought the napkin to her face, holding it tightly at her mouth as her eyes blinked back tears.

"The veil has been lifted, Mother, and I am no longer blind to your true nature. Our relationship may never be the same, but I refuse to be a pawn in your game any longer."

"You may be an earl now, but I am your mother. How dare you speak to me in such a disrespectful manner," she retorted, her tone laced with indignation.

Theodore believed his mother might have a chance at stage acting should she ever gave up her pretense at playing a society matron. Unmoved by her display, he continued with his plan. "Sadly, that is true. It is the only reason I haven't had you thrown from the house. I have a proposition, Mother. At your next at home, you will come forward and admit that you were trying to harm Miss Catherine for your own reasons and that you were the one who spread the lies. I also want a public apology to Miss Catherine from you at the upcoming ball. If you do not, this will be your last season in town under my largesse."

"How *dare* you request something so ridiculous of me. I am the Countess of Matlock." Standing so swiftly, she knocked her chair back to the floor. She spoke in a condescending tone, making it clear that she felt superior to him. Head tilted back, she attempted to look down her nose at him. "I am one of the leading ladies of society and you want me to apologize publicly to that Bennet chit? She is no one and has no respect for the bounds of society. She is full of pervasive ideas. It was bad enough when your cousin married her sister, but I refuse to let her corrupt our family." The table shook as she pounded on it, causing the silverware to clatter.

Theodore returned to eating his meal, as if unaffected by her outburst. Mrs. Goodwin had outdone herself. The meat was cooked to perfection, and the brussels sprouts were roasted to a crispy, golden brown. He did not want it to go to waste. "You may feel however you want about the situation, but you seem to forget that I own this house, not you. It is within my rights to state that those who reside here must comply with specific expectations. At the forefront of those standards is kindness. I expect kindness, Mother; no more treating people the way you have. If you find it is not something that you can comply with, you are more than welcome to remove yourself to the home that you received in your marriage settlement."

"But that is in Wales!" His mother's voice reached heights that caused the dogs in the street to shudder and howl.

Theodore found it was surprising that he turned out so well, considering his mother was one of his models for behavior. He managed to reply without sounding condescending, but his true feelings were evident in the slight raise of his eyebrow. "Yes, I believe it is. You will be happy to know that Cedric had the foresight to have it redone recently. I have just today sent a message to the steward to make sure that there are staff there and ready to serve you should you choose to relocate."

"I would never choose to relocate to Wales." His mother's facade of grace crumbled, replaced by whining and uncontrollable shrieks. "There is no society there. The people are practically primitives. It is unthinkable!"

"I put a decision before you, Mother. It is your choice to apologize and conduct yourself with kindness. Kindness to everyone, mind you. Cruel gossip will be a thing of the past. You will admit your wrongdoing and apologize to Miss Catherine or move to Wales." As Theodore looked at her face, he could see the defiance in her expression, so he spoke softly to try and make a connection. He was giving her one last chance. "I understand that may not be within your capacity to do, so I have made sure that you have a comfortable second option. The home is comfortable, and I will even make sure your expenses are taken care of."

Screaming, his mother picked up her plate and threw it at the wall before rushing from the room. Theodore watched her go, then tucked back into his meal. He couldn't help but think it was sad that someone else hadn't had a chance to enjoy the meal. It was a missed opportunity, as the meal was a delectable treat that deserved to be relished.

***

MARCHING UP THE STAIRS, Lady Matlock fumed. If her son thought to direct her behavior, that he knew what to do, he had seen nothing of her abilities thus far. Making her way to her room, she meticulously crafted a cunning plan. With the door closed behind her, a wicked smile played on her lips.

Chapter Nineteen

She was unsure as to when she had developed the habit, but Catherine realized that when her emotions were high, she painted. At the moment, she was elbow deep in paint. It was the same painting that she had been working on since Cedric's death and it was almost complete.

Originally, it had been a momentary inspiration born from the desire to bring Theodore some comfort. Even though she was angry at him for his decision to end things between them, she would not stop working on what would be his gift. The pressure was on as she worked tirelessly to complete the intricate details of the art piece. She would never be a painter with any renowned pieces but like most artists, she felt the need to work sometimes, and this was one of those times. Cedric had such love for him, and she was afraid that he was losing sight of it. Maybe her project would touch Theodore's heart and help him through his struggle.

It had only been two days, but the ache in her heart made it feel as though time was standing still without him. She was well aware of Theodore's inner turmoil, but she couldn't make sense of his decision to let her go, despite his clear affection. He had not lied when he had told her he loved her; she knew that much.

Pausing, Catherine stepped back from her work. Studying it intently, she realized that it was all but complete. It needed to dry some before she added one or two highlights and her signature in the corner, but it was finally done. Wiping at her forehead with the back of her wrist, she smiled at what she created.

Picking up a rag on the table next to her, Catherine began cleaning her hands. She rolled her neck trying to relax the muscles in her shoulders. Despite the joy that painting for hours on end brought her, her heart still ached at the void left by Theodore's absence.

Looking around, she spotted Lambert sitting in the corner mending something. "Would you care to go for a walk, miss?" Lambert asked. Having been Catherine's maid for some time, she was aware of her habits when she started painting.

"Yes, I do believe some nature might help me regain my equilibrium. Let me just get cleaned up and we can go."

It was only a matter of time before she and Lambert were leaving the house and heading at a sedate pace towards the nearby park. Seeking solace, she was determined to find a tranquil place where she could confront her shattered emotions head-on.

***

TIMMY MOVED THROUGH THE shadows, heading towards the Darcy place. Few people paid attention to a scruffy child moving about with a purpose. Though he tried to keep clean and relatively presentable, it was nearly impossible to succeed with no home. As he got to the house, he noticed the nice Miss Catherine leaving with her maid. Careful to stay out of sight, he avoided her attention; he was not ready to let her know that he was interested in going to the farm she spoke of.

He had nearly decided to come forward, but not yet. For the first thing, he was going to help with the laundry, and secondly, Miss Catherine did not look like herself. The only day he had actually spoken with her, she had been no less than a force of positivity. Everything about her had spoken of light and hope. Today it was like a rain cloud was blocking her sun. He was certain she was not having a good day.

He decided he would talk to her another time, but that did not prevent him from noting that she was leaving her house with only her maid. He had watched her leave the house before and knew there was normally a footman with her when she left.

He decided to follow her for a while, just to make sure that she was safe. You never knew about things in the city. She was a pretty woman with only her maid. There was no telling what could happen. He hadn't followed her very far before he noticed someone else was following her. Timmy knew instinctively that whatever the man wanted was not good. Freezing in place, he felt his stomach clench. The man's smile was evil as he leered at Miss Catherine.

Timmy could not help but worry as he watched the man creep after Miss Catherine and her maid. It was entirely possible that he was not following her and was simply going the same way, though it did not take long before Timmy knew without a doubt that the man was following Miss Catherine. He was only nine years old and not a very big nine. What could he possibly do about a grown man?

That's when he remembered the gentleman from across the square. He could not remember his name, but he knew where he lived. He took off like a shot, no longer caring about blending into the shadows. In his time on the streets, he had come to trust his instincts, and they were screaming at him. He had to get that man, and he had to do it fast.

***

CATHERINE LEANED HER HEAD back against the tree trunk behind her. She had a decision to make. What was she to do about Theodore's actions? She had always told herself that if she found a love like Elizabeth had found in William that she would fight for it. Look at all that her sister had overcome. Despite Darcy's outwardly aloof and unsociable behavior, she saw a shy and vulnerable side to him. She fought to save his life and had even been pushed off a cliff for him. Despite their father's disapproval, she had chosen to follow her heart.

Catherine could do no less for her own. Love was like a delicate butterfly, its beauty and essence easily damaged if not shielded from harm and she was resolute in her decision not to let it pass. Love was too precious to let slip away, and she was ready to use force if needed to make Theodore see what they had. It was, after all, for his own good. She knew he would be miserable otherwise.

Theodore's stupidity would not stop her from loving him, though it did hurt. Her heart ached at the thought that Theodore could put away his love—their love. She would push past that and come up with a plan.

"Miss Catherine, your eyes are so red. Why don't I go get a handkerchief wet in the stream? A cold compress might help," Lambert offered. They had gone to a solitary section where Catherine might pine in peace. The peacefulness of the area was complemented by the presence of trees, shrubs, and a softly murmuring stream.

Reaching up, Catherine felt her wet cheeks. How long had she been crying? She had hoped a walk would help clear her head, but clearly her thoughts and emotions were still muddled. Agreeing with the idea, Catherine mustered a smile that lacked true enthusiasm. "That would be wonderful. Thank you, Lambert. I really must get myself together if we are going to walk back home."

"We will have you put to rights in a trice." Lambert moved off between the shrubs to reach the stream. Catherine watched her go, grateful to have such a loyal friend in the woman. When she had met Lambert for the first time, they had just left Longbourn behind and everything had been so different from what she knew. Of course it was better, but that did not make it any less different and confusing. Lambert had been nothing but kind and supportive, helping her to step into a different level of society with grace.

Reaching out, she took up her reticule and begun rummaging in it for her own handkerchief. Without warning, a voice devoid of warmth pierced the silence, sending a chill down her spine.

"I told you that you would regret your choice to disregard me."

Catherine felt the bottom drop out of her stomach as she locked eyes with Viscount Deerhurst's sneering face. She quickly realized that he was in the position of power and froze in place. She was hemmed in with the tree at her back, and Deerhurst was hovering over her menacingly. There were only a few options available to her for dealing with him. She understood that she had to keep a clear head, and that her best option was to provoke him into making a crucial error. "Lord Deerhurst, I am beginning to question your level of comprehension. When a lady turns you down for a dance, it is usually best not to seek her out at other venues."

Deerhurst extended his hand and firmly grasped one of the low branches of the tree above her. With a forceful shake, a flurry of petals descended upon her. "Coming to the park by yourself was not a good idea. A woman's reputation is like glass, fragile and easily shattered. Perhaps growing up in the countryside, you may not be familiar with the behaviors expected of women here." As he leaned closer, a wicked smile spread across his face, and he gently brushed a petal off her shoulder.

Despite her efforts to remain composed, Catherine's body reacted involuntarily with a shudder as his hand brushed against her shoulder. "Are you intoxicated? You cannot possibly feel that trying to accost me in public is a good idea."

"I am Viscount Deerhurst. I do not have bad ideas."

Catherine could not help but roll her eyes at his comment. Did he really think he was incapable of having bad ideas? Of course, she had her own bad ideas. Why had she only come with a single maid? She knew that Lambert was somewhere out of sight and that she was smart enough to stay hidden, but if Catherine tried looking to spot her, things would only go badly for them both. "My mistake. I suppose bad ideas are only the domain of mere mortals, not viscounts."

Deerhurst caught her eye roll and, with a glower, continued with his speech. "Lady Matlock has bemoaned your involvement with her son to all that could hear. I, always willing to lend a hand, have offered to help her rid her son of his distraction. Should it be revealed that you are compromised by another man, he would quickly abandon any thoughts of pursuing your ill-advised courtship." Taking another step forward, he leered down at her.

"Don't make the mistake of underestimating Lord Matlock," Catherine rebuked Lord Deerhurst with a glare of her own. "Or should I say Colonel Fitzwilliam, as he was referred to by those who served alongside him. He is not the sort of man you are familiar dealing with." Catherine's hand had never come out of her reticule, which was of benefit because she had several important things in the bag. Among her belongings, she carried a few pounds, a handkerchief, a packet with a needle and thread, and, most notably, the bronze penknife given to her by Theodore.

Ignoring Catherine's statement altogether, Deerhurst continued to close in on Catherine. "I will get five thousand pounds from Lady Matlock for helping to free her son. Then, between your dowry and whatever money I can bleed off that prig Darcy, it will set me for years. I will have enough funds to settle my debts and restore our family estate." With a swift movement, Deerhurst reached out and undid the ribbon on Catherine's bonnet, pushing it back to expose her hair.

"Everything is falling into place like a beautifully wrapped gift, and I love opening my presents."

Catherine remained still while her fingers moved urgently around her bag. "I am neither a gift nor yours. I believe you should leave before you find yourself in a position you regret." Sweat trickled down her brow as Catherine bided her time. She would only have one chance if she was to attempt what she had in mind.

Hands worked their way into her hair and started to knock her pins free.

"There is nothing about to happen that I will regret." Dropping to a knee, he crouched before her.

Gratefully, Catherine recognized that his attention was too much on her cleavage to notice anything else. Having worked the sheath free, Catherine gripped the penknife in her hand like a lifeline as she began to pull her hand free of her reticule. "Life can surprise you."

When Deerhurst's large hand moved to try to rip the front of her gown, Catherine brought her penknife around and plunged it into his thigh. A high-pitched screech burst from his mouth as Catherine shoved him back and jumped to her feet. Taking a few steps away from his shrieking form, Catherine first strived to get out of his reach. She had hoped that if she aimed for his leg, he would not be able to pursue her, and it looked like she might be successful in her plan.

"Mistress, we must run." Lambert appeared out of nowhere and began tugging on Catherine's arm.

Wordlessly, Catherine nodded her head, eager to get away from the despicable person who had threatened her so. Gripping Lambert's arm in her own for support, she rushed with her out of the group of trees. They had not taken a dozen steps before Catherine found herself bouncing off the solid form of a person she hadn't seen while looking back over her shoulder. A strong hand gripped her arm to prevent her from falling.

"Miss Catherine, are you well? We heard a scream." Mr. Burgess's voice brought Catherine around to the fact that she had run into friends. Glancing around, she spotted Selene not far behind him.

"Deerhurst," was all Catherine managed, finding she could not begin to explain what he had been attempting. She pointed behind her to where she could see his form, still trying to get up.

"Burgess! What are you doing? Unhand her!" Theodore came rushing up with young Timmy trailing behind him. Both looked rather concerned.

Selene quickly intervened on behalf of her younger brother. "He was only trying to help her and prevent her from falling. Save your male aggression for the true villain in this situation." She pointed to the injured Lord Deerhurst sniveling on the ground by the tree.

As Theodore approached Catherine, he took her into his arms. He clasped her to his chest for a long second before pushing her back and inspecting her face with concern. "Kitty! I know that I have so many apologies to make, but first, I must know, are you all right?" Theodore's shaking hand ran through Catherine's mussed tresses before moving to frame her face in both of his large hands.

"I will be fine. I stopped him before he managed to do what he wished." Looking behind her, Catherine shuddered, seeing Deerhurst glare at her from the ground. Turning to Theodore, she gave a feeble grin. "Have I told you how grateful I am that you got me that pretty little penknife?"

Theodore glared at the miscreant. "What were you thinking trying to accost Miss Catherine, Deerhurst?"

Catherine may have found Deerhurst's sneer more intimidating if she was not being held so comfortingly in Theodore's embrace. With a toss of his head Deerhurst barked, "You may be an earl, but I do not have to answer your questions. Thanks to that wanton chit, I am in rather urgent need of assistance."

Theodore gave Catherine one last squeeze before stepping back. "Kitty, my dear, would you mind going with Lambert and Miss Burgess? I think I must have a conversation with the idiot viscount." The tone of voice he used made Catherine think the conversation might involve more than simple verbal communication.

"Do not think you must hold back on my account. He deserves much for his assumptions and ill-advised behavior. He believed that if I was compromised, you would abandon me without hesitation." Glaring at the man, Catherine scoffed, "Apparently, he was under the impression that he could pay off his debts by ruining and then marrying me."

"*What*?" A fierce growl escaped Theodore as he moved away from Catherine and toward the man who had intended to harm her.

Deerhurst, despite his inability to stand, mustered a snarl as he forced himself onto his knees. "She should not have crossed me. I told her she would regret it."

"Such the gentleman," Selene's commented as she drew close to Catherine and put her arm around her friend.

Catherine leaned into her friend with gratitude for the emotions she had gone through were exhausting. It was as if she had walked through a maze of emotions, starting with depression, then fear and anger, only to now settle into contempt. "My choice to not dance with you remains unchanged. Are you beginning to regret your actions as you realize that trying to exploit me was a poor choice?"

"I would say so. If he has not, I am more than happy to explain how it is not wise of him to target you, or frankly, anyone else." Theodore rolled his neck and squared his shoulders.

Deerhurst moved his hand to hover over the blade in his flesh. He curled his lip at it, as if it was the embodiment of all the ills in his life.

Watching the man's hand hover dangerously close to the small blade, Theodore spoke up. "I would not remove the knife if I were you. We need to summon a physician before we remove it. We also need to get a magistrate. There will be consequences for your actions."

"You cannot tell me what to do!" Reaching down, Deerhurst yanked the blade out of his thigh. When blood started gushing from the wound, his eyes rolled back into his head.

Chapter Twenty

"Devil take it!" Theodore rushed forward, but he did not make it to Deerhurst's side before the viscount crumbled to the ground. Witnessing the blood starting to pool beneath Deerhurst transported Theodore's thoughts back to the horrific scenes of the battlefields he had endured. Frantically pushing those thoughts of screaming and death to the side, he tried to assist the man that he could not help but hate with all that he was. "He must have nicked something when he pulled out the knife."

Catherine hurried to where Theodore was kneeling. "What can I do to help?"

Theodore's hands were clasped tightly on the man's leg, trying to keep as much blood as possible inside his corrupt body. Ignoring the man's moans as he came back around Theodore said, "Untie my cravat. We need to see if we can stop this bleeding. He is a fool. There was a reason I told him to leave the knife alone."

From behind them, they heard Mr. Burgess say that he was going for help followed by the sound of receding footsteps. Theodore did not have the time or inclination to wonder who might be able to get there in time to help the swiftly fading Lord Deerhurst.

Catherine's fingers hurriedly began to unwind his cravat, careful to avoid strangling him in the process. "This is not what I intended when I stabbed him. I only wanted to be able to get away."

Taking the folded cravat Catherine had handed to him, he pressed the bandage on the wound. "Do not take this onto yourself. He would have been fine had he not gotten the bright idea to pull out the knife. It is always better to pull out a knife with a physician present."

"Your mother is not paying me enough for all this." Deerhurst's words were slow and slurred.

Theodore's world stilled. The breeze running through the trees quieted down, along with the bubbling from the brook. "My mother?"

"Five thousand pounds. It seemed like a good idea." Deerhurst paused to breathe for a moment. "Could pay off the creditors in town."

Theodore forced his mind to stay focused on the life slipping out between his fingers and not his mother's betrayal. "We need a strip of cloth to tie a tourniquet. I think it is the only option we have to stop all this bleeding."

The sound of ripping cloth had Theodore turning to spot Catherine ripping a strip from her petticoat. "Where do you want me to tie it?" she asked without hesitation.

"Above where my hands are." Theodore fell in love with Catherine all over again watching her put everything aside to help him save a life. Despite the grim circumstances, he couldn't help but marvel at her desire to always help others. He kept his hands pressing hard on the wound, feeling the warm, sticky blood seeping through his fingers.

His eyes remained fixed on Catherine as she tightly wound the strip of cloth around the viscount's thigh in attempt to stop the bleeding. "Make it as tight as you can."

"That is duce painful," Deerhurst complained but refrained from struggling against their efforts. "Are you certain you are not just trying to make me suffer?"

Theodore's lip curled into a sneer as he fixed a piercing glare on Deerhurst. Despite the heroic act of saving his life, he was resolute in ensuring the man faced justice for his despicable activities. "If you do not want to bleed to death before help can get here, then you will be grateful for our efforts. I would let you bleed to death, but I do not want Catherine to have to carry your miserable life on her conscious as I know she would."

Looking at Catherine, he noted her grim determination. Her hair was mussed and her bonnet was missing and still she was glorious. What better woman could there be? Not only had she been able to defend herself against Deerhurst, but she was willing to save his life after he so stupidly endangered it. Her fingers deftly created a slip knot that she pulled tight before doing something to twist it into place.

Grunting in pain, Deerhurst complained once more. "Isn't there a better way to stop the bleeding?"

"As you decided to accost Miss Catherine in a park, we do not have a lot of options. If we were on the battlefield, I might be able to cauterize your wound with a hot iron. That normally works, and only sometimes festers. But like I said, you haven't left us with a lot of options." Theodore growled and wondered where Mr. Burgess was with the physician and possibly the magistrate.

Needing to focus on something besides his desire to rend the man lying in the grass to pieces Theodore looked around the small clearing. Theodore spotted Lambert standing to the side with the little boy Timmy at her side. As he stepped out of his home that morning, the little scamp's concerned face caught his attention, clueing him in on the potential for trouble. A rushed conversation about a dangerous man following Catherine into the park had sent him running. The little boy had hurried to keep up with him. Undeterred by the curious gazes, he reached the park with ease, quickly locating Catherine amidst its sprawling grounds.

Anger churned in his gut as he noted that despite her calm facade, she must be distressed by the events of the morning. She might have done what she had to in order to protect herself, but that did not mean she was not affected. It was not easy to harm someone else, despite how necessary it might be to protect yourself or others.

"I say! I was uncertain of what I would find when the gentleman said I was needed, but this was far from what I expected." A man with a bag had arrived and rushed to Theodore's side. "What happened?"

"That is a longer story than we have time for. Long story short, this cur has a knife wound in his thigh. I have been applying pressure, and we tied a tourniquet to attempt to stem the flow of blood."

"It sounds, and looks, as if an artery may have been cut. It might require some more care than we can provide here, but it looks like you managed to save his life." Opening his bag, the unknown man began looking for something within its contents.

"I will have you know I am Viscount Deerhurst!" The complaint was feeble, yet Theodore was sure it grated on the nerves of everyone secretly hoping he would lose consciousness.

"That does not prevent you from being a cur! Be glad I did not let you bleed to death," he said, his voice dripping with menace, "after what you were attempting to do to a lady in broad daylight in public."

"It sounds like we have a wrong'un then." A new voice commented and Theodore looked up to spot Mr. Burgess approaching with three rather burly men. The one in front seemed to be in charge. "I am Justin Wright. My men and I are Bow Street Runners. Mr. Burgess said you were needing help with a villain."

"Thank you for coming," Theodore greeted quickly before returning his attention to Deerhurst's leg.

"You may move your hands, sir. I will take care of the wound now." The physician moved his hands into place as Theodore took his away.

The moment he could move away from the miscreant, Theodore moved to check on Catherine. He was uncertain of how his attention would be received, but he could not force himself to stay away from her. "Are you truly well?" He wanted to cup her face in his hands but did not for more than the fact that his hands were covered in blood.

"I am well enough, though I fear the penknife you gifted me is rather soiled now." Catherine wrinkled her nose in disgust.

Looking over at the blood covered weapon in the grass, Theodore was ever more grateful he had found the beautiful blade and gifted it to her. "I would never have imagined you would have to use it in such a way, but I am glad it was there for your protection in my absence." Shoulders suddenly slumping, he lowered his gaze with a contrite expression. "I cannot apologize enough for my stupidity."

"While I am happy that you appear to have come to your senses, I do not think this is the time nor the place to have the conversation that we need to have. I will be fine. Speak with the increasingly frustrated looking gentlemen over there. It is time to take care of the matter at hand."

"As you wish, my lovely Artemis." Giving Catherine a smile and a nod, he turned to the men behind him. He considered shaking the men's hands, but decided against it due to the blood that coated his hands.

Justin Wright nodded in thanks before saying, "I can see that the current situation is under control. I will need something to put in my report." Looking down at the moaning man, he made a face of disgust. "From your conversation, I am assuming we are not here to hunt down the person who stabbed the cove?"

"No, I stabbed him," Catherine spoke up as she stood with Miss Burgess's help.

Rushing forward, a shaken Lambert stood in front of Miss Catherine as if to protect her from arrest. "He was threatening her. She was only trying to protect herself. It was only right that she do so with what he was trying to do."

"Yeah, he said he was given five thousand pounds to hurt her. He deserves to be stabbed. Miss Catherine is a good lady," Timmy added, approaching the men.

"Do not either of you worry. We are not going to take the young miss away." The gentleman at the front of the group tousled Timmy's hair before turning back to Theodore. "We will need to get everyone's names and an idea of what happened."

"I am Colonel Theodore Fitzwilliam, the current Earl of Matlock. The moaning wretch is Viscount Deerhurst. He admitted before you came that he was offered five thousand pounds to compromise the woman I am courting, Miss Catherine Bennet." Looking back at Catherine where she stood, her hair loose and disheveled, it was obvious that she had endured something, yet her posture was straight, and her gaze was determined. She was a goddess, her beauty and fortitude radiating like a celestial beacon, leaving him in awe. How had he ever lost sight of that? "I can only be grateful that she managed to prevent his attempt with her penknife. Mr. and Miss Burgess and I came upon the scene shortly thereafter. Despite being advised that he should leave the knife in place until a physician could be summoned, Deerhurst pulled it out. I can only assume that he damaged something, causing a large amount of blood loss."

The Bow Street runner gave a low whistle. "That is quite the lady you are courting." Turning, he gave a smart nod to Catherine. "I wish my own sister would have as much nerve. Good on you, miss, for putting such a cad in his place."

"Cad! I am Viscount Deerhurst. I will be respected." The weak complaint only received a series of eye rolls and hard looks.

Studying Theodore for a moment, Justin seemed to draw some conclusions before speaking. "So, Lord Matlock, are you wanting to press charges against the *cad*? Most lords want things handled quietly, but I am thinking you are not one of those lords."

"No, I want him to face the harshest punishment allowed by law. Make an example of him, as they say. We need fewer people like him in the world. People should not think they can get away with horrible behavior because of who they are related to," he declared emphatically. Theodore's voice quivered with anger as he clenched his fists, the blood staining his hands a stark contrast against his pale knuckles. He still felt the need to pummel the man on the ground behind him.

One of the men behind Justin cracked his own knuckles and looked down at Deerhurst. "He was doing this at someone else's behest. Do you know who was out to hurt Miss Bennet? Or would you like us to find out for you?"

"No, he admitted that it was my mother, Countess Matlock. I presume she was unhappy with my choice of wife." His voice was hard and devoid of emotion as he openly admitted to the fact that his mother was indeed a horrible person. There was a long minute where everyone merely looked at one another. What could one really say to such a confession?

Looking Theodore in the eye, Justin asked what needed to be asked. "Are you interested in pressing charges against her as well?"

Squaring his shoulders, Theodore barreled forward despite the pain in his chest. "I will not allow my mother to think that she is above the law." Theodore refused to compromise his morals on behalf of his relationship with his mother. As far as he was concerned, he no longer had a relationship with his mother.

"Very well, governor, we'll get things underway. Here is my card. I will be in touch as things progress. We will make sure the cad is taken care of. You need not stay." Looking over at the intrepid Miss Catherine, he nodded to her. "I do believe the young miss would be best served by having a cup of hot, sweet tea."

"Thank you for the suggestion." Theodore looked at Catherine closely and saw that though she was still maintaining a strong facade, she was paler than usual. It would be better to get her back to her home. "Let us all head back to Darcy House." A hand on his sleeve stopped him from going directly to Catherine. He looked at Lambert with his eyebrows raised.

In a quick and gentle manner, she spoke up, her words barely reaching his ears. "Might I suggest that you wash your hands of the blood, my lord? There is a stream just there." Lambert pointed to the body of water that bubbled tranquilly not ten feet away.

Nodding his head, Theodore first picked up the dirty blade and then went to the water and began scrubbing the blood off his hands in the cool water. It gave him a moment to collect his thoughts before he had to face everyone again. Done with his hands, he cleaned the blade as best he could. So many things were running through his head, recriminations among the foremost. There was also a tremendous amount of relief that Catherine was well and, for the most part, unharmed.

"While he is doing that, I will help you with your hair and bonnet." Selene had picked up the bonnet as well as Catherine's reticule before helping her get the bonnet back on her head. Hopefully, nothing would look so very amiss as they made their way back to Darcy House.

Once her bonnet was back in place, Catherine kneeled in front of Timmy, who had begun to look uncomfortable and out of place. "Timmy, thank you for coming to my aid earlier."

"It weren't nothin', Miss Catherine." Looking away, he blushed. "I am just that glad you are safe. I will let you folks head to your home now." As he made to go, Miss Catherine quickly stopped him by embracing him tightly.

"I would hope that you would come home with me. I would like to introduce you to my family. They will be very grateful to meet the boy who was so helpful to me. If you do not want to stay, you do not have to, but I know they would like to show their gratitude as well." Catherine held the boy out from her and looked into his face.

"Well, if you want me to. I suppose I can come with you for a while." Timmy gave a small smile.

Returning from the stream with less blood on his person, Theodore offered his arm to Catherine, who took it without hesitation. They all left the clearing by unspoken agreement, and no one bothered to look back at the group seeing to the injured Lord Deerhurst.

At the exit of the park, Mr. Burgess spoke up. "Lord Matlock, I see my carriage waiting. Would you be opposed to taking my carriage to Darcy House? I do not think we can all fit, but at least Miss Catherine shan't have to walk among the crowds."

Looking at Catherine, Theodore saw her nod of approval. "Splendid idea, thank you, Mr. Burgess." He watched as the tall gentleman moved through the cacophony of carriages to summon his own.

There was not much talking as they waited for the carriage to make its way over. What did one say in such a situation? Theodore figured they were all, for the most part, still shocked by the events of the morning.

Looking down at Catherine, he was once again stymied by her stylish bonnet. He could not catch her expression as she stared straight ahead, effectively blocking his view of her face and her glorious hair. He knew intrinsically that he had much to atone for, but he hoped with all that he had in him that he had a chance of redeeming himself in her eyes. It had to be a good thing that she had so easily taken his arm, right? He would hope that there was hope for them still.

The carriage pulled around and Lambert and Miss Burgess shepherded Catherine into the interior. Theodore judged it to be a fairly roomy. "Mr. Burgess, it might be tight quarters, but do you suppose we might all cram into the convenience? I think it might fit for the short distance we need to travel."

Looking up at the carriage, Timmy's eyes widened in both fascination and apprehension as he found his voice. "I can ride up top."

Mr. Burgess leaned down, smiling kindly at Timmy and patted him on the back. "That is kind of you, young man. Here, let me give you a hand up."

Timmy let Mr. Burgess grip him under his arms and hoist him up to the driver. "Thank you. I wasn't right sure how one got up there."

Theodore hopped into the carriage while Timmy was getting situated and introducing himself to the driver. He was pleased to note that Catherine was making room for him to sit next to her. Lambert sat by the window, while Catherine sat in the middle, creating a cozy space for him on her side. He sat next to her and felt relieved when she leaned on him almost immediately.

He was not sure what he was going to say to her or how he was going to apologize, but he knew it was not best to try having the conversation in a crowded carriage. So they all passed a quiet few minutes before arriving at Darcy House.

Disembarking, he helped the ladies out of the carriage while Mr. Burgess helped Timmy down. It appeared the lad had more fun than he had expected, and his grin was infections.

The footman at Darcy House saw the group exiting the carriage and opened the door ahead of everyone. Theodore entered the building, his arm linked with Catherine's. Spotting a servant, he requested they get Darcy and Elizabeth. Lambert quickly scurried away, seemingly on a mission to ensure that Catherine had everything she needed.

Timmy was trailing behind everyone, seemingly overwhelmed by the fancy surroundings. "I do not know if I should be in here. I think it would be better if I were to go round back to the servants' entrance."

Releasing his arm, Catherine knelt down in front of Timmy. "I am so grateful that you were thoughtful enough and brave enough to get Theodore for me. I couldn't care less what others may think about it, you are welcome in my home. My brother-in-law William will be glad to say the same."

"What is it that I am rumored to have said?" Darcy walked into a tableau of people in the entryway.

Theodore went to his cousin. "There is a lot we need to discuss, Darcy. However, to answer your question, Catherine has been trying to reassure young Timmy that he does not need to head to the servants' entrance."

Darcy looked at Theodore, his brows furrowing with mounting concern. "If Catherine wants Timmy here, then by all means he does not need to rush off. Though considering it, I am going to guess that Timmy would be best served by being rewarded for his good service with a hot meal."

Looking up at Darcy with a confused expression, Timmy questioned him. "You don't even know nothin' about what happened. Why are you so willing to be generous with me?"

"Well, if Catherine wants you here, I am sure she has her reasons. A meal is not so dear that I would not be willing to offer it to you while we sort out what happened." Darcy gestured to the butler, who had come to offer his assistance. "Rutherford, please show this young man to the kitchen. He is our guest. I would like him to have a hot meal. Please ensure that he is thoroughly taken care of as he has done our family a great service."

"Of course, sir. I would be honored to see to the young man." Turning to the boy, he flashed a warm, toothy grin to make him feel at ease. "Right this way, young sir." With a grand gesture, he escorted Timmy away from the group.

Meanwhile, Darcy glanced around at everyone still in the entryway and gave them a grim smile. "I am unsure of what transpired, but I would like to know and since this is not the place to hold a conversation, I suggest we all head to the upstairs sitting room."

"On that note, I do believe it is time for us to leave you to this discussion. If you have any need of me or my brother, please do not hesitate to send a note around." The Burgess siblings stood and moved to leave, but not before Selene walked over, extended her hand, and gave Catherine's hand a comforting squeeze, silently conveying her presence and support. "Please know that I am here to help support you. You can count on both me and my brother," she emphasized, her tone warm and sincere.

Theodore once again offered his arm to Catherine, and they joined the procession of people heading to the sitting room. At the top of the stairs, Catherine's sisters descended onto the scene, taking her away from him and enveloping her in a flurry of feminine reassurance.

Chapter Twenty-One

CATHERINE HAD BEEN STRONG, but the moment Mary and Lydia enveloped her, she felt her hard outer shell cracking. So much had transpired, with nearly none of it being good. With what had the making of a long and difficult discussion before her, she struggled to keep her emotions in check. She did not have time for tears. There were things to do.

"One of the maids will bring up some tea, Jane's special blend. I have a feeling we may need its soothing influences." Tucking Catherine under her arm, Mary walked with the group into the sitting room. "Lizzie will be upset that she was not here, but she was needed at her charity and she and Georgiana should be back soon."

Catherine noticed that Lydia kept up with her sisters but occasionally turned back to glare at Theodore. Lydia had always been determined to protect her loved ones from pain. "I would very much like to know why my sister has come home from her walk in the park looking dazed."

"Do not worry, Lydia," Darcy said confidently, "we will be told in quick order."

The room was large enough to seat the gathering of people with ease. Catherine found herself sandwiched in between her sisters. They each reached for one of her hands, offering their immediate and unwavering support to their cherished sister. There was an uncomfortable silence as everyone looked at one another, trying to figure out how to start explaining all that had gone before. Catherine could not stand the building anxiety and so she blurted out what first came to mind. "I stabbed Lord Deerhurst in the park with my penknife."

"Lord Deerhurst, the gentleman from the rumor circulating about you that claims he attempted to drag you onto the balcony at a ball?" Mary spoke up from beside Catherine. "What did he try to do this time?"

"He admitted he had been paid five thousand pounds to compromise me. Furthermore, he had devised a scheme to marry me and seize my dowry. He continued to say that he would blackmail William for whatever else he could get out of him. I managed to keep him from following through on his threats by stabbing him in the thigh."

Lydia's arms encircled Catherine's arm, her eyes burning with determination as she surveyed the group. "He should be glad it wasn't me. I would have stabbed him somewhere he would have regretted more."

"Yes, Lydia, we all know that anyone who tried to hurt you or your sisters would regret it." Reaching out, Mary patted her hand. "What happened after he forced Kitty to defend herself?" Mary asked the room her brows raised.

"Selene and her brother came upon me and Lambert, and shortly after that, Theodore and young Timmy arrived." Catherine's voice cut through the tension and filled in some of the gaps for the people in the room.

Theodore took over from there. "Timmy had noticed Deerhurst following Catherine and came to get me, hoping that I could help her."

"Theodore, I assume that you did not leave him to go free," Darcy questioned as he settled into his chair, his brow furrowed in deep concentration.

"He stupidly pulled the knife from his thigh, causing some pretty severe damage to himself and almost bled to death before help could arrive. Mr. Burgess went for help while Catherine and I went about trying to save his worthless life." Theodore let out an audible grumble, clearly frustrated. "A physician arrived to take care of his wound. Several Bow Street runners also came and took him in hand. I told them I wanted Deerhurst to be charged with whatever possible."

Mary's brows furrowed, a look of confusion crossing her face, as she turned to her sister and asked in a hushed tone. "Kitty, you mentioned that someone paid Deerhurst to harm you. Who could want to hurt you that much?"

Clearly noting their hesitation, Darcy spoke up. "May I presume that the fact the Burgess siblings left means you know who paid the dastard and we will not like it?"

Rising from his seat, Theodore made his way to the sideboard and carefully poured himself a finger of smooth, amber-colored whiskey. Taking a long gulp, he sighed heavily and then made his way back to his chair, drink in hand, to give his response. "In an attempt to sabotage our relationship, my mother paid him to compromise Catherine."

"Lady Matlock did *what* exactly?" Elizabeth questioned. She had just come in the room and had only been present for the tail end of the conversation. Rushing over to her sister, she dropped to her knees in front of her and inspected her for damage.

"I am fine, Lizzie, or at least I am doing better than Lord Deerhurst. I told him he would regret bothering me. He said he never had bad ideas, but I fear he was wrong." Catherine's giggle escaped her lips, but it carried a hint of sadness, as if it were on the verge of turning into a sob.

From where she knelt on the floor, Elizabeth turned to Theodore. "I apologize for the unfortunate revelation of your mother's malicious intentions. I know you and William will need to talk, but I think I should get Kitty into a hot bath and then bed." Standing, she wrapped her arm around Catherine and ushered her from the room.

***

DARCY NARROWED HIS EYES as he watched his much-loved cousin. Theodore was obviously distressed and rightfully so. The revelation of his mother's involvement likely left Theodore with a storm of conflicting emotions. Darcy found it difficult to decide what to say. On the one hand, he wanted to comfort him, but on the other, he had hurt Catherine only days before.

When Catherine had come back from speaking with Theodore in tears, her sisters had quickly united to find out what had happened. Catherine had been piled with hot chocolate and biscuits while the sisters had bad mouthed Theodore's behavior for the rest of the day. It was an understatement to say that they had all become quite angry on her behalf.

He knew Theodore loved Catherine, but that did not negate that he had shattered the poor girl's heart into a million pieces. Elizabeth had been so very upset when she found Catherine sobbing that it was all he could do to keep her from marching across the square to confront Theodore.

"Have you realized how much of an idiot you are yet?"

Running his hand through his hair, Theodore sighed in frustration. "I realized that evening, but I have been trying to figure out what to do to fix things in the meantime. My mother was behind the gossip, and I realized I had to put my foot down. I told her she had to apologize in public and change her behavior."

"You know that your mother will never do that. She is too proud." Darcy stretched his feet out in front of him, his gaze fixed on his cousin.

"I acknowledge that, but I wanted to grant her the possibility of changing her behavior. I told her she had two options: behave how I want or move to Wales." Theodore sighed and leaned back in his chair. "I gave her the chance to be a better person, and she plotted with Deerhurst to ruin Catherine. It seems like her choice is clear. It's time for me to reach out to my solicitor and initiate the necessary steps to have her removed from my home and my life."

"I am sorry it has come to this. I know you were hoping that with the loss of Cedric, you could grow closer to your mother. She has proven herself unworthy of the title. Do you have a timetable in mind?"

"That is actually hard to say. I told the Bow Street runner that I did not want her to hide behind her position and he should prosecute my mother and Deerhurst to make an example of them. No one should be able to feel they are above the consequences of hurting someone." Slumped over with his head in his hands, Theodore seemed to have lost his normally positive demeanor. "I cannot bear the thought of her in my home, but I will need to find out if she needs to stay here for a trial."

Darcy started to tap his finger on his leg, pondering how he would be able to help his cousin out of his morass of problems. "That does complicate things. Do you have a plan on how to proceed from here?"

Theodore started using his fingers to mark off the tasks he had in mind. "I need to speak with the solicitor and the man from Bow Street and see how things will proceed. My biggest priority, however, is to talk to Catherine and admit how foolish I've been. I have to make amends and try to win her back."

"At least you have your priorities straight now. I must tell you, however, that it may be more difficult to win Catherine back than to deal with your mother and Deerhurst. Elizabeth and her sisters are probably going to close ranks. You may have to get through them before you get a chance to speak to her." Darcy stopped and rubbed the bridge of his nose. "You may come this evening. I am hoping that the situation here will have calmed down sufficiently so that you will be able to find an opportunity to speak with her."

***

CATHERINE LAY ENSCONCED IN the softest blanket she had and surrounded by her sisters. She was clean of all the blood from the morning's trials, but that did not mean it was not invading her mind. Deerhurst had attempted to hurt her—ruin her, in fact—effectively steal her dowry, and blackmail Darcy. Why was it that she still felt so guilty washing his blood from her hands?

Years ago, she had faced similar turmoil when she had shot the horrible Wickham with an arrow to protect her sister. It had felt different, though. Though she would never hesitate to shield someone she cared for from harm, prioritizing her own safety felt less innate. The experience of protecting someone else was somehow different from the experience of protecting herself.

Could she have done something else? Something less violent? Was stabbing the man the only option she had?

By firmly clasping Catherine's hand, Elizabeth effectively brought her focus to the present moment. "I can see your mind spinning faster than a wayward top. What is going through that pretty head of yours?" Reaching out, Elizabeth smoothed some of Catherine's hair out of her eyes.

Biting her lip, Catherine confessed, "I was wondering if I could have found another way to protect myself. A man nearly died because of what I did."

Lydia snorted in a very unladylike fashion. "The man nearly died because he was too stupid to take the wise advice offered about leaving the knife where it was until a physician arrived."

Mary, who was sitting at the foot of the bed, smiled sadly at her younger sister. "It seems to me that we, as imperfect humans, always ask ourselves what if? What if I had chosen my words better? What if I had done that? It is my opinion that it is a very dark path to wander down."

"I do not know why, but I am finding it hard to justify harming someone else merely to protect myself." Catherine shook her head fitfully. In that moment, there was a conflict between her logical mind and her emotions, and she couldn't determine which side was prevailing.

Elizabeth spoke softly to her younger sister. "When you shot that arrow at Wickham, did you feel that it was the right thing to do?'

Sitting up in the bed, Catherine turned to face Elizabeth. "Of course! He was trying to hurt you. I was not about to let him harm you if I could help it." Reaching out, she clasped one of Elizabeth's hands in both of hers. The moment she had seen Wickham trying to drag her injured sister away, she had felt something change in her. She could not have let him abscond with her any more than she could survive without breathing.

Elizabeth tilted her head in question. "How is it different? You still hurt someone."

Catherine's brow furrowed in puzzlement, distorting her face. "I was protecting someone else. Protecting someone else from pain is something stronger, I think, especially if you love the person you are protecting."

"Then I do not see this situation as anything different." Elizabeth's face was carefully blank, as if wanting her sister to draw her own conclusions.

"What do you mean?" Catherine asked, her unease mounting.

"How do you think all of us would have felt had we found out Deerhurst had hurt you, or if you had married him and he mistreated you?" Pausing, Elizabeth waited a moment before continuing, allowing the depth of her message to sink in. "I can tell you for a fact that I would have been devastated to learn that you had been harmed in any way by that scoundrel. So, in effect, you were protecting us from harm by protecting yourself."

Catherine sat in silence for a moment, unable to form words as her mind spun like the top that Elizabeth had spoken of. It was true that her sisters would have been devastated had something happened to her. If something similar had happened to any of her sisters, she would have thanked God that they had come out safely. The severity of the man's injuries would have mattered little to her if he had tried to harm her sisters in any way. Why was she any different? Why should she hold herself to a higher standard than she would anyone else?

The struggle within her mind finally subsided, as if a whirlwind had settled and left behind a calm stillness. The act of hurting someone to defend herself might evoke feelings of guilt in her, however, it was a means of shielding her sisters from emotional pain. Catherine's muscles seemed to unclench as she finally accepted what she had been forced to. "I would never let him hurt any of you," she declared firmly, their mutual protective instinct palpable.

Elizabeth's hand gently grasped Catherine's, bringing her closer and enveloping her in a protective hold. "No, my sweet girl, we sisters fight to protect each other in every way that we can."

"I do not know what I was thinking." Catherine's words were muffled when she talked into Elizabeth's shoulder.

"We all forgive you for being distressed. It is only expected. You had a very hard morning," Georgiana spoke up from where she sat next to Lydia. She may not have exhibited the exuberance of some of the sisters, but she was still very supportive. "What I want to know is what are we going to do about my wayward cousin."

Lydia bumped her shoulder into Georgiana. "That is certainly a better topic to consider. Deerhurst has no redeemable qualities and we would be best to forget him. Colonel Theodore, on the other hand, may be redeemed."

"He said he was going to apologize. Or rather, he had many apologies to make and then later he said that he could not apologize enough for his stupidity."

"Well, that is a start. It is always better if someone can admit how stupid they have been. It makes for better groveling," Mary said, her face lighting up with a smile.

A giggle escaped so suddenly, Catherine gasped in surprise. "Mary, I never would have expected you to be one for groveling."

"It is better that someone knows they have done wrong and must apologize. The bible does speak of asking for forgiveness when necessary. I am not different from any of you. I do not take well to people hurting my sisters. He made you cry. It is only fair that he grovels." Mary's prim humph, in turn, made every one break into a relieved laughter.

"Are you going to forgive him and take him back, so to say?" Leaning forward in her chair and bouncing slightly, Lydia was clearly eager to find out.

Catherine pushed herself up to the head of her bed so that she could lean against the wall and look at all her sisters. Anticipation filled the air as all four of them awaited an update on her romantic journey. She pondered, trying to come up with how to explain how she felt. "Before everything went horribly wrong, I had decided that I could not let him go. Even if I was going to have to hit him over the head with something hard, I was going to get him to come to his senses."

"Well, it sounds like you will be forgiving him." Georgiana smiled, always happy when people got along as opposed to fighting. Catherine knew that most of all, she was happy when those she loved were happy.

"Do not let him get away with his idiocy too easily." Lydia, young and brash, was clearly unwilling to let Theodore's transgressions slide so easily. "Though I am angry at him for hurting you, I agree that you belong together. With everything happening, it is almost as if the hand of fate has reached out to help you two along your way."

With a sudden jolt of surprise, Catherine jerked her head back, her eyebrows shooting up. "Really? How has any of this been propelled by fate? His mother has been treating him horribly since his brother died. She even tried to pay someone to ruin me."

Lydia started using animated gestures with her hand to explain. "And yet it will not keep you apart. Not in the bigger scheme of things. I would imagine that the obstacles you have encountered will only serve to strengthen the love between you. It is allowing you two to see more of the other than you would typically get to see during a courtship."

Catherine nodded, seeing the supporting facts behind her sister's argument. "I always thought love was something ephemeral, and that you had to catch it before it passed you by. Love can be within your grasp, but you must act swiftly or lose it forever." Catherine began twirling her hair around her finger, thinking about her conclusions. "You also have to nurture love once you have it, or it can wither."

Georgiana sighed and leaned against Lydia who was sitting next to her. "I think that is a very nice sentiment, Kitty."

"Whether it's written in the stars, good fortune, or kismet, I am committed to catching this opportunity and not allowing the love of my life to elude me."

"William said that Theodore asked to see you this evening, perhaps after supper?" Elizabeth said. "Perhaps this will give you the opportunity you need to catch fate as it were."

"It would be better if she could catch kismet. It sounds more romantic that way." Lydia laughed when two of her sisters threw pillows at her.

***

IT WAS CLEAR THE household staff was all very fond of the family, including Miss Catherine. Almost immediately after Timmy reached the kitchen, they became aware of his actions to assist Miss Catherine. As a result, they immediately adopted him as their own. He was promptly offered a meal and a change of clothes better than any he had ever owned, even before he had been orphaned.

Timmy could only marvel at the change in his circumstances. He emerged from his bath, feeling invigorated and snug, his freshly washed clothes providing an added layer of comfort. The food had been copious and delicious. It appeared that the staff ate just as well on a regular basis. He had been debating taking the family up on their offer to go to their country property, but now he had pretty much decided.

Looking up from where he sat in the corner of the kitchen observing things, he saw the well-dressed man from before. Trying to be on his best behavior, he slid down the chair and smiled at the man nervously.

"They tell me you are Timmy," the gentleman said with a smile as he approached.

Standing straighter, he nodded and replied, "Yes sir."

"I am Fitzwilliam Darcy," he introduced himself, his voice noticeably laced with kindness, "and I wish to extend my heartfelt thanks for the help you provided to Miss Catherine."

Delight washed over Timmy as he blushed, overwhelmed by the unexpected gratitude from a man of such high social status. "She is a nice lady I could not let something bad happen to her. Not if I could help it."

"It seems as though they have taken care of you while we were seeing to Miss Catherine. Do you need anything?"

"No sir, the food was good, and they gave me new clothes. I even got a pair of boots! I do not know what else I could need." Looking down at his new shoes in wonder, Timmy grinned before looking back up to catch Mr. Darcy's own smile.

"Some of the staff have asked if we could find a position for you. And while I would be more than happy to offer you some kind of role here, I would first like to know what you would like."

Biting his lip, Timmy hoped he was not about to be too bold. "Miss Catherine mentioned you have a farm that needs help. I have never been on a farm."

"We will be in London for at least another month of the season, and then we will be returning to Pemberley in Derbyshire. If you want, you can return with us, and I would be more than happy to have you help at the home farm." With a thoughtful expression, Mr. Darcy brought his hand to his chin, deep in thought. "The family who have been running it recently had two of their sons leave home to start their own endeavors. I think they can use the help if you are interested."

Timmy feared his eyes might bulge out of his head and responded the only way he knew how. "I am."

"Well, in the meantime, would you be at all interested in helping the grooms? Working with the horses? Along with a generous wage, you would also receive food and lodging."

"Really?" Timmy could not believe his luck. This was so much more than just a meal; this was more than he had ever dreamed of.

"Yes, really," Mr. Darcy grinned.

Chapter Twenty-Two

THEODORE HAD SPENT THE rest of his day in a frenzy of visits to people he rarely saw. He had gone directly from Darcy House to the address on the card he had gotten from the Bow Street runner. It was there that he had learned that Deerhurst had survived his trip from the park to his home. At first, Theodore had been concerned that Deerhurst would try to escape, but then he had learned one of the runners was going to be stationed outside his house to monitor him and prevent him from running. The doctor had advised that he remain in bed for two weeks at a minimum to allow his leg to mend adequately.

It sounded like he might be prosecuted for the threat he made against Darcy, and a charge of blackmail seemed to have a greater likelihood of success in court compared to other offenses they could bring to book. Theodore's anger grew as he contemplated the lack of consequences for Deerhurst's actions towards Catherine. He was outraged by the lack of laws that adequately protected women as he believed they deserved.

The runners said they had all that they needed and would keep him in the loop. He made sure that they knew he would fund everything as necessary. It seemed that his mother could not be prosecuted for the role she played in the whole situation. Lady Matlock had proven to be too clever to pin down legally. Without hard evidence, it would merely be a matter of Lord Deerhurst's word against Lady Matlock. Despite that, he was determined to make sure his mother did not get away with her actions.

His next stop had been going to his solicitor. It had been a fairly simple matter to arrange for his mother to be cut off from all Matlock funds that she was not entitled to. He also arranged with the man the strictures he would put in place for her time in Wales. Before he had found out that his mother had acted so horribly against Catherine, he had been willing to support his mother in a manner to which she had been accustomed. That was no longer the case. She came into her marriage with a set amount in her settlement, and that was all she would be receiving. With it invested in the four percents, she would get roughly a thousand pounds a year. That thousand pounds would have to cover all the estate's expenses, including the steward that would be in place to manage everything.

At home, he went through all the bills that had been forwarded to him from the shopping that his mother did. He wrote every proprietor a message stating that from that day forward, he would not cover his mother's debts. As he added up all her clothing expenses for the year, it seemed like a small fortune. It was more than she would receive from that point forward. She would certainly need to adjust to a different lifestyle. He asked Barnes to get him a tray for he would not go to supper with his mother. Instead, he kept to his rooms and the study. He knew that if he saw his mother, he would explode, and he wanted to speak with Catherine before he confronted her. Catherine had a right to be there when they put her in her place if she so chose.

When it was finally time to go to Darcy House and beg for forgiveness from Catherine, he felt physically and mentally exhausted. He felt as if he had just fought a grueling battle, and maybe it was so. It just wasn't the type of battle he had grown used to.

Tugging self-consciously at his waistcoat, he waited in the entryway of Darcy House. Part of him thought he might be turned away, that Catherine may have come to her senses and decided he was not worth the effort. Forcing himself to stand and wait instead of giving in to the desire to pace, he waited to see if Catherine would come.

The sound of footsteps on the stairs had him glancing up in eager anticipation. Catherine was coming down the stairs arm in arm with her sister, Elizabeth. It was apparent that the day had been hard on her equanimity. Catherine did not look quite like herself. He was also certain that his stupidity from earlier in the week did not help matters to begin with.

Elizabeth stood in front of him, her arm wrapped protectively around her sister. "Theodore, Catherine has agreed to speak with you. You may talk in the sitting room. Lambert will be in the room with you and a footman will be standing in the hall."

Nodding with a solemn seriousness, Theodore replied, "Thank you, Elizabeth."

After giving her sister a warm hug and a gentle kiss on the cheek, Elizabeth patiently waited for her to exit the room. She then faced him with a stern expression. "My sister is determined to speak with you, and I am respecting her wishes. However, I want you to know I am not pleased by the fact that my sister spent days crying over your words and actions. She has told me that you wish to apologize, and I am willing to allow that. Just know that I will not stand idly by and allow you to hurt her again."

He had always gotten along well with Elizabeth even before she had married his cousin. His heart ached knowing that his own foolishness may have harmed his relationship with her, as well as all the Bennet sisters. "I am sorry, Elizabeth. I will do everything in my power to make it up to your sister. Please know that I love your sister deeply and I want only the best for her."

"Do not force me to find a way to hurt you. You know, we Bennet ladies protect our own." Elizabeth stared at him with a hard, penetrating gaze. Then, with a slight smile, she added, "I would rather have you for a brother than an enemy. Now go reassure my sister."

"Yes, ma'am." Theodore hurried to the sitting room, nodding to the footman standing next to the open door.

Catherine was sitting in a chair by the fireplace. His heart shuddered in his chest as their eyes met. How had he summoned the audacity to crush her heart with his actions?

Moving slowly, he settled on the chair near her. "Are you recovered from this morning?"

"It took some time, but my sisters helped me to recover somewhat." Catherine smiled, but it did not travel all the way to her eyes. She somehow seemed wary, as if she feared he might hurt her again.

Remorse settled deep into his gut. He had put that wariness there. "Yes, the bond you share with your sisters is remarkable." A few moments passed by without conversation. Theodore had a million thoughts swirling in his mind, making it difficult for him to choose where to begin.

Catherine closed her eyes and then opened them after taking a deep breath. It was as if she had found her balance and returned to the conversation with a heightened sense of strength. "You said you had apologies to make."

"Yes, apologies, so many apologies. I was wrong about so many things. I was wrong for assuming that you were incapable of overcoming the gossip of the ton. I was afraid of letting you get hurt. Somehow, I felt as if it was my fault that you were in pain." Scrubbing at his face, Theodore fought to forget the haunting image of her expression at the ball.

Tilting her head, Catherine frowned. "You thought I was crying because I was hurt?"

Pausing, Theodore looked at her in confusion. Why else would she have been crying? "Yes?"

"You may not know this about women, but we cry for many reasons. We can cry because we are sad or depressed or happy. That night I cried because I was so furious, and I had no easy way of expressing it. You may move on to your next mistake." Catherine offered a small smirk as she shifted in her seat, crossing her legs at her ankles.

He was taken aback by his own stupidity. Theodore only hesitated slightly before continuing. "Lydia was right. I was allowing my mother too much influence over me and my life since becoming earl. You were right. The weight of trying to fill my brother's shoes was causing me to lose sight of who I really was. More than anything else, I was wrong about my mother. I foolishly believed that my mother was telling the truth when she said she wanted to help me adjust to my new responsibilities. That she wanted to grow closer."

Reaching out, Catherine clasped his hand until he looked her in the eye. "I know the pain of betrayal is worse when it is perpetrated by someone who should love you. You know how hard I struggled. How hard all my sisters and mother struggled under my father's domination. Despite everything, I am sorry that you had to see her for what she is."

Returning the gesture with a squeeze of his own, Theodore smiled halfheartedly. "Thank you for showing me empathy and understanding, especially in light of my own stupidity. Though I by no means want to excuse my behavior, I want to explain how I have been feeling."

Catherine nodded in encouragement as she returned her hand to her lap. "I noticed that you were struggling even before Cedric died. Tell me what is going on in that head of yours."

"It is odd, as if I am waking up from another one of my nightmares, only to find that it carried over into my real life. I feel like I have been detached from myself for so long." Trying to figure out how to explain how lost he had become, he stood up and paced the room, the sound of his footsteps filling the silence. "Even before my brother died, I had felt lost and had been trying to find my way. I had expected nothing but pain and eventually death in battle, and then suddenly, I was not in the regulars anymore. I did not have an estate or any prospects."

"Is that what you were worrying over before Cedric died?" Catherine's voice came softly from where she still sat.

Finally settling into a defeated stance in front of the fire, Theodore watched the flames flicker. With a slow shake of his head, Theodore forced himself to continue. "I had finally admitted to myself and my brother just how badly I had been struggling. Then he died, and I was drowning in responsibilities and my mother pretended to be a lifeline. Only she was a snake just waiting to devour me."

"You have been struggling on your own for far too long. I hope you realize now that you are not alone in this. The only reason my sisters and I managed to overcome my father was the fact that we drew together and not apart. You have people who want to help you—allow them that. Allow *yourself* that. Even in battle, you did not fight alone. You had an entire group of other soldiers fighting with you."

With a heavy heart, he turned and looked at Catherine, his shoulders drooping. "You are right. I did not look for help when

I should have and when I did look for help, I went to the wrong person."

"Yes, well, you will also have to admit that I might just be smarter than you at times." Despite Theodore's dejected state, Catherine smiled, seeming to wait for him to realize something.

Noticing her expression, Theodore began to perk up. Was it possible that he had not entirely ruined what could be his only chance at happiness and love? "I wholeheartedly agree. I should have realized that as a mere colonel, I should have appealed to my general for help."

Wrinkling her nose playfully, Catherine responded, "I am not fond of the designation of general. I prefer Artemis."

"Yes, how could I forget? As a mere mortal, I should have looked to my goddess for guidance." Approaching Catherine with hope in his heart, he could see the laughter in her eyes as he reached out to take her hand. "Can you ever forgive me?"

Fighting a grin, she replied, "Well, let me think about your errors. In short, your understanding of how to honor your brother's legacy was flawed. The disconcerting fact was that you were losing touch with your own identity. You were incorrect in trusting your mother. Most of all, you were wrong to assume I was incapable of facing the ton and their lies." Though it all sounded grim, Catherine did not seem at all disturbed by the list of his errors.

Nodding his head in agreement, Theodore concurred with her assessment. "All correct. I am so sorry."

Catherine tilted her head, revealing a mischievous smile, and eyes filled with laughter. "Mary told me you should grovel."

Drawing closer, he knelt in front of her, his broad chest brushing her knees. "I will. I am determined to say or do anything necessary to remove the wariness I observed on your face earlier," Theodore affirmed.

Taking up Theodore's other hand, she held them both in her own. "I do not need you to grovel. I need you to do something that might be harder. Trust in me and have faith that we can confront and conquer anything that comes our way, hand in hand. I need you to reach out and grasp love tightly, hold onto it with both hands, and cherish its essence alongside me."

"Hand in hand?" Theodore intertwined his fingers with hers, creating an intimate connection. His thumb ran along the underside of her wrist and he felt her shudder.

With a visible swallow, Catherine responded shakily. "Yes, I want to work together with you in a partnership. In case you hadn't noticed, I am not your typical society maiden. I do not need to be shielded from life. I demand to be a part of it."

"If you are so eager to demand your part in my life," he wondered aloud, "does that mean I am forgiven? Can you ease the agony in my heart and bring me solace with your mercy?"

"Your heartfelt apologies have left me with no choice but to forgive you." Catherine's forgiving gaze met Theodore's, their eyes locking in a moment of understanding. "It is just as well as I cannot fathom my life without you by my side."

Theodore clutched her face in his hands and rested his forehead against hers. He took a moment of simply breathing in the love that she so freely offered, and that he had stupidly cast aside. With the certainty that he had not lost his chance of a happy life filled with love, he felt a surge of joy that made his head spin.

Pulling back, he gazed into her eyes and, emboldened by what he saw there, Theodore made a snap decision. Settling back on his heels, he took up Catherine's hands once more. "Now that you have granted me clemency, I must beg for another favor. I have learned the perils of shouldering too many responsibilities, and I realize that my current approach is unsustainable. I need help. I cannot take on everything alone as I have been doing. Leaning on my mother's advice is out of the question. I need the help of someone I love, someone who loves me." Bringing Catherine's hands up to his mouth, he kissed her wrists where her pulse seemed to thud crazily. "Catherine, my Artemis, my heart, I love you more than I ever thought was possible. Though I have proven myself eminently stupid, will you have me, idiocy and all? May I have the privilege of your support and companionship for the rest of our days?"

Pulling her hand free of Theodore's grasp, she cupped his cheek. "Well, someone must take you in hand. I suppose since I love you beyond reason, I must commit my days to your care."

With a surge of energy, Theodore pulled her to his chest and buried his face in her hair. His life had gone from devastating to delightful so quickly that it was making his head spin, but he did not care. Pulling back, he went to kiss Catherine but froze at the sound of a throat clearing.

He had completely forgotten that Lambert was sitting in a chair in the corner. Looking over, he saw her glance over the edge of her book at him, an eyebrow raised. Convinced that he was blushing, he gazed into Catherine's eyes, which were crinkling with amusement. "Do you suppose we could sit on the settee together and talk?"

"Of course." Catherine stood with his assistance and moved with him to the settee facing the fire. "So, what have you done since we so sadly parted ways?"

"I have done many things, but the first thing I did after I realized what a great dunderhead I had been was write your mother. I wrote to her about my error and she sent me a letter in return. You will appreciate its message, I think." Taking the letter out of his coat pocket, he presented it to Catherine. She took it with ease and opened it to read it with a smile on her face.

Theodore,

It pains me to know that your mother's manipulation has caused you suffering, and I wish it wasn't so. I would never wish that pain on you or anyone. For your mother to do this at a time when you were grieving, your dear brother is beyond the bounds. I trust that you will handle the situation with her in a way that demonstrates both firmness and kindness. Do not let her dictate your life. Find your own way to be happy.

I know how difficult it is for you to have the earldom and its responsibilities thrust upon you. Your place in the world and what you should do may be unclear, but trust that I have confidence in your judgment. You survived years at war and saw to your men. You have proven you know how to take care of people. The scale of an estate is irrelevant when considering the fundamental truth that it is made up of individuals who require attention and care.

Among my daughters, Kitty has displayed the most noticeable growth. She spent most of her life cowering under her father's shadow, but once she stepped out into the light, she found the strength to flourish. She will never go back to living in the darkness again. Society will never shape her to fit its expectations. The birth of my son may have heightened my emotions, but my belief in my daughter's abilities remains steadfast. You need never worry that she would wilt under the pressure of being your countess.

All that being said, I am sure that your quarrel with my daughter probably concerns you the most. I have to admit, you've really gotten yourself into a mess this time. While I know you are an honorable gentleman with a good heart, you have made mistakes. Now that you understand as much, you must apologize to my daughter post haste.

Dear boy, happiness is fleeting, and we only have a limited number of opportunities to seize it. Don't let those chances slip away by failing to make an effort. I would love to call you son, but that will only happen if you get off your backside and do something about breaking my daughter's heart.

Your possible Mother,

Fanny

PostScript. Give my Kitty all of my love.

Folding the letter back up, she placed it on her lap. "I think it will please her to learn that she will gain you as a son. She has always favored you. You were a great aid to her when we managed to become liberated from my father's dominance."

"She has offered me many pearls of wisdom in that letter. I'm looking forward to having her as my mother, because I no longer want to accept mine." With a sigh, Theodore crossed his feet at the ankles and positioned them closer to the flickering flames.

Wrapping her arm around his, Catherine snuggled into his side. "How are things with your mother?"

"They will not charge her with anything, but I refuse to have that woman in my house. In any house that I inhabit. She can have her settlement money, but I will not support her in any other way." Theodore looked into the flames as they danced and compiled his thoughts before continuing. "Before Cedric died, he had the estate that Mother gained in her settlement refurbished. He was afraid of her reaction to his getting married. He wanted to have a place to send her if things became unbearable. She will be leaving for Wales as soon as may be."

"She will not be best pleased by that." As Catherine laughed, her soft chuckles conveyed a deep sense of comprehension. "Though oddly enough, I have always wanted to travel and see places in Scotland and Wales and Ireland. I hear there are many great vistas, and I would love to have the opportunity to paint them."

Grinning widely, Theodore looked at Catherine, eager to dream of their happy future together. "Then I will make sure you will have every opportunity while traveling together. Perhaps we can go on an extended wedding trip and check on the estates I have inherited."

"I would be thrilled with such a trip." Catherine rested her head on his shoulder before asking, "When are you telling your mother of these changes?"

Resting his head on hers, Theodore realized he needed to take care of their current problems before they could get to their happily ever after. "I was hoping that we could do it together. I would like to present a united front. Mother has been trying to divide us, and I would like to show her how much she has failed."

"I am willing to join you. In fact, I have an idea that might help you." Sitting up, she offered him a mischievous grin and asked, "Does your mother read the paper at all?"

Chapter Twenty-Three

CATHERINE WALKED WITH LAMBERT across the square. It was a glorious morning, and she was ready for the battle ahead. Reaching Matlock House, she smiled at the footman who opened her door. "Thank you, Jones."

Barnes came to her immediately and bowed. "Miss Catherine, may I say just how glad I am to see you here?"

"I am rather glad to be here." Catherine grinned at Theodore's batman. Lambert had confessed that she had spoken with Barnes, and he had seemed bothered by Theodore's recent actions. It was reassuring to discover that he had been silently rooting for her, like a hidden ally.

"Lord Matlock asked that you join him and his mother in the breakfast parlor. If you follow me." Turning, he led the way to where Theodore waited for her.

Upon entering the room, Catherine noticed Lady Matlock was sitting at the table drinking tea. There was toast with jam on a plate near her saucer, and she was working her way through a plate of eggs.

As Theodore saw Barnes bring her into the room, a smile instantly spread across his face, lighting up his eyes. His breakfast of tea and toast sat untouched. "Kitty, I am so glad you were able to come for breakfast." Getting up, he came over to her and kissed her on the cheek. "Come sit with me. Would you care for some tea?"

Catherine sat in the chair that he pulled out for her and smiled warmly at him. "Yes, I would. You know how I like it." Looking across the table, she did not miss the look of shock flash across Lady Matlock's face. The lady never would have expected Catherine to show up so calmly at breakfast. Her plan had failed. Catherine would not be suffering the dreadful fate of being forced into marriage with Deerhurst. Not that she would have wed the cur no matter what he did. It would be interesting to watch how Lady Matlock reacted to her failure. She did not strike Catherine as the sort who liked to lose.

"Really, Theodore, the girl can get her own tea," Lady Matlock scoffed at her son. With a subtle hint of doubt, she altered her tune, her soft smile lending a softness to her next words. "She is not as delicate as you might suppose."

Catherine took the teacup that was offered and took a grateful sip before turning to smile at Lady Matlock. "Thank you for your support, Lady Matlock, but I do like it when your son chooses to spoil me so."

Taking his seat once more, Theodore smiled at Catherine over his own cup of tea. "And I love spoiling you, so it works out for the best."

Catherine looked around the room while she waited for the battle to begin. It was a pleasant space, even if slightly ostentatious. The food on the sideboard was plentiful and she might have enjoyed some if she did not have something to do instead of enjoying the morning. The morning paper sat on the sideboard next to the food. It was unassuming but held the key catalyst to the morning's events. Catherine desired to get things moving, so she spoke up. "Would you mind if I looked at your paper? With so many people at my home, I have to wait my turn to read the day's happenings."

Lady Matlock stood and went to the sideboard, instantly taking up the paper and moving back to her seat. "Of course, dear, as soon as I finish with it. I always read it first thing. You would not know this, but a person of my status simply must be kept up to date on all the goings on."

"By all means, please do read it. Tell me if you see anything of note." Turning to Theodore, she smiled at him, her heart racing with anticipation. They had wanted his mother to see what they had arranged to be in the paper, but she knew they could not simply ask her to read the paper. They had discussed the fact that Lady Matlock may try to twist things unless they presented their engagement as a done deal. She would also need to be shown their commitment to her absence from their lives. They did not have to wait long before a high-pitched shriek disrupted their quiet conversation about Artie's latest antics.

Lady Matlock slammed the paper down on the table before her. "Theodore, this is not to be born! There is an announcement here in the Morning Post that is simply outrageous. You must contact these people and tell them of their errors. It is egregious."

***

"WHAT ERROR, MOTHER? WHAT did you read that was so very upsetting?" Theodore put his teacup down and leaned back in his chair.

"There is an announcement of your engagement to Miss Catherine. You are courting the chit, not marrying her. They obviously have their facts wrong. It even says that Lady Matlock is relocating to Wales and will not be present for the wedding to be held at Pemberley but wishes her son every happiness. I have no desire or need to move to Wales or anywhere else." Clearly realizing his lack of intentions to do her bidding, Lady Matlock made a strangled sound of frustration. "You must go there immediately and set them straight."

"The announcement is correct, actually." He reached out to Catherine, who was sitting next to him, and as their hands met, he pressed a gentle kiss onto her knuckles, a gesture filled with affection. "I have humbly asked Miss Catherine to be my partner in life, and she has bestowed upon me the privilege of her hand."

Lady Matlock gaped at them, mouth open and expression bewildered, but then her expression hardened. "You did not see fit to come to your mother with this news?"

Catherine gently placed her hand on Theodore's, providing reassurance, before she spoke. "We announced it at supper last night at Darcy House. Our news was received with great enthusiasm, and everyone was thrilled to hear it. You were invited to come last night, were you not? My sister said she invited you personally." Catherine smiled innocently at the woman who had plotted her demise. They had all known she would not attend. Lady Matlock had not come to a single family dinner. Apparently, she thought herself above such things.

Despite appearing chagrined for a brief moment, Lady Matlock pressed on seemingly undeterred. "Yes, well, beyond that. They obviously still got things wrong. I am not going to Wales." Once more, his mother could not maintain her deceptive act, and her tone was on the verge of reaching the extreme end of the screech spectrum. She would soon make the dogs howl.

As he intertwined his fingers with Catherine's on the table, he met his mother's gaze. "Mother, do you remember our conversation when I told you I knew you had been the one spreading rumors about Catherine? I emphasized the need for you to apologize and rectify your actions."

Lady Matlock sniffed and looked haughty. "I remember that conversation and I have every intention of—"

"Pretending to apologize. Yes, I know that you would do something of the sort. But that option is no longer open to you, not when I know that you are still actively attempting to hurt Catherine."

Lady Matlock slammed her teacup onto the table as she tried to defend herself. "I do not understand how you could believe such a thing about me!" In a sudden shift from rage to sorrow, she added, with tears welling up in her eyes, "I have been trying to draw closer to you. Has this woman been turning you against me? Against your own mother?"

In the face of his mother's dramatic and ever-changing behavior, Theodore stayed composed and responded with a calm demeanor. "If you had read further, you would notice that Lord Deerhurst is being prosecuted for blackmail, among other crimes. He told us that you were paying him to ruin Catherine."

Lady Matlock cried, her hand clutching her heart as she desperately tried to elicit their empathy. "What!?! And you would believe his lies over your own *mother*?"

"Yes, Mother," he confessed, his voice trembling with anger. "I can't deny that I suspect my own mother of paying someone to injure the woman I hold dear. I will not tolerate the deceitful behavior that you have consistently displayed. This is not up for debate, and I will not argue with you about it. From this day forward, I will no longer have you in my home or, for that matter, any of my properties."

Lady Matlock's mouth flapped for a moment, and then she let out a shrill, incomprehensible sound that made Theodore and Catherine cringe in unison. Theodore watched her carefully; it was obvious his mother was trying to come up with some plan to stymie him. She had painted herself into a corner and had been found out. There would be no escape from the consequences of her actions.

Ignoring his mother's attempt at interruption, he continued. "The maids are packing your things, and you will be on the road by mid-day. There is enough light in the day for you to get several hours out of town by nightfall."

"I am your mother. You cannot do this to your nearest relation." The warmth and emotion drained from her voice, leaving behind a hollow emptiness that exposed the artificial tears she had been using.

"I protect those I love, Mother, and while I thought I could love and trust you, you have proven me wrong. I no longer acknowledge you as my mother. Thankfully, in just over a month, I will be marrying an incredible woman." Looking to Catherine, he gazed lovingly at her. "Her mother has graciously given me permission to call her my own, easing my feelings of being an orphan."

Standing up, Lady Matlock stomped her slippered foot. It was quite ineffectual. "That woman is the daughter of a solicitor! Nobility runs in your bloodline. You cannot possibly be glad of such a relationship!"

"There is no questioning the amount of respect I have for Mrs. Hawkins. Formerly known as Mrs. Bennet. I will gladly take her as mother over you." Theodore stood up, his fists pressing into the table as he faced the irate woman. His gaze was as frigid as the coldest winter's day. "You are a disgrace to the title, Mother."

Theodore could feel the warmth of Catherine's hand on his arm. When he turned to her, she smiled reassuringly. Without a word she was showing him that he was not alone in his struggle.

"You are running out of time, Mother. You will be in the carriage in a few hours. I suggest you change into traveling clothes and supervise the packing of any items you want to bring. You may take anything *you* own. All items that belong to the family must stay at Matlock House. Any personal belongings that cannot be packed today will be sent to you separately."

With one last screech, Lady Matlock angrily hurled her teacup towards her son, narrowly missing him. Her anger was evident as she stormed out of the room, her footsteps resonating with intensity. The crash of a door slamming closed soon followed.

Theodore turned and looked at the man who had been standing behind him throughout the entire encounter. "Barnes, could you follow her with the butler and make sure she neither steals anything nor starts breaking things? I would hate to lose a family heirloom if we can help it."

"Of course, sir." With a bow, he left, following the sounds of discord.

***

CATHERINE WATCHED THEODORE ALMOST deflate. It had been a lot to confront his mother about her transgressions and finally force her from his life. She knew she needed to help him but finding a way to divert his attention from the events of the morning proved challenging. Getting up, she looked at the food still on display. Wasn't the way to a man's heart through his stomach? "So what should I try? I did not eat before I came over. It all looks delicious."

Coming out of his daze, Theodore smiled at Catherine. "Mrs. Goodwin is amazing. Her baked goods are a perfect balance of sweet and savory flavors that always leave me wanting more. Though to be fair, I have never found myself disliking anything she made."

Catherine filled two plates with random bits of food, paying special attention to the baked goods. Bringing them both to the table, she put one in front of him and one at her spot. She ignored propriety for the moment and gave Theodore a hug. He seemed to need it desperately. "I know you did not eat before I arrived. You need to eat."

"Yes, my love." Nestled in her arms, Theodore inhaled deeply before responding. "In the years to come, I foresee a peaceful and harmonious existence. You will instruct me for my own benefit, and I will unquestioningly comply."

Pulling back, Catherine rolled her eyes, but a smile tugged at her lips as she looked at the man she loved. "Eat your scone, you silly man."

"Yes, dear."

Neither of them could remain serious and they both burst into raucous laughter. When she was finally able to catch her breath, Catherine noticed Lambert smiling where she sat against the wall. It seemed they were all happy about how things were proceeding.

***

THE MORNING PASSED BY slowly. Catherine remained with Theodore as they waited for Lady Matlock to leave. He had told her she could go, that he would be well, but she pointed out that they were entering a partnership, and she would not leave him to take on his mother alone. After they finished their meal, they relocated, settling into the downstairs sitting room. Lambert stayed with them, as well as a footman, for propriety's sake.

They used the time to engage in deep conversations and craft ambitious plans for their future together. Theodore finally admitted to himself, and Catherine, that parliament just was not for him. He could not abide the posturing and rubbing elbows with people to gain their votes. Catherine freely supported his decision.

Tilting her head seemingly in thought, Catherine said, "You know, if you want to do good, you could create your own charity. It is not like you won't have the means."

"Like the one Elizabeth is working on?"

"Similar, but I was thinking something you would do well is starting something for wounded soldiers. The war in France is not yet over and the number of wounded men is ever increasing."

Stretching his legs out in front of himself, Theodore pondered the possibilities. There were many men out there who could do with a good dose of help. It was what his brother was trying to wrangle from parliament, but it was possible that he could skip the middleman and help himself. Turning back to Catherine he asked, "Yes, but wounded soldiers are not going to want to be simply cared for. How would that work?"

"Just like with the children, find a way to help them find jobs. If a man can no longer work in the fields due to having lost a limb, help him learn another way to support himself. Teach him to read and write, help him become a clerk. Or if it his mind that needs time to heal, have him work with horses or dogs, away from the hustle and bustle of the city."

Standing, he began to pace as ideas began forming in his mind. "You are right. It is not as if I won't have enough land and property to set something up somewhere. I can reach out to a few of my old contacts from the regulars and have them let me know of men in need. This could work. It will take time and we might have to miss a season or two getting things set up, but I do not think we will mind." Walking back to Catherine, Theodore reached down and grasped her hands, pulling her to him. Holding her close he whispered, "Have I told you how brilliant you are?"

"Not that I recall." Catherine smiled up at him, her eyes full of mischief.

"Well, you are. You are brilliant and brave and beautiful and probably several other things, but I have run out of b words for the moment." Theodore grinned watching Catherine chuckle at his antics. "Have I told you that I love you?"

"I believe you have once or twice," she breathed in reply.

"That's good, because I love you beyond all reason." Closing the distance between them he claimed her lips with his own. Theodore was lost to everything but the tiny sound that Catherine made the moment their lips touched. Sadly, the kiss did not progress as far as either would have liked before a loud clearing of one's throat was heard.

Pulling back slightly, Theodore looked down and spotted the slightly dazed look that remained on Catherine's face and nearly leaned in to kiss her again. Before he could follow through on his impulse, another throat clearing had Theodore looking over at Lambert who sat there with eyebrows raised. The footman standing by the door merely grinned. It probably was not the best time to proceed as he would wish.

Giving Catherine a kiss on her blushing cheek, he tugged her with him back to the settee. Holding hands, they continued to talk of plans. Once they were married at Pemberley, they would start an extended tour of his newly gained properties. Eventually, it was decided that they would go to Matlock first and then move on to the properties in Scotland. They would keep an eye out for a good location for the soldier's charity project.

Eventually they lapsed into staring happily into one another's eyes. Realizing where things would head if they stayed as they were, Theodore stood. Pulling her to her feet Theodore said, "Let me show you around."

Theodore led her below stairs, introducing her to the staff with a smile, knowing they would soon address her as Lady Matlock. Catherine was very careful to ask all their names in hopes of learning them all, which was something the current Lady Matlock had never done. The care and concern for everyone that Catherine displayed went a long way towards winning the staff over. To ensure their well-being, she went so far as to request a tour of their living quarters, inquiring about their comfort and whether they were properly maintained. The staff, particularly the senior staff, were aware that she would be inspecting the house as the future mistress. However, the fact that her foremost priority was their comfort left a profound impression.

The morning had passed pleasantly until the reality of their situation crept back in when it came time for Lady Matlock to leave. In the end, there was less of a to do than either Theodore or Catherine had expected. Lady Matlock marched out of the house, head held high, refusing to acknowledge either of them as she left. She said not one word to her son, who she might never see again. Having gambled and lost, her pride left her with no other choice.

After Lady Matlock had left the premises, Theodore walked Catherine back to her home. They started working on the plans for the wedding with Elizabeth and her other sisters. Needless to say, it was a very merry afternoon.

***

DEERHURST DID NOT FARE well. His father had never been fond of his oldest son and his latest behavior had proven too much for the older gentleman. Though his father managed to bear enough weight on the courts to keep him from the gallows, he quickly disowned his son. As a result of some intriguing legal maneuvers, he not only lost his viscount title but was also banished to Australia, vanishing into obscurity.

Life became a swirl of dress fittings, dinners, and morning calls. Gossip had been rife for all of three days. Deerhurst's trial and eventual sentence allowed the rumor Lady Derby started to take hold. She put it about that Deerhurst had been put off by Miss Catherine's very wise refusal to have anything to do with him. She implied that he then tried to ruin her reputation by spreading lies about her. Between that and Catherine's refusal to act ashamed, the talk soon stopped. It did not hurt that she was soon to be a countess.

By the time the Earl Deerhurst approached Catherine and her family in public, the lingering scent of scandal had dissipated completely. His kind apology for the horrible behavior of his son was not necessary but appreciated, nonetheless. The Deerhurst, Darcy, and Fitzwilliam families would never be close, but they would not be enemies.

By the time they departed London, even Catherine, who had a keen sense of style, had grown weary of the endless fittings and pursuit of new dresses. She had at least been able to enjoy the evenings she had spent in Theodore's company. It was a common sight to see her and Theodore attending events they both loved, always enjoying each other's presence. Theodore did not go to a single boring dinner again.

In no time at all, they were all headed to Pemberley to coordinate the wedding. Young Timmy rode in one of the carriages with the other servants and they kindly let him sit by the window, allowing him to indulge in the mesmerizing view of the countryside passing by.

Chapter Twenty-Four

Theodore fidgeted as it seemed like an eternity before Catherine appeared. Darcy grinned at him from where he stood. Not so very long ago, Theodore had ribbed him as they stood at the front of the same chapel while Darcy was waiting for Elizabeth to appear.

It was not so very different from last time as most of the same people were there. Elizabeth was there, though this time she was on the front pew with young Artie on her lap. He was waving happily at everyone and was certainly adopting a more extroverted approach to life, a departure from his father's preference for solitude. In that, he took after his mother.

Kiernan sat beside Elizabeth, home on a break from Eton. He was glad to make it to another one of his "sister's" weddings. As always, he was happy to entertain Artie as necessary. As he picked up the toy Artie had carelessly tossed, he handed it back with a gentle smile and playfully tousled the child's hair. The boy had entered another record growth spurt and would soon be as tall as some of the women he had so lovingly adopted back in Hertfordshire.

Kiernan had met Timmy before the wedding and thanked him for helping Catherine. The two had gotten along well despite their age difference, which was good because Kiernan's family had taken Timmy in. They could use the extra help on the home farm and Kiernan's mother always had an abundance of motherly nurturing to dole out. Timmy had been wary at first but was starting to let the family into his heart.

Jane and Bingley had come sometime before the wedding, happy to socialize with the ever-expanding family. This time, they had their small, blue-eyed bundle of joy in tow. Mr. and Mrs. Hawkins sat nearby with their own son, Mathew, who, strangely enough, was only two weeks younger than his niece. Mrs. Hawkins was beaming, not because her daughter was becoming a countess, but because her daughter was happy to be marrying a man she loved. Above all, her greatest desire was for her daughters to find happiness in their marriages. That Theodore was now an earl was immaterial.

There were new people present. Miss Burgess had been eager to come see her friend wed and, of course, her brother was in attendance as well. Theodore did not miss how he kept looking at Lydia. They were both young enough and Lydia was not even out yet, so there should be some time before another wedding should they continue along those lines. Mr. Goulding had come as part of the house party that had been thrown together. He was gazing longingly at Mary whenever he thought no one was looking. Theodore made a mental note to talk to Darcy and Bingley before he and Catherine left for Matlock that afternoon. He had an interesting idea that might help the two star-crossed love birds.

Lord and Lady Derby were also in attendance as well as their son and daughters. They were quite fond of their cousins, the Gardiners, all of whom were also in attendance. Before they had left London for Pemberley, Theodore had become closer with the Derby family. It was a relief to receive insight about being an earl from someone who possessed a genuinely kind demeanor and no underlying motives.

He might have lost his dear brother and his traitorous mother, but he was not alone. His life had become enriched by the presence of many wonderful individuals, all brimming with love and goodness.

Theodore's musings stopped the moment he saw movement at the back of the church. There, being escorted down the aisle by her Uncle Gardiner, was his bride. Catherine's smile was glorious, and in a room full of joyful individuals, her radiant smile outshone them all.

How had he succeeded in securing the companionship of such an awe-inspiring woman for the rest of his life? He had nearly let it slip through his grasp, but somehow love found a way, like a delicate butterfly landing on his fingertips.

And then she was there, walking to him. He could not say what she wore besides noting that whatever it was, it complimented the glow that she seemed to exude. With every step she took, he felt his breath catch. It was a splendid agony watching her approach. He was torn between wanting her by his side and prolonging the intoxicating effect of witnessing her approach which set him ablaze.

Then, finally, she was next to him, and he could not stop himself from reaching out and taking her hand. He brought it to rest over his thudding heart. Ignoring the curate who was ready to start the ceremony, Theodore focused only on Catherine. Smiling down at her glowing face, he whispered, "I thought you would never get here."

Catherine looked up at him with a teasing glint in her eye. "I was never very far away."

Theodore observed Catherine, captivated by the genuine happiness radiating from her expression, surpassing the power of any spoken language. "Any time you are not by my side, you are far too far away." They were finally going to be able to start their life together and they would not be separated again. Not if he could help it. A rather loud throat clearing finally got their attention back to why they were all there.

"If I may begin?" the young curate questioned them both, eyebrows raised.

Theodore looked at the man, and he had the decency to blush before responding. "By all means. The sooner she is my wife, the better."

Laughter echoed through the chapel as, once again, the curate had to wait to gain the attention of those gathered before beginning the ceremony. In the end, it did not take them long to be joined in holy matrimony.

Chapter Twenty-Five

CATHERINE HAD BEEN SO busy accepting well wishes from guests that she had not eaten anything at all at the wedding breakfast. She had also lost track of her husband. Looking amongst the crowd, she searched for him with anticipation in her eyes. When she finally spotted him, he was walking toward her with a full plate of scrumptious delectables. "How did I manage to lose sight of you? You are a great, tall kind of a husband."

"I am unsure. Maybe it is because you are shorter than many of the people here?" He gently pressed his lips against her cheek. "I know that you have not eaten. Come sit with me and eat something."

"Yes, my love." With a giggle, Catherine went with him to a nearby table. Sitting, she giggled again when he temped to press a piece of strawberry to her lips.

"You will need to eat before we leave for Matlock," Theodore said with a mischievous grin.

"I am perfectly capable of eating without assistance," she assured him. Taking a bite of the warm scone, she chewed slowly, feeling the crumbs melt on her tongue as she leaned against him. After a few more bites enjoyed in silence, Catherine spoke up. "I want to show you something before we go. I had it brought with me from London, and it is going to be taken to Matlock as long as you approve."

Theodore remained still, allowing Catherine to stay snugly nestled against his side. "It will be your home, too. You can put whatever you want in it."

"Yes, I know, but it is a wedding gift for you. I want you to pick where it goes." Smiling to herself, Catherine finished the scone and brushed her hands of the crumbs. "I have it waiting for you to see whenever we are ready to sneak away for a moment."

"I think once we are done eating, we will have a few moments to ourselves."

Eager to show him the gift she had worked so hard to give him, Catherine sat up. "I am done if you are."

A low bark of laugher from Theodore was quickly followed by him sneaking his arm around her waist and him pulling her back into his side. "You barely ate one scone and a strawberry. There is no rush. We will see your gift soon enough. Eat."

After a pleasurable few minutes of finishing the breakfast he had gathered for her, Catherine was walking down the hall with her husband. They made it into her sitting room where on an easel, carefully covered with a cloth, her masterpiece remained hidden, a product of countless hours of dedication. Bouncing on her toes next to the artwork, Catherine was suddenly terrified. She hoped he liked it, but what if he didn't?

Theodore looked at her and then at the covered easel. "You painted something for me?"

With a nervous gesture, Catherine pressed her teeth into her lower lip before she whispered, "Yes, and suddenly I am afraid that you will not like it, but I hope... I hope that you do."

Shaking his head in denial, Theodore responded. "Of course, I will like it. You made it for me." Pulling the fabric away from the easel, Theodore froze in place, visibly stunned by what he revealed. In the painting, Cedric and Theodore were frozen in a moment of happiness, with Cedric's arm casually draped around his brother's shoulder, his proud eyes fixed on Theodore. It was from that night, before Cedric's heartbreaking death, when everything was still sparkling and bright. It was the perfect expression of a brotherly affection, a reminder of the love his brother had for him, the pride.

"What do you think?" Catherine asked, her voice still hushed, but now with solemnity. She hoped the shocked expression on Theodore's face was a good sign.

"I have no words." Theodore's voice was rough with unshed tears.

"Do you like it?" Sensing his appreciation for her gift, she reached out and wrapped her arms around his waist.

"I love it." Pulling her into his side, he pressed a kiss to the crown of her head. "And all I got you was jewelry."

As she laughed, Catherine had a moment of realization that she might be the only new countess unmoved by the idea of jewelry. "Well, now you know next time to get me more paints."

Joining in her merriment, Theodore chuckled. "If this is the kind of masterpiece that you make me, I will buy you your weight in paint and canvas whenever you wish it."

"I love that my husband knows just what to offer me." Standing on her tiptoes, she gently pressed her lips against his cheek. She was just short enough that it was not easy, but worth it. Theodore ran his nose along the tip of hers, and Catherine's breath caught in her throat as she became captivated by the storm brewing in his eyes. She felt his strong arms encircle her, pulling her tightly against his chest, and sensed the frantic thudding of his heart that mirrored her own.

"I love that you know just what I need." Leaning down, he proceeded to devour her lips with his own, only pausing long enough to stop for breath and to trail light butterfly kisses along her jaw.

They might have continued without the notice of time passing them by if not for the startled maid walking into the room to gather the last of Catherine's things. Pulling apart reluctantly, they grinned at each other before turning to the maid. Catherine smiled at the poor girl. "Thank you, Grace. Could you please make sure that the painting is securely wrapped and ready to be transported?"

"Yes, Miss, or... I am sorry. Mrs., or um...Lady? I am so sorry." The maid stood there, her cheeks turning a deep shade of red, nervously twisting her hands together.

"Do not worry, Grace, I am hardly used to it. I think we will all need time to get used to the change." Catherine was quick to try to reassure the maid before turning to Theodore. "So, would you like to bring your painting to Matlock?"

"Yes, I would like that very much." Leaning down, he whispered into her ear, careful not to be overheard by the already timid maid. "I would also like to bring you Matlock. Do you think we can leave yet? I would like to be away with my new bride."

Stepping back from Theodore, Catherine tried to think of where her maid might be. "We can say our goodbyes and leave soon, but first I need to find Lambert so that I can change into my traveling clothes."

"We do not need Lambert. I can help you change." Theodore's eyes sparkled with amusement as he gazed down at Catherine.

Catherine tried to look stern but found it impossible. "I have this nagging sensation that if you were to *help* me change, we would experience some sort of delay."

Theodore's booming laughter echoed through the room and down the hall, reaching the ears of everyone in the vicinity. It was something those who knew the pair eventually got used to. Theirs was a marriage, a partnership that would always be filled with love and laughter.

Epilogue

Theodore jerked awake. Sweat soaked his brow, and his heart raced. Forcing himself to hold still, he attempted to catch his breath and slow his heartbeat. The dream had been horrible, and the smell of gunpowder and blood still lingered in his nostrils. Where he had once had simple dreams of the horrors of battle, they had morphed recently, becoming much worse. Since his marriage to Catherine over a year ago, his dreams had slowly started to feature her, lost and hurt on the battlefield.

Theodore lay there, his forearm pressed against his eyes, trying to recover from his nightmare. This time she had been bleeding and calling for his help and no matter how hard he tried, he could not get to her. The only benefit of his vicious nightmares of late was that it was now much easier to overcome them than his dreams of before. All it really took was for him to roll over.

If he rolled over, he was able to see his darling Kitty lying in bed next to him. Her presence was a balm to his aching soul. Shifting onto his side, he watched her sleep. Her unruly hair sprawled across the pillow, seemingly torn between curling into waves or staying sleek and straight. Reaching out, he wrapped a strand around his finger and let it slide against his skin.

She needed her sleep, but he found he had a desperate need to be connected to her. He was uncertain how long he lay like that, watching her sleep, but eventually, he noticed her eyes were open, and she was watching him back. Even in her drowsy state, her eyes were focused and aware, and a serene smile passed fleetingly over her lips. "Did you have another dream?"

"Yes." He didn't need to say another word; a knowing glance between them spoke volumes. She always understood.

Stretching languidly, she yawned, "Do you want to snuggle until it is time to get up?"

"You need your sleep," Theodore's protested softly. There was no one to wake, but they still whispered as if trying to preserve the night.

Rolling her eyes, Catherine slowly wiggled closer to him and settled in to the crook of his arm, using him as a pillow. "I am not the one who is going to help with the harvest today. I will have time to nap later if I need to." Setting her back to his front, she relaxed into him and drew his arm across her body, laying his hand against her swollen abdomen. "Besides, your child has decided that it is time to play."

Smoothing his hand against her belly, he was able to feel their child move even through Catherine's silky nightgown. "She must think the middle of the night is the best time to practice her archery."

"Is she a girl tonight?" Catherine giggled softly.

Amazingly, a little limb pushed hard at its mother's abused flesh and Theodore could almost imagine seeing a little footprint. Rubbing at the slight bulge, he tried to soothe the worn skin for his dear wife. "I would love another Artemis to spoil. I am already having so much fun with her mother."

"What about your need for an heir? I would have thought you would want a boy first." Catherine's voice was curious, but soft with sleep.

"It is not like it was very hard for us to start this little one, and I am not opposed to practicing with a few daughters before we get a son. I am in no rush." As he used circular motions to soothe their active child, a smile formed on his face as he buried it in his wife's hair. Theodore hoped he could get Catherine to fall back to sleep. The delivery was fast approaching and the larger their child grew, the more difficult it was for her to get around. By midday, she would frequently find herself drained, her fatigue evident in the droop of her shoulders and the weariness in her eyes. After tea, he would usually convince her to rest, but not always. His wife insisted on being a very busy woman.

She often wrote letters to all of her sisters and oversaw certain aspects of their new charity project. It turned out that his brother's property had the ideal setup for injured soldiers to overcome their limitations and learn to work with large animals through a horse breeding program. They also used the manor house there to give lessons in skills the men could use to become clerks or office workers. He knew Cedric would be proud of their efforts and was grateful his brother was still able to make a difference in the lives of others.

She painted also and they had a whole hall of paintings of family here at Matlock Manor. Of course, the painting of him and his brother had a place of honor in the center of the collection. That was on top of the fact that she oversaw all the household duties and made sure their tenants were well cared for. He recently had to encourage her to let the housekeeper go on some of the visits to the see the tenants. She was simply too far along in her pregnancy to be waddling all over the property.

With a yawn, Catherine nestled closer into his arm, her voice muffled. "How many daughters are we talking about?"

"Your mother had five daughters and I think you all turned out wonderful. We can spread them further out if you want." Their child had finally settled back to sleep or whatever it did between bouts of exercise. His arm snuck around Catherine, and he leaned over to kiss her on the back of her ear. "What do you say, five daughters and two sons over the next twenty-two years or so?"

Humming softly under her breath, Catherine yawned again. "I say you are a crazy, crazy man and I love you." Drifting off, she murmured something unintelligible about puppies.

Theodore's grin widened as he cherished the comfort of holding his wife close, feeling their hearts beat in sync. After they got married, it had been a startling revelation learning that Catherine talked in her sleep. While she rarely made any sense, it was always interesting.

And just like that, the haunting memories of his nightmare dissolved, leaving him with a renewed sense of clarity. The overwhelming presence of love in his life made it impossible for any ghosts from his past to find a place to haunt.

He knew the coming day would be a long one as he was helping with the wheat harvest. Hopefully, Catherine would remain indoors, engaging in light and effortless tasks to avoid exertion. There was no telling, but he would definitely assign Lambert and Barnes the task of looking after her. With only one month to go, he did not want to risk anything. Theodore eventually succumbed to sleep once more, soothed by the steady rhythm of his wife's breathing.

***

Normally when Catherine woke, she was either alone or her husband was laying there watching her. This morning, however, he remained asleep. She carefully rolled over so that she could watch him. She rarely saw him so at ease and still.

Their baby had woken her with its persistent kicking of her bladder. She would have to get up soon, but for that moment, she would enjoy the stillness of the morning. Catherine had always loved the way his hair fell against his forehead when he lay on his back.

His nightmares still bothered him but were coming less often. She was happy for him. The more she discovered about his wartime hardships, the stronger her resolve became to spare her sons from the same fate as Theodore. None of her sons would be treated as he had been. They would all receive an estate, or some means of supporting themselves and whatever families they had.

Soon enough, she could not ignore her bladder any longer. Slipping out of bed, she shuffled to the table where her wrap lay and went to take care of business. On her way back, she caught sight of the stack of letters on the table. Recalling the preposterous contents of each letter, Catherine rolled her eyes and chuckled softly. Lady Matlock had overspent her budget purchasing dresses and was demanding more money. After some discussion, Catherine and Theodore had come up with an appropriate response. They had simply responded to Lady Matlock's letters by telling her no and then they had contacted the steward. They told him that to come up with the difference in funds, he should start having Lady Matlock be served the same food as the servants, and he could also see to whatever other economizing he deemed necessary. Lady Matlock might learn to spend better next quarter after living on stews, brown bread, and tallow candles for a while.

When she returned to stand beside the bed, she found Theodore stretching and rubbing the sleep out of his eyes. "You are up early. Are you well?"

Smiling broadly at Theodore, Catherine reassured him. "I am well enough. Your child was stomping on my bladder, so I was forced to take care of matters."

"We can't have that." Theodore crawled across the bed and to her side. Sitting on the edge of the bed, he pulled her into the v of his legs and took her belly in his large hands. Leaning down, he kissed her belly and then began talking into her skin. "You in there. I know we have not been properly introduced, but I am your father. We will get to know each other later, but for now, we must have a talk."

Catherine could not help but giggle. It was just too cute, and his lips moving on her skin tickled. "That tickles."

Glancing up at her, he teased, "Excuse me, I am having a conversation with my son or daughter." Then focusing back on her belly, he continued with his one-sided dialogue. "Now, before I was so rudely interrupted by your mother, we were having a conversation.

I know that you are living in there rent free, but that does not, however, mean that you can damage the property. As a lord or lady, you will simply have to learn better manners."

Reaching down, Catherine ran her fingers through his hair, loving the way he loved her and their child. "Have I told you today how much I love you?"

Kissing her belly again, he replied, "Well, you do talk in your sleep, but I did not catch that particular phrase."

Her smile grew wider as she gazed lovingly at her husband. "I love you more with every breath I take."

Leaning his cheek against the gentle rise of her abdomen, his eyes met hers and his gaze was filled with such love and wonder. "That is good because I love you so much, I ache. The intensity of my love for you is beyond measure, to the point where I am occasionally astonished there is space for any other emotion within me. I am completely filled with my love for you."

With tears running down her face, Catherine looked at her husband in wonder. Not for the first time, she was grateful she had the courage to chase after love, to capture it. Catching kismet had not been easy, but it had been worth it.

Acknowledgements

Before you go, I would like to express my gratitude for reading *Kitty Catches Kismet*. It's been a joy to create this work of love, but without readers, it would be an exercise in futility. If you found this book enjoyable, kindly consider leaving an honest review on your preferred website to help others discover it.

Cooming Soon

The act of writing has completely consumed me, and I cannot stop. I am currently immersed in writing another full-length Pride and Prejudice Variation, which is set to be published in May 2024. Coming Soon: Mary's Daring Demand.

Kitty's mother, Fanny, is the subject of my short story, Fanny's Strength. It tells the tale of how she found the strength to raise five amazing daughters and find her own happily ever after. By subscribing to my newsletter through the link below, you'll receive a free copy, as well as exclusive updates on my upcoming releases and other exciting content.

https://dl.bookfunnel.com/66ax5bftkb

About the Author

My journey with words started out as a painful one. The letters on the page seemed to taunt me, and I spent countless hours with my mother trying to decipher their meaning. Our reading journey started with Little House on the Prairie and continued with other books, mostly in the historical fiction genre. Slowly but surely, I started reading independently, advancing from historical fiction to fantasy and science fiction.

The stories I found in the books I read held me captive, and I often lost track of time. The realization of the true power of the written word inspired me to pursue writing. Unfortunately, I had to put it on the back burner in order to deal with pesky things like paying for food and housing. Then a dare from my sister brought back memories of my passion for writing in high school. It was a passion that I was determined to rekindle.

When I got back into writing, I turned to my latest reading addiction for inspiration, Pride and Prejudice Variations. My mind was fixated on the regency era and the romance of Elizabeth and Darcy, making it hard to write anything else. So I went with it and here we are.

I graduated from college and promptly realized that a degree in American Sign Language was not as helpful as one would hope.

Moving from working as a sign language interpreter to home health and hospice care and mental health services, I have had a diverse career.